Chase and Charlie

Jessica Scott Romano

To Charlie, who taught me that there's a way out of any situation, as long as you have the guts and the brains to keep believing in yourself.

And to Sarah and Daniele, who never let me give up on myself or my dream. This book is for you.

1

My big brother is awesome.

Sure, brothers and sisters are supposed to fight all the time, but Chase and I never have (don't worry, my parents don't understand it either). Chase is two years older than me and, despite his enormity (he's 6'6" and 310 pounds) and my petiteness (I'm only 5'5"), a lot of people mistake us for twins, possibly because we do everything together. We go places together, we watch movies together, we finish each other's sentences, we read each other's minds...well, sort of. In our conversations, there's never a "Chase" without a "Charlie," never a "him" without a "me" right after it; we're so close that my mom says we're basically one soul living in two bodies.

Chase is my best friend—which is why I had to try to clear his name when he was framed for murder.

It happened at the movie theater, of all places. Chase and I had gone to see the new *Star Trek* flick two nights before his college graduation. It was supposed to be our last hurrah—our symbolic last night of fun before he had to go off and join the adults in the "real world," where he had already landed an internship as a physical therapist at the YMCA. To start our night off with a bang, we had gone to Chuck-E-Cheese, where we had won enough tickets to combine and exchange for an enormous, life-size Chuck-E-Cheese doll and a handful of disapproving looks from the younger kids' parents. Next came the movie (we left Chuck waiting in the passenger's seat of the car to guard our leftover pizza) and after that, we had planned to go to an all-night mini-golf course, where we were going to play until one of us got a hole in one (which probably never would have happened, due to my appalling lack of coordination and the fact that Chase's hands made the putter look like a Barbie doll accessory).

Our night was supposed to be epic. Instead, it was epically awful.

"Ugh, I hate previews," Chase groaned as we filed into two seats toward the middle of the theater.

"What, you don't like movies about talking dogs?" I asked, plopping down in my seat and pouring my box of Sno-Caps into our gigantic communal bucket of popcorn.

"No, I just don't want to see all of the funny parts of a movie in the trailer." He emptied his box of Sour Patch Kids into the mix as well. "Half the time, the movie they're advertising only has about three funny parts in it altogether, so they show those in the previews to market it as a comedy and get you hooked—"

"—then you pay to see the movie, expecting it to be hilarious, but it's actually some dramedy about a girl who gets impregnated by some dude she met in a club," I finished.

"Exactly."

We had had this conversation before, many times. Chase and I loved movies. We had seen every movie that had come to that theater since we were ten years old, even if we had had to scrape together all of our birthday money or do extra chores around the house to finance our trip. When we weren't at the real cinema, we'd watch movies at home on cable or DVD, or on one of the hundreds of old VHS tapes our Grandpa Max had left us when he died. Films were our passion, and just one of the many things that brought us together when that pesky "real world" kept threatening to pull us apart.

The lights dimmed a bit lower as the more impressive trailers began to play, reducing the visibility of the theater to "can barely see my hand in front of my face" levels. I leaned back in my seat and shuffled my feet to unstick my sneakers from the floor, then I fearlessly plunged my hand down into our trademark cesspool of movie theater snackage.

"Ugh." I grimaced as my hand squelched against the soggy popcorn. "We put *way* too much butter in this." I took my hand back out to show it to Chase and we both watched as big, fat teardrops of golden butter glinted in the light from the cartoon movie preview on the screen and splashed back down into the paper bucket.

"I'll run and get some napkins," Chase sighed, rolling his eyes as he squished his extra-large soft drink into his cup holder and stood up.

"What am I supposed to do while I wait?" I asked, waving my dripping hand at him.

"Just stick your hand back in there and mix the butter in with the rest of the popcorn," he said, shoving my hand back into the soggy mess. "It's already all gross anyway."

"Thanks." I smirked.

He stuck out his tongue at me in reply, then began his slow, hulking, disruptive shuffle to the end of the row of seats. A few of the Trekkies behind us shouted angrily that he was blocking their view of the whole screen (which, admittedly, he probably was), but he was eventually able to sidle past everyone to the end of the aisle and down the carpeted stairs.

I did as Chase suggested and stirred the popcorn, mixing in the butter with the melting Sno-Caps. Half-drooling with anticipation of its gooey goodness, I grabbed an enormous handful of greasy popcorn, oozing chocolate, and sticky Sour Patch Kids. Just as I was about to shove the delicious disaster into my salivating mouth, the lights went out completely, plunging the theater into complete darkness.

I dropped my popcorn back into the tub.

It was normal for the house lights to go down at the start of a movie, but the movie wasn't playing. The screen was just as pitch black as the rest of the theater, and I couldn't even make out the shape of my sticky hand anymore when I waved it in front of my face.

All around me, people began to shift in their seats, whispering nervously to each other, as if the darkness imposed some sort of volume limit.

"What's going on?" A man yelled from behind me, sounding oddly panicked (apparently he didn't know about the volume limit).

"Yeah, where's the movie?" called a gruff-sounding woman toward the front of the room.

"Chase?" I squeaked, completely inside the noise parameters. It was a little known fact (except to Chase, of course) that I was—and am, to this day—deathly afraid of the dark. It seems irrational, yes—until you consider what kind of things could be lurking in said darkness, especially in a shadowy movie theater full of possible perverts and rapists. "Chase?" I whispered again, my heart pounding so hard in my chest that I was sure that the Trekkies behind me could hear it.

Slowly, people started to remember that they all had cell phones. Soon, the theater was filled with tiny, floating squares of blue light, all bouncing toward the exit. It didn't help me see any better, however; it only dazzled me, stinging my eyes and reminding me of a swarm of lightning bugs bobbing across an empty, black abyss.

Suddenly, there came the sound of a scuffle from up by the screen.

The quadrilateral fireflies flocked in that direction as I rooted myself to my chair, cowering in my fear of nothing and straining to keep myself from hearing what was going on.

"Help!" a muffled male voice cried out, as most of the fireflies reached the end of their thirty-second lifespan and flickered out. There was a loud grunt and a clang, then the sickening, splattering sound of a pumpkin being smashed to pieces across the carpeted floor.

Several people screamed, but I didn't know why.

Who cares? I thought. *It was just a pumpkin!*

Wasn't it?

My mind was too alert, too many thoughts were racing through my brain for me to figure out what was really happening, and the bright, burning, blistering cell phone lights couldn't even begin to penetrate the cloying, suffocating darkness around me. There was more grunting, more thumping, more cracking, more screaming. Just as one last, loud, agonized moan reached my ears, the lights came back up, this time to their full brightness.

Everyone gasped.

All of the people in front of me were staring at the platform beneath the screen, covering their mouths in horror and disgust. Some were crying, others were stoic and emotionless as they stared ahead of them with blank faces, as if they were in shock. One of the Trekkies behind me stumbled to the aisle and threw up.

I couldn't see anything. I didn't *want* to see anything. I didn't know why, but I was sure that my sense of foreboding, for once, should be heeded, and that I should not, under any circumstances, look at the platform below. Every neuron in my brain was telling me to just stay seated, to just wait, to just sit still and stay quiet until my big brother came back to get me.

But I was standing up.

Against my will, my numb, tingly body brought me to my feet, to stand atop my jelly-legs.

I took a deep breath and looked down at the platform.

I felt the popcorn bucket fall to the ground, brushing wetly against my pant leg, as I met Chase's eyes beneath the blank white screen.

It was him. He had been the one grunting, the one groaning, the one smashing the pumpkin (it *was* a pumpkin, right?). He was what everyone had heard, what everyone was gaping at with a mixture of fear and anger.

He was holding a bat. A shiny, silver, aluminum baseball bat covered in something that not even my delusional brain could confuse with pumpkin guts.

"Don't look, Charlotte," Chase plead, in a whisper that carried to me through the now-silent theater as well as if he had shouted it. "Please, don't look."

But I looked.

I looked at his red-stained clothes, at his wide, panicked brown eyes staring out at me from the depths of his pallid, blood-streaked face. I looked at the bloody bat in his hand. I looked at his once-white, now-crimson tennis shoes. Most of all, though, I looked at the battered, bleeding, broken body of the man that lay on the floor at his feet—the man that everyone in that theater knew had just been killed by my big brother.

That's when I fainted.

2

I HAD NEVER FAINTED in my life, but I fainted then, and I fainted hard. I fainted so hard that I didn't even know where I was when I woke up...probably because where I woke up was nowhere near where I had passed out.

"Chase?' I muttered as I came to, unsticking my fuzzy tongue from the roof of my dry, cottony mouth as I squinted around at the lobby of what appeared to be a police station. My head was in my mother's lap (I could tell it was her because, even in the face of adversity, she still smelled like warm chocolate chip cookies and laundry detergent), and police officers swarmed around us like busy worker bees, fluttering their paperwork wings and buzzing questions at her so sharply that they physically stung her.

"Mrs. Chapman, has your son ever physically assaulted you or your daughter?" one of the officers demanded, his pen suspended over a clipboard as he stood in front of her, his belt buckle just even with my nose.

"Of course not!" Mom exclaimed, her hand flying up to her neck to touch the crucifix necklace that my dad had given her when they were teenagers. From the position I was lying in (face

7

up, staring at the bottom of her chin), I could see that her jaw was clenched in distress, and her long, pale fingers were trembling.

Mom had always been fragile. She had been sick a lot as a kid, and now she rarely left the house for fear of catching another debilitating illness. Her hermit-esque lifestyle had never really bothered me—having her home meant that I was never lacking for a female confidant or a plate of warm brownies —but it bothered Chase. While Dad treated Mom like she was a tiny glass butterfly that could be shattered by the slightest jostle or raised voice, Chase thought that Mom should get out into the world and experience things.

Somehow, though, I don't think that a murder investigation was exactly what he had in mind.

"Chase has never assaulted anyone," I grunted, sitting up. Mom grabbed my shoulders as I swayed, wincing as the blood rushed to my head so fast that it felt as if someone was hitting me in the head with a baseball bat.

Oops. Poor choice of words.

Just then, there was a scuffle and a loud, clinking shuffle of chained feet as Chase was dragged roughly into the police station. My mother gasped, covering her mouth with her porcelain fingers like a scandalized woman in a black and white movie.

I felt my own chest constrict with shock and horror as I got a closer look at my big brother, shackled between two rough-looking cops like a dangerous, Hannibal Lecter-like criminal. His white polo shirt was stained with dark, blackish-purple blood and his well-worn jeans still dripped with the stuff. Bits and pieces of bone and flesh and God knows what else peppered his pant legs and crunched beneath his feet as he crossed the shiny white linoleum floor, his sneakers making a sloppy squelch with every clanking step he took. His bare arms were coated in chunky, sticky-looking clumps of gummy, jelly-like fluid that glittered and glistened beneath the bright fluorescent lights, and the skin on his face looked as if it had been airbrushed with maroon spray paint, with specks of dark blood scattered across his cheeks like rusty red freckles.

But that wasn't the worst part.

His eyes, his once-wide, once-kind, once-innocent, brown eyes were wild and round, filled with some sort of odd, disconnected look that made the hairs on the back of my neck stand up.

"Where...where are you taking him?" I stammered, getting to my feet. Mom clutched the side seam of my jeans as if to steady me, but in reality she was probably afraid that I would do something stupid (which, admittedly, would not have been out of character).

"Interrogation room," the cop to Chase's right informed me, his voice curt and his thin, brown lips barely moving. His dark eyes stared straight ahead, not looking at me, as if he were afraid that seeing the humanity in me would lessen the evil he needed to see in my brother.

"Right now?" I asked, tasting bile. "Doesn't he need to see a lawyer first? Or make a phone call?"

"He doesn't deserve a phone call," snarled the other cop, a young, clean-shaven rube with the face of a twelve-year-old combatting a nasty stomach virus.

"Watch it, Lieutenant," snapped his older, wiser, wearier-looking counterpart.

"Hey," I called, helplessly, as they kept walking, passing us now. "Hey, that's my brother!"

Chase hadn't looked at me before, but he looked at me then. His big, empty brown eyes focused on me for a moment, piercing me with a strange sort of strangled intensity, communicating a thousand desperate, wordless messages I couldn't even begin to decode.

"Can I just...can I just talk to him for one second?" I begged, blinking furiously as they just kept on walking, dragging my brother farther and farther away from me.

"Charlotte," my mother whispered, her voice choked with tears, "Sit down here and—"

"NO!" I shouted, growing more and more frantic with each clink of the chain and each squelchy, squeaky footfall.

"Ma'am, we need you to calm down," the lieutenant called over his shoulder, throwing me a dispassionate smirk that only frightened me further.

I needed to see my brother. I needed to hug him, to touch him, to tell him that everything would be alright. I needed to make that distant, tortured look in his eyes go away, and I needed to tell him that I loved him and that I knew he hadn't killed anyone, no matter how bad it looked or sounded to everyone else.

But they just kept walking.

The blue-uniformed officers led him through the lobby to a door on the other side. Suddenly, inexplicably, my heart filled with dread and a deep, dark, soul-shattering fear. Somehow I knew that, once he passed through that doorway, once he crossed over that threshold to meet whatever lay on the other side, the brother I knew would be gone, never to be seen again. And I would be left there alone, with no one to look out for me.

Before I knew what I was doing, I broke free of my mother's limp, feeble grasp and took off running, bounding across the bright, blood-slick floor, dodging desks and chairs and trashcans and startling all of the on-duty cops. I was just sliding up to Chase when someone finally gave a shout to announce my presence.

The two policemen holding my brother flinched in unison,

turning around just as I jumped in front of Chase and leapt up to throw my skinny, shaking arms around his neck.

"I know you didn't do it!" I cried, hot, burning tears streaming down my face as I hugged him tight, praying that it wouldn't be the last time.

"Charlie, get down," Chase said gently, his deep voice thick with pain as it rumbled through my chest cavity.

"NO!" I yelled again, as one of the cops grabbed me around the middle and tried to yank me off him. I leaned my head back to meet Chase's eyes, and was heartened to see that, though full of anguish, they were also full of life now, as that horrible hollowness began to ebb. "Chase, I need you to know that I believe in you!"

I wasn't sure why, exactly, but I knew that, in that moment, there was nothing in the world more important than for him to know that someone, somewhere, still trusted him, still looked up to him, still had complete and utter faith in him and everything that he did.

Chase's eyes softened as they filled with affection and the same fond, brotherly pride I had seen in them so many times before.

"I know you do, Charlie," he murmured, a ghost of a smile pulling at his lips.

Reassured, I nodded as I returned his semi-smile. Then, with a final squeeze of his big neck and a kiss on his blood-spattered cheek, I let go, allowing the pissy young lieutenant to haul me away.

3

Okay, I knew that Chase was being framed, but why?

My brother was big and bulky, yes, but he wouldn't hurt a fly! He was an enormous teddy bear: putty in the hands of a child or a stray dog or an old lady who needed help carrying her groceries in from the car. Many a small, furry life had been saved by Chase's sweet, giant hands and gentle attentiveness, and many a girl had fallen for him and his shy, quietly compassionate disposition. Chase Chapman was the nicest guy in the world, no contest, and I couldn't come up with a single reason why anyone would want to hurt him.

Being his proud, adoring younger sister, however, I was a bit biased. Maybe the childlike eyes of youth had blinded me to a secret he'd been keeping or a darkness in his past that he'd been hiding?

I doubted it.

Nevertheless, I spent the next three days ransacking his room, looking for the slightest hint that he had an enemy that I didn't know about. I dug through all of he drawers, sifting through gym socks and t-shirts and boxer shorts with pictures of little yellow ducks and happy-go-lucky Disney characters on them (most of which had been gag gifts from me) and I pulled out every dress shirt and barely worn suit jacket that hung in his tiny closet, shoving my hands deep into each and every pocket, seam, crevice, or buttonhole I came across. I checked under his mattress, where I knew he had hidden a dog-eared photo of his childhood love, Millie Lawrence, who had moved to Toledo when they were thirteen. Her raven hair and Invisalign smile held no secrets, however, so I put the photo back, wondering if she was stashing a similar picture of my brother beneath her own bed in Ohio.

After that, I checked under the box springs and beneath the bed frame, which took much longer than necessary due to the fifteen years' worth of dusty, dirty, discarded toys and old issues of *Car and Driver* magazines crammed between the bed and the floor (as well to my paralyzing fear of touching mouse poop or a dead spider). Eventually, I found a shoebox full of old love letters from his high school sweetheart, Lindsey Hardison, but even those were too sweet and innocent to arouse suspicion of anything worse than a stolen glance in geometry class or a kiss behind the bleachers at a football game five years ago.

As expected, I found absolutely nothing that implied that my brother had the capacity to kill anyone. In fact, based on the evidence I had just accrued, I think that someone would have had an easier time nominating him for sainthood than sending him to jail.

There was just no reason for anyone to suspect him of murder (aside from his presence at the crime scene and his possession of the murder weapon, of course...), and there was even less reason for someone to want to set him up. I had to have missed something. I had to have overlooked a clue or a suspect at the movie theater that night. There had to be something, some sort of logical explanation, that would prove his innocence, and I had to find it—fast.

Chase had to know more than I did. There had to be something that I wasn't seeing or intuiting, and he had to know what it was. I needed to talk to him, but how? When? When he wasn't locked up in solitary confinement in the county jail (with bail set at a price higher than the one Donald Trump paid for his tower), he was meeting with the slick, weasely lawyer my dad had hired to defend him at his hearing the next week. I wasn't allowed to see him (possibly due to my behavior at the police station after he was arrested...) and calling him was completely out of the question (apparently you can't use your cell phone in jail. Who knew?).

The helplessness was agonizing, and the questions and theories and possibilities running through my mind were driving me insane. It didn't help that my parents both believed that Chase was guilty. That was par for the course, though. Mom and Dad had never been of much use in a crisis. While my father gave a problem the very least amount of effort before either ignoring it or giving up on it all together, my mother inevitably dissolved into a puddle of tears and fainting and indecision. That time wasn't much different. While Mom had spent the past three days sobbing her brains out and baking enough cookies to give an obese giant a heart attack (cooking soothed her, I'll never know why), Dad had been calling lawyers and politicians and priests night and day, trying to figure out how to get Chase to roll over and plead guilty to avoid the electric chair (or whatever corporal punishment consists of these days) and just spend the rest of his long life in prison.

So it was up to me—kooky, geeky, plucky Charlie Chapman: quirky screw-up and loyal little sister—to save him.

I couldn't think of a worse person for the job.

4

ON MONDAY MORNING, four days after the incident at the movie theater, we got a phone call.

As usual these days, my father forbade me to answer it, assuring me that it was a lawyer or a judge or someone calling about Chase's case. As luck (and deviousness) would have it, Dad and I "just happened" to pick up the phone and put it to our ears at the exact same time.

"Hello?" came Dad's voice from the den, rough and ragged from three sleepless nights and four days of horrified acceptance of the fact that his first-born child was a "bad seed." His words were loud as they boomed through the extension, making me wince as I held the receiver of my hamburger-shaped rotary phone away from my face.

"Mr. Chapman?" answered another man. He sounded gruff and arrogant, and a little like Humphrey Bogart's character in *The Maltese Falcon*.

"Yes, this is Greg Chapman."

"This is Chief Hudson, of the Jefferson County Police Department. I'm calling about your son."

My palm grew slick against the plastic sesame seed bun.

"I'm listening," choked my father.

"There has been a recent...change...in terms of your son's preliminary hearing. It had been scheduled for this Thursday, correct?"

"That's right."

"Well, due to the fact that Chase seems to recall nothing that happened on the night of the murder, as well as to an insistent urging for leniency from the victim's estate, the hearing has been cancelled."

I gripped the burger with wet, cold fingers. No hearing should have been good, right? No hearing meant he was coming home!

So then why were both men acting as if Chase had just been given a death sentence?

"Wha...what does that mean?" Dad asked slowly, with growing indignation, "My son doesn't get a fair trial? He doesn't even get a chance to try to prove his innocence now?"

Go, Dad! I thought fiercely, relieved to know that, for the moment, at least, we were sharing the same outrage.

"Not exactly," mumbled Bogart's sound-alike. "Instead of sending Chase to prison, we are sentencing him to six weeks of intense psychological evaluation and treatment at Gray's Institute for Mental Health."

My heart stopped.

My brother was being sent to a mental institution? An insane asylum? The loony bin?

"...we'll be transporting him out there right away. I'm afraid there'll be no time for you and your family to see him before he goes, and any contact after his admission will be discouraged."

"But why—"

"I assure you, Mr. Chapman, that if there is even the slightest chance that your son is innocent, the doctors at Gray's will find it. And if he isn't—"

"What? You'll just send him straight to jail without a trial?" my dad blustered.

"—they will be able to correct whatever mental instability caused him to commit such a—"

I slammed the phone down.

5

My brother was not crazy.

If either of us was crazy, it was me. I spent hours after that phone call pacing my room, rubbing tracks in the lavender carpet with my bare feet as I traced and retraced the same path from my unmade bed to my scuffed-up dresser. At first, I was mad. I couldn't think of a single word that wasn't an obscenity, and I couldn't unclench my pale white fists for more than a few seconds at a time. After that, I was desolate, completely shattered emotionally by the fact that my sweet, kind, heart-wrenchingly innocent brother was locked up in a place that not even The Joker from *Batman* would want to call home. Then I was angry again—so angry that my chest burned with rage and injustice and my eyes stung with red-hot tears of indignation.

Next I was hungry.

Making sure that my father was still locked in his bedroom, consoling my ever-weeping mother, I snuck into the kitchen and gathered up an armful of her peanut butter and grief cookies to take back to my room. I piled them up on top of my polka dot bedspread and turned on my small, blocky, 13-inch television set, hoping to lose myself in a few *M*A*S*H* reruns or blathering talk shows long enough to gain some perspective.

My attempt to distract myself failed miserably, however. Instead of partaking in the mindless array of daytime specials about chubby little beauty queens or cartoons about brightly colored kids with triangle-shaped heads and nasally singing voices, I became immersed in the world of crime shows. What started off as one episode of *Law and Order* quickly turned into hours and hours of criminals and policemen, killers and convicts, dramatizations and reenactments and "ripped-from-the-headlines" murder cases.

Over the next three days, I watched (and lived and breathed) so many cop dramas and procedurals that I started to dream about rapists and cadavers and fake psychic detectives, and I began to speak in outdated cop lingo snatched right of the script of *Dragnet*. It wasn't until I finished my third *NCIS* marathon, however, that I finally found what I had been looking for.

After scanning through the channels in search of a court show or another *JAG* spin-off, I came across and old, completely unrelated sitcom from the sixties called *Hogan's Heroes*. Hogan, I soon discovered, was a U.S. army colonel, and a prisoner of war in a German camp during World War II. He had been placed there, along with a ragtag crew of multi-ethnic cellmates, to help smuggle secrets to the Allied forces back home.

He also helped people escape.

Now, I wasn't going to try to break Chase out of the mental institution (I wasn't *that* crazy...yet). But I *could* find a way to get inside myself. I was certain that if I, like Colonel Hogan, could infiltrate the facility and blend in with the other "prisoners" there, I could get close enough to Chase to find out what really happened at the movie theater that night. Then, drawing on my newly embraced, Hogan-inspired ingenuity and a bit of sibling Wondertwin powers, I could escape with the secrets that would free him and contact the police to relay whatever information I had obtained from my covert mission.

Would it be dangerous? Yes. Illegal? Probably. Stupid? Of course! But I could do it, I was sure of it. Chase needed help, and I would gladly be the one to give it to him. All I would have to do is go down to Gray's Institute of Mental Health and convince the doctors there that I was crazy too.

After a whole week of living off cookies and cop shows and thinking of nothing but violence and conspiracy theories, how hard could that be?

6

THE NEXT DAY, I left home right after lunch and took a bus to "The Institute" on the outskirts of town. I left a note on the kitchen table, informing my parents that I was either running away to join the circus or to go stay with my phone-less, shut-in Nana Georgette, depending on the traffic. It didn't really make much difference where I was, though—my parents had been ignoring me for the past few days anyway. They wouldn't notice if I was gone, and if they did, they'd have no trouble believing that I really was with my kooky grandmother uptown, eating stale chocolates and brushing her two-dozen cats.

I would have taken the family car to the asylum, but I wasn't sure how long I'd be gone, and I figured that the pseudo-hobos and creepers that usually rode the cross-town bus could teach me more about being crazy in thirty minutes than Jack Nicholson could have taught me in a year. Unfortunately, after an hour and a half of riding, all I learned was that the midday bus crowd was made up almost entirely of elderly women shoppers and truant teenagers, neither of which were much help to me in the crazy department.

The closest bus stop to the mental institution was over a

mile away from it, but I could still see its three enormous, ominous, grey towers looming in the distance as I stepped off the kneeling bus. I waved to the world-weary driver, who nodded dimly in acknowledgement. I half-expected him to shout a warning at me about getting too close to the old insane asylum, but he stayed mum and drove away, unaware of the fact that we had all just become characters in a real-life horror film.

In keeping with the scary movie clichés, I felt a chill caress my spine as I began to walk toward the towers. Of course, it was a balmy sort of day, full of sun and just the slightest hint of a warm, late-summer breeze, so I knew immediately that the chill had to be a supernatural thrill of foreboding.

I was enjoying this too much.

I knew that what I was doing wasn't a game. I knew that it was a matter of life or death, guilt or innocence, prison or freedom. But as my pink and black sneakers crunched over the gravel and broken glass scattered across the cracked city sidewalk, I felt invigorated. For once, I was actually *doing* something. I wasn't just sitting around in my room, living vicariously through Sandra Bullock or Mariska Hargitay while I ate Cheetos and wondered what I should be doing with my life. For once, I was taking action. For once, I was helping someone. For once, I had a purpose.

Anticipation (both fearful and exciting) sizzled in my veins as I half-walked, half-jogged toward the monstrous, villainous-looking building. Gray's Institute for Mental Health, I had learned during a morning of thorough internet research, had been established in 1849, and had originally housed patients afflicted with anything from migraines to multiple personalities. These days, after much modernization and a facelift from the rich new owner, the hospital mainly boarded patients with anxiety disorders, depression, mild cases of schizophrenia, and/or suicidal tendencies. The goal of the doctors was to rehabilitate these people, or at least to help them to manage their conditions well enough to re-acclimate to the realities and hardships of everyday life before releasing them back into society as "normal" citizens.

From what I had read, however, very few of these patients ever actually made it out. For one reason or another, most of them either required long-term treatment or elected to stay in residence of their own accord, claiming that life "on the outside" was just too hard to take.

Tell me about it.

I also found out that The Institute devoted a large wing of its 200,000 square foot facility to the housing of the criminally insane. I assumed that was where they were now holding my brother. Unfortunately, I wasn't sure I could muster either the intensity or the credibility of a potential homicidal maniac, so I would be going in as a regular old run-of-the-mill crazy person.

When I finally reached the tall, grey stone building, however, I still wasn't entirely sure what my plan was. For a moment, I just stood there, paralyzed by stupidity and poor planning, beneath the enormous stone archway, looking at the large, rounded glass doors. "Gray's Institute for Mental Health," read a set of straight, perfectly-sane looking white letters stamped on the glass, "Visitors not allowed after 5:00 p.m."

Strange. The police chief had implied that no visitors were allowed at all, regardless of the time.

Maybe that rule only applied to falsely-accused criminals.

Still, I could almost feel Chase's strong, calming presence in the air as I stood outside the entryway. He was there, just on the other side of the glass and down a hall, waiting for someone to help him.

Then a thought hit me.

Maybe he wasn't waiting at all. So much time had passed, maybe he had given up hope that anyone would come for him.

Maybe he believed that we had all forgotten about him, or had convinced ourselves that he really *was* the cold-blooded killer that the police had made him out to be.

I grabbed a hold of the cold, steel door handle and let myself in.

7

There was a low, electrical buzz to signal my entrance, but no one came rushing to greet me.

Good, I thought. My heart was pounding so hard and so loud by that point that I wasn't sure that I could have heard someone welcome me anyway.

I seemed to have walked into some strange, futuristic sort of cafeteria. At least ten rows of shiny silver tables filled the room like long, skinny, chair-less chemistry lab desks, all bolted to the floor and each supported by one round, skinny metal pole in the middle. The floor was a dizzying, dazzling white that reflected the oddly blue fluorescent lights hanging from the ceiling above, and two of the four long, blocky walls were composed almost entirely of glass. Squinting, I tried to peer through the back wall/window, but I could see nothing but distorted refractions of light and my own wavy silhouette bouncing back at me.

That time, the chill that tickled my spine was genuine.

"Can I help you?"

I jumped.

I heard the rattle of a janitor's cart as a young man about mine or Chase's age walked up to me. He was dressed in powder-blue scrubs and white, lace-less sneakers that the detective in me found very suspicious.

"Do you work here?" I frowned as he shifted a few Lysol bottles around on his clunky plastic cart.

"No, I just like wearing this outfit. It really brings out my eyes."

"Oh, a smart-ass!" I cried, throwing my hands up in mock relief, "Just what I was looking for!"

His tanned face flushed a bit beneath the weird blue lights.

He had been right, though. Those scrubs really did bring out his eyes. He had dark, deep blue eyes the color of something expensive like sapphires, or something cheesy, like the sea after a storm. They were a bit hard to see, though, through his shag of dark, brownish-black hair. He wasn't bad looking, overall, and he had a nice, boyish, genuine-looking face smattered with a few wild freckles here and there that I found rather adorable. He looked trustworthy and honest and shy—kind of like a more mature, more manly Zac Efron.

"Can I help you?" Fake Zac asked again, sounding tired now.

I bit my lip as I considered his offer.

"Well?" he urged.

"How crazy does a person have to be to get a room in here?" I asked finally, deciding that a bit of recon was necessary before I set my still-practically-nonexistent plan in motion.

"What do you mean?"

"Like..." I started, walking over to one of the shiny, metal tables, "let's say—hypothetically—that I wanted to go under-cover here as a crazy person. What would I have to do to convince the doctors to admit me?"

"Well, first off, you can't use the phrase 'crazy person.'" He frowned, looking strangely intrigued by my question. "People here find that pretty offensive."

"No 'crazy' talk." I nodded. "Got it."

"And I'm pretty sure you can't just walk in here and expect them to think you need treatment."

"So..."

"So... I'm gonna need more information," Efron the Orderly told me, abandoning his cart and following me to the table. "What's this about?"

"I'm an undercover cop," I lied, running a finger along the mirrored surface of the cold steel. "I'm working a case."

"Bull."

"Okay, I'm a rival asylum owner, looking for some tips on how to run my business."

"Try again." He smiled, obviously amused by my horrible lying skills.

"Would you believe that I'm doing research for a book?"

"Nope."

I sighed.

I clambered up to sit atop the hard, slick table and I motioned for him to move in closer as I dangled my legs over the side. Hesitantly, he tiptoed over to stand in front of me and I glanced dodgily around at all the reflective surfaces.

"Can anyone hear us?" I whispered, and he leaned in even closer. He smelled like Old Spice and Lemon Pledge. Not a bad combination.

"No, not as far as I know. Now what—"

"I came here to see my brother," I burst, my eyes darting around in anticipation of an angry guard or an overly inquisitive doctor.

"Alright, visiting hours—"

"No, you don't get it." I shook my head so hard that a few ringlets of my straw-colored hair fell out of my ponytail and into my face. "I can't *visit* him. He's like a prisoner."

"Oh..."

"I'm not trying to break him out or anything," I said quickly, sensing him pulling away, "but I really need to see him. Well, talk to him, actually. He's innocent, but no one can prove it, and no one is trying but me."

"And your idea of 'trying' is to pass yourself off as a mental patient so you can get close enough to talk to him?"

"Well...yeah."

"What happens if you get caught?" Faux Zac asked, his voice low and disapproving. "Then you'll both go to jail."

"Yeah, but at least I would have *done* something!" I growled, much louder than I had intended. I looked down at my fists, clenched atop my lap, and was once again reminded just how unfair and unjust this whole thing was.

The orderly was quiet for a moment, thinking it over. Then, just as I was beginning to think of a way to sneak past him and go on with my plan without his help, he finally spoke.

"You're sure he's innocent?"

I looked up at him, blinking the sting from my wide green eyes, and said, with all of my conviction, "I'm sure."

He looked at me for a few more seconds, as if he were sizing me up. Then he held out his hand and said, "Come with me."

"Wait, just like that?" I asked, incredulous, but letting him help me down nevertheless. His palm was rough and warm, and I felt a strange swooping sensation in my stomach as he folded his fingers around my hand.

I hoped that was just the thrill of adventure.

"Yeah," he replied, "just like that."

"But why?" I insisted, "You have no reason to help me!"

"Maybe I do, maybe I don't," he said cryptically, shrugging as he led me back toward the front door.

As we reached the entrance, I stopped, digging my heels into the linoleum and taking back my hand. "Wait a minute," I demanded, "I know what you're doing!"

"What's that?" He seemed puzzled.

"You're tricking me! You're going to lock me outside or call the police or—"

"No, I'm not," he interrupted, his voice suddenly so sincere and intense that I had to stop being indignant and listen. "I am really going to help you. You've got my word on it."

I thought it over for a minute, searching his big blue eyes as my stomach did a few dozen back flips.

Damn adventure.

"How do I know I can trust you?" I asked finally.

"How do I know *I* can trust *you?*" he returned.

"Good point." I nodded. "Okay, lead on then, Mr. Janitor!"

"I have a name, you know," he said wearily, as he unlocked the door and held it open for me (apparently the door locked from the inside, but not from the outside. How ominous).

"Really?" I gasped, walking back out onto the black asphalt parking lot. "What a coincidence! So do I."

"I think you are the most sarcastic person I've ever met." He chuckled, closing the door behind us as he shook his head.

"Thanks, I try."

He rolled his eyes. "Alright, I'll tell you mine if you tell me yours."

"Okay, go ahead," I encouraged, contemplating giving him an alter ego or pseudonym instead of my real name.

"Hogarth James."

I snorted.

"*Hogarth James?*" I repeated, shaking with laughter. "What kind of a name is that?"

"A bad one," he admitted, chagrinned. "Alright, now tell me yours. If I'm going to be a co-conspirator in some sort of crime, I need to know who I am going to be co-conspiring with."

I regarded him once more, evaluating his level of trustworthiness again. Eventually, I decided that, if the universe had already stuck you with a name like "Hogarth," you couldn't afford to be a liar.

"Charlotte Chapman," I said proudly, holding out my hand for a handshake, "but everyone calls me Charlie."

"Charlie Chapman?" He grinned, grabbing my hand and making my stomach flutter again. "And you think *I* have a stupid name?"

"I never said it was stupid!"

"Yeah, but you thought it, though," he assured me. I wanted to deny it, but my obnoxious snorting earlier had already given me away.

"Is that really what people call you though?" I asked, still fighting an attack of the giggles, "*Hogarth?*"

"That's my name." There was a sparkle in his azure eyes now. "What else would they call me?"

"I don't know..." I paused for a moment to mull it over. "What about 'Hoagie?' Like the sandwich?"

It was his turn to snort. "Hoagie? Really?"

"Sure, why not?" I shrugged. "It sounds a heck of a lot better than Hogarth!"

"I can honestly say that, of all the names I have been called in my life, that is by far the most original."

"Why?" I wondered, not seeing what was so original about it. "It seems like a logical choice to me."

"Fine," he sighed, still chuckling. "You can call me Hoagie if you want."

"Good. That's what I was planning to do anyway," I replied, with a saucy grin. "So, tell me, what's the plan?"

"The plan for what?"

"For breaking me in!"

"Oh, that." He nodded, faking solemnity with a deep faux frown.

That time, I couldn't blame the stomach flutters on the thrill of adventure.

He was both cute and funny—a deadly distraction to a geeky novice gumshoe like myself.

"Alright," he began, getting a little more serious now as he leaned in conspiratorially, "I've been working here for a long time, and I know just about everything there is to know about this place and the doctors who work in it."

"Okay…"

"The most important thing to remember is that you can never underestimate them. They're smart. Way too smart to buy any of that secret-agent-slash-writer-slash-asylum-owner junk you were peddling back there."

"Alright, Obi Wan, so what do I do?"

A mosquito buzzed past my face and I wondered if it was being attracted by the blush in my cheeks or the anxious thudding of my racing heart.

"First of all, you stop talking."

"Well, *excuse* me!" I snapped, offended, "I didn't realize I was being such a—"

"No, no, no, not to me," he amended hastily, waving his hand as if to erase his last statement. "You have to pretend that you're mute. If you don't talk, they can't tell you're lying."

"Am I really *that* bad a liar?" Colonel Hogan would be so disappointed.

"Yes." He laughed. "One of the worst I've ever seen."

"Wow, thanks."

"Don't mention it," he replied cheerfully, clearly enjoying watching me reevaluate my life. "But anyway, what we'll do is this: I'll take you in and say that I found you wandering the streets by yourself, barefoot—"

"Aw, man! But I love these shoes!" I whined, pointing at the neon pink stripes on my dirty black sneakers.

Hoagie let out a long-suffering sigh. "I'm not going to throw them away, I'm going to hide them somewhere and give them back to you later."

"Oh, okay." I perked up, eager for action once more. "Then what do we do?"

"Like I said, I tell them I found you, and that you won't say a word. They'll ask you a bunch of questions, but you can't answer any of them. Don't even write your answers down on paper if you can help it. Then, if we play our cards right, they'll admit you."

"Just like that?"

"Pretty much. They're not too picky here. They're always on the lookout for new patients. But anyway, that's only the beginning. You'll have to let them move you into one of the dorms, where you cannot, under any circumstances, speak a word to your roommate. Not even in your sleep!"

"I'll have a roommate?"

"Yeah, every patient here has a roommate. Well, every one except for the criminally insane."

My stomach fell. "Like Chase," I said quietly, suddenly overwhelmed by the thought that he was so alone in the world that he didn't even have a mentally unstable roommate to keep him company.

"Is Chase your brother?" Hoagie asked, looking a bit troubled by my expression.

"Yeah."

"What's he in for?"

I hesitated.

Should I tell him the truth and risk ruining my only chance to get inside?

"Um... I'd rather not say," I mumbled vaguely, looking down at my shoes.

"That bad, huh?"

I tilted my head back up to find him wearing a pained

expression, as if he could really understand the strange combination of hopelessness, desperation, and fear I had been feeling for the past week.

"The police say he killed someone," I told him, unable to stop myself. "A *lot* of people say he killed someone."

"And you say he didn't?"

"Of course I say he didn't!" I bristled. "My big brother is not a murderer!"

"Okay, okay, I believe you," he said quickly, holding out a placating hand. "Trust me, I know all about believing in something when no one else does."

I searched his eyes for further explanation, but he turned them away.

"Anyway...you'll have to take part in all the daily rituals and things they do here, like chow time and therapy and all that. But the biggest problem is going to be the pills."

"The pills?"

"Yeah. At every meal, they give every patient two little white pills, whether their condition requires medication or not. I don't know what they are, but I know they make everyone really quiet and listless and weird. So, whatever you do, don't swallow any sort of drug they may give you."

"Now you're starting to scare me," I admitted, feeling a bit queasy.

"Hey, we don't have to do this if you don't want to," he told me, putting a bracing hand on my shoulder.

"No, I have to do it." I gulped, my throat dry and cottony with second thoughts. "For Chase."

"Are you sure?"

"I'm sure."

"Are you really sure?"

"Yes, I'm really sure."

"But are you really, really, *really*—"

"Hoagie, I'm sure!" I laughed, and he smiled, looking relieved.

"Atta girl. Now there's no need to worry, because I'll be nearby pretty much all the time."

"Except at night, when I'll be all alone with my psychotic roommate." I smirked, feeling a bit sick again. What was I getting myself into?

"No, I'll be here then, too," he said, his smile falling,

"Why?" I asked slowly, getting suspicious again. "Oh no, don't tell me you're really a patient here."

"No, but I do live on site," he responded heavily. "My uncle owns the place."

"Oh, crap!" I yelped, jumping backward in horror. "Oh, crap, I'm sleeping with the enemy!"

"Take it easy, nobody's sleeping with anybody! I'm a gentleman. I'd at least take you out to dinner first," he replied, attempting to deflect my accusation with humor. It didn't work. "But anyway, I'm not the enemy."

"Oh, yeah?" I shouted, feeling a bit hysterical, as I backed away across the blacktop, cursing my own naiveté. "Says who?"

"Says me."

"Okay." I shrugged manically. "So, tell me, if you're not the enemy, then who is?"

"My uncle."

I stopped moving.

"Why do you think I'm trying to help you?" he asked me, scooting closer as he lowered his voice. "Why do you think I already had all this stuff planned out? You're not the only one 'undercover,' Charlie. There's something going on here with the patients, and I've spent the better part of the last four years trying to find out what it is! And apparently I can't do it alone, so I need your help."

I blinked stupidly at him.

"And, in exchange, I'll help you get to your brother, and I'll do whatever it takes to help you clear his name. So, what do you say?" He held out his calloused hand again. "Are you still in?"

His expression was hard, but there was a hopeful, almost pleading look in his eyes as he waited for my answer. I thought of him, searching for truth all alone in that creepy place, and I thought of Chase, caught in a web of lies and misconceptions, cut off from everyone he loved, and I knew that there was nothing else for me to do.

"I'm still in," I said firmly, taking Hoagie's hand.

8

"I don't think this is very convincing," I commented dryly, standing in my sock feet in a patch of grass at the edge of the parking lot as Hoagie rubbed dirt and dead leaves all over me, attempting to make me look like some sort of woodsy hobo.

"Take one of your socks off then," he suggested, dropping a pile of mulchy dirt on top of my head before rubbing it into my now-loose, now-tousled hair.

"Yeah, that'll fool 'em."

"Do you want me to help you or not?" he demanded, sprinkling my head with bits of grass and tree bark now.

"I want you to help me get a room in an insane asylum, not an audition for *The Walking Dead!*"

"Hey, your cover is a lost girl who's been wandering around in the woods for days! How else are you supposed to look?"

"You sure have given this a lot of thought," I observed, as he gave my wavy/curly, blonde/brown locks another good shake to spread out the clumps and chunks of debris.

"Well, you have a lot of time to scheme when you're mindlessly pushing a broom all day in a building full of people who are either too stoned or too mentally disturbed to talk to you."

"Are the patients here really that bad?"

He scooped up another handful of sandy brown dirt and spit on it, rubbing the mixture around in his palm to create a gloppy, glue-like concoction.

I made a face.

"No, I don't think they're bad at all. Most of them, anyway. It's hard to tell, though, because they're all so doped-up. It's pretty scary, actually. *They* should be the ones auditioning for *The Walking Dead*."

"So, you think the doctors are over-medicating them to keep them quiet?" I asked, feeling the tingle of excitement again as I channeled my inner Sherlock Holmes. Two mysteries to solve were always better than one.

"That's one of my theories," Hoagie replied, folding his lips down into a deep frown. "Here, let me rub some of this stuff on your face."

"The stuff you just spit on? No way!"

"Come on, I don't have germs!"

"Germs aren't the problem!"

"Just let me do it," he insisted, laughing at my wrinkled nose and disgusted grimace.

"Alright, fine," I conceded, "but I'm spitting on you later to make it even."

"I'm looking forward to it." He winked.

I laughed and leaned in to accept my slobbery mud facial. I half-expected him to just slap it all on my face, smearing it across my cheeks like a clown with a cream pie. Instead, though, he dipped his clean thumb into the mess in his left hand before lightly, gently stroking the gritty paste over my right cheekbone. Then, just as gently, he dabbed some above my left eye, atop the bridge of my nose, and under both my ears. I watched him, holding unnaturally still, as he got some more goop on his finger and rubbed it onto my chin, sliding it down my neck to my collarbone. He was biting the tip of his tongue in concentration, and his eyes were so intent on my face that I wondered if he was even seeing *me* at all, or just a canvas for him to paint his nature-inspired art upon.

I also wondered if he could feel me blushing.

"Okay, that should do it," he said finally, stepping back to admire his work.

"S-So..." I stuttered, suddenly self-conscious, "how do I look?"

"Crazy," he replied, looking satisfied. Then his blue eyes glinted roguishly as he poked my arm and added, "Crazy-cute."

I snorted again. "Wow, that was cheesy!" I giggled, my awkwardness dissipating.

"Hey, I'm a cheesy guy," he said with a shrug. "It's not every day that a girl lets me rub dirt and spit on her face!"

I laughed again, and he handed me some crud to rub over my clothes. Once my Freddy Krueger-ish red and black striped t-shirt, raggedy cut-off jean shorts, and one remaining neon green sock were sufficiently dusted with specks of grass and sooty dirt, my transformation was complete. I almost wished I could see myself the way Hoagie saw me. I was pretty sure that I looked hideous...or at least a little like Pigpen from the *Peanuts* cartoons.

"Alright," Hoagie said with a grand, sweeping gesture toward the building, "your audience awaits!"

My stomach churned, but I nodded dutifully.

"Do you have any last words before we go in?" he asked me, looking a bit green himself.

"Hmm..." I pondered, tapping my dingy finger against my dirty chin, "how about, 'Tonight we dine in Hell!'"

He laughed. "That one seems a little intense, don't you think?"

"True..." I acknowledged. "What about, 'FOR NARNIA!!'"

He laughed even harder. "I don't think that one's really appropriate either..."

"'Veni Vidi Vici?'"

"Overused."

"'Here's lookin' at you, kid?'"

"Overrated."

"'Nobody puts Baby in a corner!'"

"Now that one's just silly..."

"'Yippee-Ki-Yay, Mother—'"

"No."

"Okay, okay," I sighed, pausing for a moment to gather my thoughts. "Alright, I think I've got it this time."

"Let's hear it."

I took a deep breath and drew myself up to my full (probably unimpressive) height and said, with all the confidence and solemnity I could muster, "See you on the other side."

9

Not talking was much harder than I expected.

Hoagie and I had agreed that when we reached those rounded glass doors, I would officially go mute. As soon as we entered the building, however, a million burning questions sprang to my lips. Why was there so much glass? Why were the tables in the cafeteria made of steel instead of wood? And where were the chairs? Were people watching us through the walls? Were the walls really two-way mirrors like the ones in the police station? Had someone heard or seen us plotting outside? Where was Chase? How long would it take to get to him? How long would I have to stay? Would my roommate be a psycho? What was the next part of our plan? Would the doctors draw blood from me? Did they have medical degrees? Would they try to use me for experiments? Would I *let* them use me for experiments? Could Hoagie tell that I was shaking like a sweater-less Chihuahua in winter?

And did he really think I was crazy-cute?

All these thoughts and more were bouncing around in my brain like moths trapped in a Mason jar, making it almost impossible for me to focus. I had wanted this. I had been prepared for it from the start. But that didn't make what I was about to do any less terrifying.

I wished I had watched a few more episodes of *Hogan's Heroes* before I left home.

"Okay, this is it," Hoagie said, as we reached a second set of glass doors on the back wall of the cafeteria. Unlike the more decorative doors we had just passed through, these were tall and square and blank, with sharp edges and even sharper corners that blended so well with the surrounding glass wall that you could barely tell they were there at all. "Are you sure you want to do this?"

To be honest, I hadn't been sure of much of anything since I had left home, and things had only gotten murkier the moment Hoagie had taken my hand and offered to help me. He was holding my hand again now, his warm, work-worn palm damp with worry sweat as he looked at me much too intensely, with eyes full of anxiety and what looked a little bit like mortal terror.

I nodded.

He squeezed my hand and swallowed hard, as if he were trying to choke down his Adam's apple. "Are you sure? Because if you're having second thoughts—"

I shook my head vehemently, cutting him off. We were just wasting time now.

He sighed and ran his free hand through his shaggy hair, then through his barely-there, blue-tinted five o'clock shadow. "Geez, I don't' think I've ever been this nervous in my life!"

"You're not the one being committed," I mouthed, with a teasing smile, as I gave our linked hands a playful shake.

"How weird is it that *you're* the one reassuring *me?*" he asked, grinning wryly as he continued to look pale and dubious.

I shrugged, finding it a little adorable that he was so worried about me.

"Okay, I guess we should go in now," he croaked, his tentative smile fading. He looked a bit like he was leading me to the gallows.

It was my turn to get sweaty palms.

"Remember," he muttered, lowering his voice as he leaned in close to speak into my ear, "don't talk to anyone, not even me, unless we're alone."

My stomach squirmed a bit at the thought of us being alone together.

"And don't, under any circumstances, take the pills!" he warned, his hushed voice almost pleading now. "While you're getting checked in, I'll see what I can find out about Chase."

My squirming stomach plummeted at the mental image of Chase sitting in a lonely room in the criminals' wing.

I nodded.

Hoagie pulled back for a moment to look me in the eye, his lips parted slightly, as if he were about to say something, but didn't know if he should. Then he leaned back in, even closer this time. His lips tickled my burning ear as he whispered, "Listen, I'll be around any time you need me. I won't let anything happen to you in there, I swear."

I stepped back to get a glimpse of the sincerity sparkling in his dark, steadfast blue eyes. Then, compelled by forces that I couldn't control, I reached up and put my arms around his neck, hugging him tight, as if I had known him forever, and as if I would never see him again.

He hugged me back, wrapping his arms around my waist and pressing his stubbly cheek against mine.

It was weird, really, to be hugging someone I'd literally just met before embarking on a ludicrous endeavor that would most likely land us both in prison, but something about it just felt right. As we pulled apart, both blushing and awkwardly fidgeting with our hair and our clothing, I realized what it was. Hoagie made me feel safe—something I hadn't felt since the moment Chase had gone to get napkins at the movie theater over a week before. I was an independent woman, sure, but it was still nice to know that someone, even just a cute, cheesy, stranger someone, was looking out for me while my big brother was indisposed.

"Ready?" Hoagie asked, clearing his throat as he grabbed the narrow door handle.

I still had a thousand questions, a million doubts, and a billion second thoughts, but I pushed them all away. Then I nodded.

10

THE RECEPTION AREA looked a lot like the lobby/cafeteria we had just left. Its floors were a slick, glossy white that disoriented me with reflections of overhead lamps and my own movements, and the same strange, tingly electrical hum filled the air, making the hairs on my dirty arms stand up. Like the previous room, this one's main feature was one long, blurry-looking glass wall, but the other three walls were a blank, clinical, uniform-looking white that, in spite of their myriad doors and hallways, reminded me of the inside of a padded cell.

In keeping with the science-fiction décor, there was a futuristic-looking circular desk in the center of the room, at which sat a young blonde woman in a dress so white that it put even the creepy-clean walls around us to shame. She was typing at a super-slim, super-expensive-looking flat-screen computer, and was biting her red-lipsticked lip in concentration, completely oblivious to our presence aboard the deck of the Starship Enterprise.

Hoagie cleared his throat and I jumped. For a moment, I had forgotten he was there. I had gotten lost in the surreality of the moment, and had been wondering very seriously whether it was not a horror film I was in, but an alien-packed, post-apoca-lyptic sci-fi flick.

"Oh, hey," the blonde said, sounding a bit bored, "I didn't see you guys there. Come on in."

No wonder we had been able to plot out our entire scheme just thirty yards away from the front desk. Obviously this chick had more important things to focus on than silly visitors and pesky intruders. As we made our way around the silver tabletop to stand in front of her, she went back to whatever she had been doing, her big, brown doe eyes flicking back and forth from monitor to keyboard as she either input some data or typed up an entry for her blog.

Hoagie cleared his throat again, then said awkwardly, "I, uh... I found this girl out front. I think she's lost or something."

The receptionist glanced up at him, her pretty face blank.

"I...uh...thought she might need some help, so I...uh... brought her in."

She stared.

"She...she...can't talk, see?" Flustered, Hoagie turned to me, pointing at my throat. For a moment, I just looked at him in disbelief. And *he* had called *me* a terrible liar!

He widened his eyes meaningfully and I rolled mine. Then I pointed at my lips and turned to the blonde, shaking my head, implying that I could not, or would not, speak.

"I see..." she said slowly, her perfectly-sculpted brows furrowing beneath her movie-star bangs. "And you are..."

For a second, I thought she was talking to me. Then, with a surge of repressed laughter, I saw that she was addressing poor Hoagie, the lonely orderly.

"I'm Hogarth James," he sighed, his shoulders slumping a bit as he blushed. It was clear he had done this before. "I work here."

I wondered briefly why he didn't just tell her that his uncle owned the place, but then I decided that it was more entertaining to watch his ears turn red with embarrassment instead.

"Hmmm... is this your first day?" The blonde frowned. "I don't think I've ever seen you before."

"No, I've been here for years. I gave you a tour of the building when you got hired six months ago."

"Oh. Oh! Oh, okay," she replied with a crimson smile and a tinkling laugh that kind of made me want to punch her. "Well, it's nice to meet you, Howard."

"Hogarth," he grumbled.

I had to use all the strength in my body to keep myself from cracking up.

"Oh, *Hogarth*, that's right," she nodded, as if she were the one correcting him. "I think the boss's name is Hogarth too, isn't it? Weird. Oh, well. Anyway, so you found this girl outside?"

"Yes, and she can't speak," Hoagie told her, his friendly voice cold and dispassionate now. "She doesn't have any I.D. and she doesn't want to get the police involved, so I brought her in here. I thought maybe a few days with the therapists might—"

"Here you go!" the receptionist sang, whipping a piece of paper out of the printer beneath the desk and handing it to him with a flourish. "Take her back through that hall to exam room three and have her fill this out. The doctor will be in shortly."

Hoagie looked stunned for a moment, then he ripped the form out of her manicured hand and grabbed my wrist, leading me over to a narrow white doorway opposite the glass wall as he mumbled something that sounded like "...eighteen freaking years and no one even bothers to learn my name..."

I slipped my wrist out of his grip and slid my hand into his, giving it a sympathetic squeeze. I couldn't hide my obvious glee over his sad, Charlie Brown-esque predicament though, and when he caught my eye, he blushed even harder.

"Quit it," he said, "it's not funny." But that didn't stop the corners of his mouth from twitching.

In no time, we were standing in front of a skinny white door on the left hand side of the hall. A large, shiny, black "3" glared back at us, marking the first stop on my asylum induction tour.

"Alright, I guess you just have to go in there and fill this out. I'll go see what I can find out about your brother."

My heart stuttered as the smile slipped from my face. He was leaving me here? Alone? So soon?

I nodded weakly, my tongue dry and sticky as I took the paper from him. My legs felt like linguini noodles, but I crossed over to the door and grabbed the cold silver knob, my slick palm slipping slightly against the steel.

I had known this moment was coming. I had known I would be alone in this thing eventually. Actually, that had been my plan all along. I had never factored a partner into my strategy, except for maybe Chase at some point. So why did I have to bite my lip to keep myself from begging Hoagie to stay with me?

This was getting too intense.

I took a deep breath and turned the knob, pushing open the door with purpose and determination—and without a glance back at Hoagie. I had to be strong. I had to be independent. I didn't have room in my sci-fi/horror/adventure story for a love interest. I needed to focus on the task at hand: at being fake crazy, at helping Chase prove his innocence.

I shut the door behind me with a snap.

11

Before I even had time to miss him, Hoagie was rapping at the door. He knocked quickly, urgently, with just the tips of his knuckles, but the sound was deafening as it echoed around the bare, microscopic room I had just entered.

Worried, I quickly threw open the door.

As expected, Hoagie was standing just where I had left him, framed by the white doorway in his baby blue scrubs and lace-less white sneakers, wearing a frightened look that just about scared me to death.

"What's wrong?" I mouthed, gesturing for him to come in.

He complied, hastily closing the door behind us. "I was thinking about it and I think...maybe...maybe I should stay with you for a while...to make sure you fill out the form right and everything."

I raised an eyebrow.

"It's kind of a complicated thing, you know..."

I crossed my arms.

"...and I'll need to know what you put down so we can keep our story straight!"

I tapped my foot impatiently, stifling a smile.

"And...well, you know..."

I grinned.

"Alright, fine!" he conceded finally, waving his arms in defeat. "I'm worried about you, okay? I don't like this plan anymore."

I beamed as I watched his boyish face turn crimson.

"Stop looking at me like that!"

"You like me," I teased, mouthing the words with smiling lips.

"No, I'm concerned about you, that's all..."

"You like me."

"I do not!"

"You do so."

"Cut it out!"

"Just say it."

"No."

"Come on," I teased, poking him on the arm with a dirty finger as his cheeks burned red. Of all the times to be sworn to silence...

"No!"

I nodded, laughing like a muted hyena.

"Charlie, I'm warning you—"

Just as I was about to taunt him over this clearly empty threat, the door swung open and we both jumped back in surprise.

"Doctor Caleb!" Hoagie squeaked, taking a step away from me.

An impressive-looking man swept into the room, his white lab coat billowing around him like a cape.

"Young man," he said in reply, and I realized that he didn't know Hoagie's name either.

I had to use my grimy hand to physically wipe the grin from my face.

The doctor seemed busy. He walked briskly over to the tiny metal exam table in the corner of the claustrophobic little room and threw down a file folder full of papers. Even as he hunched over to open it, he seemed remarkably tall and straight and refined, with perfectly trimmed, salt and pepper hair and a clean-shaven face that was just tan enough that the white-walled room didn't wash him out like it did Hoagie and me. He had a strong, pronounced chin and eyes like a narrowly focused hawk as he concentrated on the paperwork before him and ignored us completely.

"Um..."

"Stacey tells me you found her outside the facility."

The doctor's words were clipped and short, as if he didn't have time to waste with pleasantries or explanations or moving his mouth too much.

"Yes, Sir," Hoagie gulped, shooting me a nervous look.

"Did she fill out the form?"

"No, Sir, not yet. We just—"

"Forget it. We don't need the form."

I was a bit alarmed as he slapped the folder shut and swung around to grab me by the throat.

At least...that's what I thought he was doing.

Driven by a primitive survival instinct (as well as the desperate desire to not be the first to die in this horror movie), I reached up with both my arms and slapped his hands away so hard that it made my skin sting.

Hoagie jumped and made to grab either me or the doctor (I couldn't tell which), but Dr. Caleb, calm and unfazed, held up a staying hand.

"I'm not going to hurt you," he told me, his voice still curt. "I'm just checking your vocal cords for damage."

It was my turn to blush.

I made an embarrassed, permissive sort of half-shrugging

motion and he reached back in. As the doctor put his strangely cold, strangely smooth hands on my neck, gently pressing against what I assumed to be my voice box, I glanced over at Hoagie. I had expected his blue eyes to be sparkling with teasing laughter as mine had been over his earlier faux pas, but instead they were wide and worried as he watched the physician's hands travel up and down my throat, feeling for damage that wasn't there.

"Alright, well, it seems to be a psychological rather than a physiological issue," Dr. Caleb declared after a moment, removing his hands.

Feeling a bit violated, I rubbed my neck where he had touched it, as if I could scrub off his touch with my own.

"You really are mute, right?"

It took me a minute to realize he was talking to me.

"Miss?"

I quickly nodded, hoping he couldn't see the lie lurking in my bulging, unblinking eyes.

"Okay." He nodded, opening his folder again to make a note. "We can fix that. We have ways of making people talk here."

I almost snapped my neck looking over at Hoagie. Did he really just say that?

Hoagie blanched.

"We have group therapy here every day at one, personal therapy sessions scheduled at various times throughout the day, and several other activities designed to open patients up and get them talking again."

I relaxed a bit. He hadn't intended to sound like a movie villain. He had just made a poor choice of words.

"Alright, Jane Doe," he said, scooping together his paper-work and straightening back up, "follow me to your dorm room."

I paused, my gaze flicking to my partner in crime, who caught on immediately.

"Uh, Dr. Caleb, Sir, I think maybe I ought to come too," he suggested meekly. "She seems to have sort of...latched on to me—"

"I don't think so, young man," the doctor said, cutting him off. "Recovery from trauma is an intensely personal experience. She doesn't need you around watching her do it."

Then, before I could so much as wave goodbye, Dr. Caleb ushered me out of the room, leaving Hoagie behind with the form I had never filled out and a million things I had never gotten to say.

12

Over the next few hours, a myriad of random, white-coated strangers fussed over me; giving me instructions and directions, asking me dozens of questions I wouldn't answer, and trying to help me to dress in a blocky, mint green hospital gown that was as chilly as it was unflattering. They gave me a physical, a shower, a hospital bracelet, and a worn white robe to wear (most likely so that I wouldn't distract the male patients with my thin, practically see-through gown), then, finally, they left me alone.

As I sat in my new bedroom, atop a pastel bedspread that matched my fabulous new outfit, I felt raw and exposed. I felt like a lab rat that had been scrubbed clean and examined from every possible angle before being thrown roughly back into its cage, where it would be observed for hours or days as a group of scientists waited for it to start mutating.

Dr. Caleb had briefly shown me my dorm (room 109) before the cleansing process had begun, informing me that I would be sharing the space with another inmate (excuse me, "patient"), ironically named Sybil. The doctor had then passed me off to the team of faceless pseudo-stylists, who had proceeded to strip me of both my clothes and my humanity. In the end, they had allowed me to undress myself, but they had seemed certain that letting me shower on my own would be dangerous to my health.

I pulled my robe closed even more tightly at the nape of my neck as I remembered the distant, detached way the one and only female doctor (or nurse, I couldn't tell) had sloughed off all the dirt and grass and debris that Hoagie had so carefully coated me with. I had felt more naked then than I had when I had first stepped into the tiny Plexiglas shower stall, as if our homemade mud concoction had been a mask I could hide behind to preserve the sanctity and the honesty of my true identity.

I wondered, as I twirled a strand of my still-wet hair around my now-spotless finger, if all of the other patients who came to The Institute had felt the same way on their first day. They must have been violated too; they must have been dehumanized and sanitized and sterilized the same way I had been. To be honest, up until that moment, I had thought of the real asylum residents as crazy—as laughable characters from a Jack Nicholson movie or a Batman cartoon. But they were people too, or at least they had been once, before they were demoralized by Dr. Caleb and his team of sadists.

My thoughts turned to Chase. Had he met Caleb too? Had he been scrubbed and stripped and poked and prodded and needled with inane questions?

Somehow, I didn't think so.

Hoagie had been right. There was something weird about that place, something off. The staff were like robots, completely disinterested in the people who needed their help. They didn't seem to care at all who came and went amongst them, and they hadn't even tried to establish my identity when they admitted me. They had probably assumed the police had already processed Chase. I wouldn't be surprised if they had just locked him up in a lonely, cell-like room upon his arrival and thrown away the key, leaving only a tiny slot in the door open so they could shovel in pills every few hours to keep him quiet.

I couldn't think about this anymore.

I stood up and began to pace around the small, mostly empty dorm room, listening to nothing but the sound of my feet slapping against the laminate. I crossed over to the other empty bed, the mirror image of my own green-quilted twin mattress, and puzzled over the neatness of its hospital corners.

I hoped they didn't expect mine to look like that in the morning.

I crossed back to my own bed, passing a tiny metal desk that was bolted to both the floor and the wall behind it. There was nothing on the desktop to signify that my as-yet-unseen roommate had either a personality or an identity. For all I could tell, no one had ever even set foot in that room before I had that afternoon.

There were curtains above the desk made out of a pale, gauzy sort of lace, and my heart leapt at the possibility of a glimpse at the outside world. My hopes were dashed, however, when I drew back the sheers to reveal nothing more than a wide expanse of blank plaster.

I felt my skin begin to crawl as I realized that I was trapped —trapped like the rat from my metaphor.

I willed myself to remain calm. I would be no good to anyone, let alone Chase, if I started freaking out now. Still, though, there was a tremor in my hands and a knot the size of a baseball in my stomach as I climbed back onto the bed and drew my robe closed so tight that it cut into my armpits.

Before I could spiral too far into insanity, however, the door to my room opened. Quietly, dully, a young woman around my age shuffled into the room, dragging her white-slippered feet across the cold floor as she made her way over to the second bed. I watched her as she crawled across the top sheet, moving like a malaised slug as she dragged herself to the middle of the comforter and lay down, flat on her back. Her eyes were blank as she stared up at the white stucco ceiling, and her wispy dark hair was spread out limply atop her green pillowcase like a clump of dying snakes.

That's when I really got scared.

What was wrong with her? Had the doctors made her that way, or had she been like that before? I had never heard of a mental illness turning someone into a lifeless zombie. But if the doctors *had* done that to her, they would certainly do the same to me! It was only a matter of time.

I sprang off the bed again and darted toward the door, which Sybil had left ajar. I was just grabbing the knob and mentally apologizing to Chase for choosing to save my own ass over his when she spoke.

"You're the new Jane Doe, right?"

I froze, rooted to the spot.

Her voice was slow and languid, much like what I imagined a turtle would sound like if it could talk. "You're the one who can't speak."

It wasn't a question, really. She must have known all about me already, though I had no idea how.

Reluctantly, I turned to her and nodded.

She hadn't moved a muscle. She was still just lying there, motionless, seemingly comatose, staring at nothing on the ceiling.

"My last roommate couldn't talk either," she went on, her voice so painfully laggard and thick that it made my amped-up brain hurt to listen to it. "She killed herself last Thursday. Right there on that bed."

That was it.

Without a gulp or a gasp or a glance back in her direction, I swung the door open and shot off down the hall as fast as my linguini legs could carry me.

13

My slick, slippery bare feet pounded against the glossy tiles as I ran, full-speed, down the hall. I skidded gracelessly around one corner, then another and another, trying so hard to put distance between me and that dungeon-esque room that I didn't even stop to think about where I was going. My heart thudded like a racehorse's hooves as my breath came in raspy gasps that had more to do with blind terror than with my clumsy running, and I could barely see through the filmy blur of anxiety that only got thicker the harder I ran.

But I kept running.

I hung a left and dodged a large, plastic potted plant as I started down another hallway, just as white, just as maddeningly claustrophobic as all the others. I reached the end of that one in two seconds flat, and was just starting to turn down another when I ran into something with a loud, bone-crunching "crack."

I bounced off and fell down, flopping onto my back like a limp fish as someone leaned over me, their breath hot in my flushed face.

"Oh, child, I'm sorry!"

I blinked rapidly in confusion, trying to recapture the wind that had been knocked out of me. After a moment, my panicked, darting eyes were almost able to focus on the face above me: a large, round, black face full of more sparkling white teeth than I had seen in my entire lifetime.

"You okay, baby?"

I frowned, wondering if I was hallucinating. The old, slightly wrinkled woman was a dead-ringer for Aunt Jemima— up to and including a weird, whitish scarf (or was it a bandage?) wrapped around her hair. This, combined with the completely overdone and offensive stereotype she was playing into, made me want to pinch myself to see if I was dreaming.

"Aw, sugar, I bet you were just hurryin' down to the cafeteria for supper, huh?" She laughed, helping me up. "You look like you could use it, you skinny little thang!"

As I awkwardly got to my feet, I noticed several things that I should have noticed long before. First, she was dressed just like me, in a clunky green gown and a thin, holey white robe. Secondly, she appeared to have smuggled in an entire drugstore's worth of makeup, most of which she had applied in copious measures to her blue eyelids and gunky, goopy red lips.

Thirdly, she was a man.

Though her smile was wide and feminine and her massive bosom was crushing my shoulder blade as she reached around behind me to beat the floor dust off my back, I could see an enormous, plum-sized Adam's apple jutting out at me between her strong chin and thick, sinewy, undeniably masculine neck.

I nodded weakly, trying not to stare at the hint of black beard stubble along her jawline.

"Well, come on then, girl," he/she boomed, his/her voice deep and confusingly gender non-specific, "let's go get us some grub!"

With that, Aunt Jemima's transgendered body double

slipped his/her arm through mine and led me down the corridor while I used my free fingers to pinch my left thigh so hard that it hurt.

Nope. Not dreaming.

She navigated the length of hallway much more purposefully and efficiently than I had. Her white slippered feet never so much as paused when she reached a cross section of identical-looking hallways, and her face never lost its benign, matronly smile as she held me close to her side, patting my elbow in reassurance.

"You're the new Jane Doe, huh?" she asked conversationally, as we entered the now-vacant receptionist's office.

I nodded, reminding myself to stay mum.

"I thought so," she said with a nod, patting my hand now. "I can always tell the newbies by the look on their scared little faces!"

I wasn't quite sure how to respond to that without speaking, so I gave her a brief, nervous smile and kept walking.

"I'm Troy Cooper."

I could feel my eyes widen in surprise, but I kept my cool and nodded, as if I talked to big-bosomed men all the time.

"But everybody around here calls me Big Momma."

That time I couldn't hide my disbelief. I glanced over at her and raised my eyebrows. Obviously I wasn't the only one who thought she was living a movie.

"Like Martin Lawrence," she explained, "in *Big Momma's House*. Get it?"

I nodded as if it all made sense, but before she could speak again, we reached the big, square, glass doors of the cafeteria. Troy Cooper/Big Momma had barely gotten them open when I slipped out of her grip and pushed past her to dart across the half-empty room in a state of complete and unexpected ecstasy.

Windows! I had forgotten about the windows!

The entire front of the room was made up of nothing but pure, uninterrupted, translucent glass, showcasing the gorgeous blacktop parking lot, the tall, majestic oak trees, and the beautiful, beautiful, *beautiful* emerald green grass just outside. I could almost smell the freedom in the early evening air as I put my slick-palmed hands against the door, peering hungrily out at the open space beyond, where nothing was closed off and nothing was small and confining and (most importantly) nothing, absolutely nothing, was painted white.

"Nice view, isn't it?"

I jumped as a deep, husky male voice crooned in my ear. I quickly turned to see a tall, gaunt-looking septuagenarian leering down at me with an odd, suggestive smile on his face and a sick, thirsty sort of look in his amber-colored eyes.

I shrugged noncommittally and attempted to move away, back toward Big Momma and the small cluster of patients who were beginning to line up around a table at the other end of the room.

"I'm Norman," the creepy man said, extending a hand. It was covered in long, curly, gray hair.

Trying not to wince, I took it and gave it a quick shake.

"Ooooohhhh," he purred, rolling his eyes back into his head, "that's nice."

I was just on the verge of slapping the perverted werewolf in the face when one of the orderlies rushed over and hauled him away.

Dripping with revulsion, it almost didn't register that the helpful orderly that had come to my rescue was none other than my very own Hoagie James. Before I could do anything with this knowledge, however, a scrawny, feeble-looking female patient approached me from the right to take the werewolf's place.

"That's Norman," she whispered under her breath, her

bright, electric blue eyes enormous beneath her shock of frizzy white hair. "He's a sex addict."

I nodded. I could have figured that one out for myself.

"I was a sex addict myself once," she informed me, her voice wistful as she wrapped her bony little fingers around my bicep, "but not anymore. Now I'm a meth addict. See?"

Before I could fully comprehend what she had just said, she spread her thin, papery lips apart and revealed a wide, toothless grin. Her gums were blackened in places, and her tongue was an odd, cottony white that kind of made me want to vomit.

I nodded quickly in an attempt to get her to close her mouth, but she kept on smiling. "I was a gambling addict once too," she went on, beaming with pride as she began to herd me over toward the back of the room with the others, "and an alcoholic, a coke fiend, a pothead..."

I stopped listening and started frantically searching the room for Hoagie. He had to be there, I had just seen him! There were about a half-dozen young men in scrubs and lace-less white shoes, all assisting the patients as they lined up along the mirrored wall, but not one of them was my blue-eyed, sweet-faced accomplice, and none of them could soothe the gnawing, anxious, frightened feeling in my gut.

I shook off my toothless cling-on as we reached the queue, and I made my way to the end of the line, feeling even more jittery than before. This was going to be my biggest challenge thus far. I didn't need anyone to tell me what was happening now; this was where they were going to give me the pills that I wasn't supposed to take, the ones Hoagie couldn't identify—the ones that had most likely turned my poor creepy roommate into a zombie.

I could see the front of the line as it slowly moved forward. Cup after tiny white cup of pills was handed out to the now-silent patients, who then had to stand before the stern, imposing figure of Dr. Caleb as they swallowed their medication. After checking their mouths, Dr. Caleb would nod authoritatively and hand them a silver tray of food, which appeared to be comprised of several piles of mashed potatoes in various colors and consistencies.

How the hell was I supposed to trick Caleb? Even standing a hundred feet away, I could see the steely glint in his eye and the no-nonsense look on his face. If I tried anything fishy, he'd notice for sure. Then my cover would be blown.

Oh well, I thought wryly, my nervous stomach doing back flips, *at least then maybe I'd get to go home.*

This pessimistic thought was oddly comforting. Home. Had I really only left it a few hours ago? It felt like days or even weeks since I had last seen my own room or sat on my own bed or breathed in the scent of my own mother's cooking.

My anxious stomach was morphing into a hungry one when suddenly someone leaned against me from behind, pressing something into my left hand.

Startled, I looked back to see Hoagie's chalk white face, inches from my own, as he scooted over to the wall beside me, pretending to wipe off a smudge with a wet yellow sponge.

"Sorry," he grunted loudly, as if we had never met, as if he didn't know how hard I had to fight to resist the urge to jump up and kiss all of his cute, little-boy freckles.

I gave him a shaky shrug and closed my hand around the small square of paper he had so subtly passed me. Maybe he would make a good spy after all.

"Put it in your pocket," he instructed, his voice a breathy whisper, as he concentrated so intently on the wall that I half expected his eyes to bore a hole in it.

I did as he said, slipping the note into the floppy front pocket of my flimsy white robe.

"And don't take the pills," he reminded me.

Then, just like that, he was gone.

14

With Hoagie's unread note burning a hole in my pocket, I slowly shuffled one step closer to the head of the line—or the end of the line, depending on whether or not I could come up with a clever ruse in the next two to four minutes.

Despite the direness of the situation however, I felt oddly giddy. Hoagie hadn't forgotten about me. He was right there in the cafeteria, mere yards away, and he was clearly watching out for me. He had already saved me from the creepy, hairy sex addict, which only reaffirmed the promise he had made me as we had entered the facility.

"I won't let anything happen to you," he had told me then, and now I knew I could believe him.

This newfound faith gave me courage, gave me strength, gave me back the spark of life and ingenuity that had almost been extinguished by the near-paralyzing paranoia and fear I had been feeling since I had been admitted.

I can do this, I thought to myself, clenching my fists in determination.

Then I grinned.

I had it: the answer I'd been seeking, the schematics to the scheme I needed to get me out of taking Dr. Caleb's drugs.

I resisted the urge to laugh maniacally as I raised my right hand up toward my face. Just as I had expected, the loose white sleeve of my robe fell open to form a large, hollow pocket on the inside of my wrist, completely invisible to anyone who happened to be standing in front of me.

My Grandpa Max, a connoisseur of tall tales and cheesy old man jokes, had spent many a summer night babysitting Chase and me when we were little. He had played with us and read to us and told us funny stories that can still make me laugh.

He also taught us magic tricks.

———

One day, when I was about eight years old, I came in from the backyard, carrying a cup full of dirty coins I had dug up from beneath Grandpa Max's old oak tree (which, looking back, he had probably buried there himself...). I had been so excited that I had climbed up onto his lap and shook the cup of change under his nose, splattering him with mud from my grubby hands.

"You'd better watch it, Charlotte Ann," he had warned me, a twinkle in his kindly green eyes, "If you don't act right, I'll make all that money disappear!"

Of course, I was hooked. Money was great, but disappearing money was magic.

"Show me, show me!" I begged him, shoving the cup into his weathered hand. "Please, Grandpa Max?"

He sighed dramatically, as if I were putting him out. "Well, I guess I could show you...if you promise to go right back outside afterward and fill up that big ol' hole you just dug!"

"DEAL!" I crowed, clapping my hands together. "Now make 'em disappear!"

As I held my breath in anticipation, my entire little eight-year-old body buzzing with excitement, he shook the cup of coins and balanced the bottom of it on his flat, upturned palm. He flashed me a look of stern concentration. "Okay," he instructed, squinting at the cup now, "say the magic words."

"ABRA KADABRA!" I shouted, squeezing my little palms together over my chest as if I were praying to the great David Copperfield, patron saint of illusionists.

Grandpa Max nodded. Then, without any further ado, he lifted the cup upward, tipped it toward his mouth, and proceeded to drink the entire batch of coins. I clapped my hands over my own mouth in horrified fascination as I heard the pennies and nickels clink-clink-clink their way down his throat and into his stomach.

"Grandpa Max," I gasped in disbelief, as he licked his lips and wiped them on his sleeve.

"Ah..." He sighed. "Delicious."

My mouth fell open.

"You want some?" he asked, proffering me the cup.

I just stared at him, my tiny little second grade mind completely blown.

"Here, hold this for me and I'll get you some."

Numbly, I took the cup and held it in both hands. Then, Grandpa Max lifted both his arms, tugging on the cuffs of his sleeves. I could still hear the change jiggling in his belly as he got situated. "Say the magic words one more time," he told me.

"Abra Kadabra," I whispered, enraptured.

Then, with an artful flourish, he held his right hand over the mouth of the cup and tilted it downward, sending a multitude of dirty coins spilling back into it from inside the sleeve of his red flannel shirt.

I approached Dr. Caleb and accepted his tiny white cup without argument.

"Those are to settle your nerves," he informed me, pointing to the two diamond-shaped pills he had just passed me. "The first night here is always stressful."

I placed the flat bottom of the paper cup in the palm of my right hand and nodded, trying not to let him see the savage, wicked sort of thrill I felt over fooling him. He handed me a second cup full of water and I nodded in appreciation. Without a shadow of a doubt in my own prowess, I shook my arm to loosen my sleeve, certain that he would assume that I was just jostling the pills into a better position. I took one last, deep, hopeful breath, then I raised the cup to my lips.

Immediately, I felt the pills tumble past my chin and down into the fold I had created in my robe, bouncing against my skin like Mexican Jumping Beans, hidden from the doctor by the angle of my arm. After the pills had settled, I leaned my head back even further and poured the cold, clear water into my mouth. I swallowed hard, then looked back at him, as if awaiting further instructions.

There was a tense moment as he just stared at me, seemingly waiting for something. I was just beginning to consider that my ruse had not been as clever as I thought when he spoke again.

"I have to check your mouth now," he said impatiently, and I relaxed.

Slowly, as if embarrassed, I tentatively opened my mouth and he leaned in, peering behind my teeth and between my gums.

"Now lift up your tongue."

I did as he said. With a satisfied nod, he handed me my tray of "food" and hustled me along so he could move on to the next patient.

As I headed over to join Big Momma at the table nearest the big, beautiful front window, I couldn't resist the urge to whisper, "Abra Kadabra."

15

Still flushed with victory, I took my self-appointed place at the end of the long silver table. Feigning an itch on my leg, I reached down to scratch at my robe, deftly slipping the unswallowed pills into my limp-hanging pocket, where they settled against Hoagie's folded message.

The "seating" arrangements in the cafeteria were fairly loose. A patient could eat wherever he or she (or he *and* she) wanted...but they couldn't sit down to do it. I had expected someone to bring out chairs before dinner started, but there was still not a seat in sight. I had no idea what motivation was behind the "no chair" rule—whether it was safety reasons or an appalling lack of state funding—but it didn't take long for the awkwardness of it to get to me. I hadn't been standing for more than ten minutes since I had entered the room, but just the thought of being on my feet for another ten or more gave me an instant rush of fatigue. My knees were aching and my calves were burning with imaginary strain as I shifted from one leg to the other, unable to get comfortable. The table, which had been about even with my navel when I came over, now seemed to have been built for a midget. I had to slump my shoulders and lean down low to scoop up a bite of green mush before standing all the way back up to pause with it near my mouth.

This must be how they keep them crazy... I thought to myself, as my ankles swelled with hypochondria and I inhaled the odd, sour scent of mashed peas or pureed pickles from my spork.

I had expected Big Momma to make conversation as we ate, but he was silent. I watched out of the corner of my eye as she raised her own spork to her mouth mechanically before gumming the thick, goopy rations like a cow chewing cud. Frowning, I tilted my head to get a better look at her.

His big brown eyes, so lively just a few minutes ago, were now dull and droopy. Her blue-shadowed lids hung low and her false eyelashes skimmed her cheekbones as she appeared to doze off, her jaw slack.

Alarmed, I glanced around the room. There were about thirty patients in all, some of whom giggled and chatted like school kids at recess as they choked down their grotesque dinner. Most of them, though, seemed to be in various stages of unconsciousness. A young woman with jet black hair and bright green eyes was leaning against her table, struggling to fight off the early arrival of the sandman. Another woman, a redhead, was staring at the window behind me, her face blank and her food untouched. Norman, the sex-addicted werewolf, had slumped over against his tablemate, leaning heavily against the second (equally stoned) man's shoulder.

As I watched with rising dread, the few remaining chatterboxes talked themselves into silence, ending their conversations mid-sentence with bland, detached looks and odd, faraway smiles that slipped from their faces as their heads rolled down onto their chests.

With a splat, my new toothless, meth-head friend fell face-first into her tray, and dinner was over.

My panic was mounting as the orderlies assembled, leading

the zombie patients back to their dorm rooms, two by two. I glanced at Big Momma again. Though she was standing right next to me, she might as well have been on another planet. Her eyes were glazed over and her shoulders were slumped; she looked as if it was all she could do just to keep standing up.

It must be the pills, I thought, feeling my own turn to lead in my pocket. *This must be what Hoagie was talking about.*

I would have to just pretend to be drugged, that's all. I would have to convince them that I had taken the medicine, or I would end up just like the others.

A tall, handsome blonde orderly was making his way to our table, and I did my best to arrange my features into a limp, emotionless mask.

That's when I heard the hair-raisingly familiar clink of chains scraping across the linoleum floor.

16

It felt as if someone had punched me in the stomach.

I didn't have to look up to see what was making that sound. I had learned it by heart at the police station. But it was louder now, and it shook me to my very core as Chase—poor, sweet, surely innocent Chase—was dragged into the room like a dog on a leash by a wide, stocky orderly whose scowl could stop a grown man's heart. My brother's hands, legs, and throat had all been shackled and one long, clunky silver chain linked him to two other prisoners, each of whom stared around the room with eyes so dead that I almost believed they were reanimated corpses.

Chase, who was at the head of the line, was dressed in a long robe and gown like mine. His, though, was covered in muck and blood and gore, and his kind, clean-cut face was swollen and bruised, as if he had been beaten with a crowbar. His left eye was hidden within a deep, dark, mass of puffy purple tissue, but somehow, as if he could sense something amiss in the still air of the mostly empty cafeteria, his right eye found me.

I felt a jolt as our gazes locked. I could see the recognition on his face as a wild, sick sort of horror dawned on him and he stopped cold.

The two other men staggered into him, and the beefy orderly shouted at him to move, but he didn't. One of the other prisoners barked at him to keep walking, but he wouldn't. He was staring at me fearfully, anxiously, as he took in my own robe and gown.

The blonde orderly had reached Big Momma and me. He stood between us and took us each by the elbow, checking our bracelets and coaxing us, his poor, stupid, drug-addled charges, out into the aisle.

I tried to keep my face slack, but I couldn't. Chase was looking at me with such pain, such pure agony, in his big brown eye that it felt like someone was shoving a knife into my pounding heart.

"Charlie," he croaked, his voice achingly hoarse as the orderly led me away, "Oh, God, Charlie no..."

I could feel the hot tears stinging my eyes, but I had to stay calm. I had to stay loose. I had to stay mute and dumb and dead to the world if we were ever going to make it out of there in one piece.

I had to be strong. For Chase.

"No..." he said, "no...please, no..."

I turned my burning eyes straight ahead, pretending to be mollified by the orderly's kind reassurances that the big scary man wasn't going to hurt us. I tried to concentrate on the slip-sliding of Big Momma's slippers as they scraped across the floor and the firm but sympathetic grip of the orderly's soft hand on my elbow, but those things couldn't distract me from the look on Chase's face, and nothing could block out the ragged, guttural scream that followed us out into the hallway as my big brother called out my name.

17

Keep it together, *Charlie*, I warned myself, barely able to breathe through the knot of self-loathing lodged in my throat.

I should have waved at him. I should have smiled at him or winked or nodded conspiratorially. I should have given him some sort of sign that I was okay! I shouldn't have let him believe that I was too far gone to recognize my own flesh and blood brother, and I shouldn't have left him there all alone, tied to a bunch of zombified cadavers that were nothing but a vision of his future self!

The blonde orderly closed the door to my dorm, and Sybil and I were left alone in a thick, cloying darkness that threatened to suffocate me as I lay atop my too-firm mattress, blinking up at the ceiling. I wanted to cry or scream or run or punch something as hard as I could (I wonder if Sybil was awake...) but instead, I slid out of bed and tiptoed over to the closed door, beneath which a tiny sliver of yellowish light was pooling on the floor.

With fumbling fingers, I removed the square of paper from my pocket and unfolded it as I lay down on my stomach on the wood-paneling. As quietly as I could, I smoothed the paper flat against the laminate and used the lemony glow from the hallway to read the coded message Hoagie had slipped me half an hour ago.

For a second, I couldn't make out any of the tiny, scrunched-up letters scrawled across the center of the torn sheet of loose-leaf. Then, finally, after some shifting and a whole lot of squinting, the message became clear.

FIRST FLOOR RESTROOM.

"'First floor restroom?'" I mouthed stupidly, too preoccupied with visions of Chase's tortured expression to think clearly. I felt like the kid in *A Christmas Story*; Hoagie might as well have sent me an ad for Ovaltine for all the good that did me.

Then I got it.

I could have kicked myself as I leapt to my feet. He wanted me to meet him! Or to make sure that I emptied my bladder before I went to bed... Either way, it would give me something to do, something to take my mind off Chase, at least for a little while.

I didn't waste a second. I yanked open the door and slipped out into the hall, too exhilarated by the thought of actually having a chance to interact with another fully-functioning human being to think to scan for any hospital workers that might be lurking around.

Luckily, there wasn't a soul in sight as I made my way down the long, narrow corridor to the skinny white door that read "HANDICAP ACCESSIBLE."

I had used this restroom earlier and then, like now, I had no idea whether the facilities were men's, women's, or unisex. It didn't matter though. It was the only bathroom I had seen on that floor, and it had to be the one where my accomplice was waiting for me.

Slowly, I pushed the swinging door open, and was startled to find that the room was pitch black. My lips were on the verge of whispering Hoagie's name when someone hissed, "Shut the door."

A thrill of foreboding streaked up my spine. Was it Hoagie who had spoken? I had only known him for a few hours, so it was impossible for me to recognize his low, hushed voice. For all I knew, it was Dr. Caleb, lying in wait with a fistful of pills to ram down my throat when I tried to scream.

I hesitated, barely breathing. Then, swallowing the objections of both my common sense and my better judgment, I took a leap of faith and stepped into the room, letting the heavy door fall shut behind me.

Suddenly the room was lit up by a bright, dazzling white light. I blinked, momentarily blinded by the searing glow of the overhead lamps, which slowly came into focus as I took one more cautious step into the room.

As my eyes adjusted, I turned to locate my could-be assailant, but found only Hoagie, standing near the row of sinks along the side wall, his hands in his pockets and a shy, worried look on his face.

"Hey, Jane," he said quietly, a hint of a smile playing across this thin lips.

And that's when I lost it.

Before I could stop myself, I had bounded across the room and thrown myself into his arms, squeezing mine around his neck as the tears that I had been fighting for ten long, agonizing days spilled out onto the shoulder of his scrubs. He seemed a bit alarmed at first, but then he squeezed me right back, his grip firm and strong and almost as desperate as mine was. "Oh, Charlie, was it awful?"

I nodded, forgetting, once again, that I hardly knew this person.

"Man," he muttered miserably, squeezing me even tighter as

I sniffled, inhaling the scent of his lemony cleaning supplies, "I knew this was a bad idea."

I pulled back then, getting a temporary grip on myself.

"No," I said, wiping my streaming eyes with the backs of my trembling hands. That was the first time I had heard myself speak in almost a whole day, and I wondered if my voice always sounded so weak and broken. "We have to do it. We have to save Chase."

Hoagie's eyes were wide as he stared at me, looking as if he was agonized by my agony.

I guess he had forgotten that we were strangers too.

"I saw him," I choked, and he instinctively reached out to grab my hand, as if he couldn't stop himself from comforting me. "Chase, I mean. In the cafeteria. He was in chains." I let out a small, squeaky half-sob. "Someone beat him up! Hoagie, we have to help him!"

By then I was bawling again, and Hoagie pulled me back into his embrace, rubbing my back as he whispered, "I know, I know."

"He saw me, too!" I hiccupped, repulsed once more by my own actions—or, more precisely, inactions. "But I pretended not to recognize him! I pretended I was drugged. I had to! But he saw me! He tried to talk to me, but I wouldn't listen. He was screaming my name when I left!"

"Shhh..." Hoagie exhaled, his breath hot against my already-burning ear. "I know, I heard him. I was there too. But it's gonna be alright."

"Why would I do that? Why would I just let him think that I—"

"Because you had to, that's why," Hoagie interrupted sharply, loosening his grip so he could lean back and look me in the watery eyes. "If you hadn't pretended to be drugged, they would have done worse to you than they did to him. Trust me. You did the right thing."

I stared at him for a moment, unconvinced. Then I sighed. "Maybe you're right..." I conceded, wiping my snotty nose on my robe. "But what good have I done him so far? All I've managed to do is not get caught sneaking into an insane asylum."

"And you outsmarted Dr. Caleb," Hoagie reminded me, a real smile spreading across his stubbly face now. "Tell me, how did you get away with not taking those pills? I could have sworn I saw you swallow them both!"

It was my turn to break into a shaky smile.

"A magician never reveals her secrets," I told him, feeling a faint echo of my earlier pride as I pulled the little diamond-shaped capsules out of my pocket and placed them in his hand.

"Holy cow," he marveled, his surprise turning him into a character from *Happy Days*. "Do you realize what this means?"

"That I'm awesome at sleight of hand?"

"No. Well, yeah. But it also means that now I can send these to a lab and get them analyzed. Then we can find out what they're *really* drugging all the patients with!"

"That's great!" I exclaimed, buoyed by the possibility that perhaps the day wasn't a total loss.

"No, it's beyond great," he insisted, his blue eyes fierce as they met mine. "Do you know how many lives you might have saved with this?"

"Well it's not like they're actually *killing* anyone here..." I countered, suddenly bashful.

"Maybe not physically, but mentally and spiritually they are, believe me."

Hoagie's handsome face had hardened, and a strange, haunted look crept into his eyes. Slowly, my fledgling detective brain connected the dots and I felt my heart swell with sympathy.

"Hoagie, can I ask you something?"

"Yeah, ask me anything."

"You knew someone who was a patient here, didn't you?"

The hardness in his face fell away, leaving a soft, sad, strangely vulnerable expression behind. "Yes," he replied, his voice full of melancholy as it echoed around the concrete room. "That's why I'm doing all this. My—"

I clapped my hand over his mouth.

His eyes widened in surprise, but I held a finger to my lips and cocked my head toward the door, urging him to listen. Heavy, shuffling footsteps were dragging themselves along the hall just outside the restroom. The steps got louder and clumsier as they got closer, and I couldn't help but picture an enormous, green-tinted, undead creature hulking its way down the hall, just looking for someone to crush to death.

Before I could blink the image of Frankenstein's monster out of my brain, though, Hoagie scooped me up, off my feet, and into one of the three large, handicapped-accessible stalls along the back wall of the bathroom. Wordlessly, he directed me to step up onto the rim of the low toilet seat as he swung the door shut and locked it. As he joined me atop the ice-cold commode, I could feel the germs squirming beneath my bare feet before crawling their way up my legs.

Maybe I really was crazy...

Just as I was beginning to wobble on the seat like a surfer losing his balance on an unruly boogie board, Hoagie made a sharp "pssst" sound and pointed at something near the floor.

At first, I thought he had seen a bug. I was just about to tell him that I was *not* about to kill it for him when I realized that he wasn't pointing at the ground, he was pointing at the stall door. The bottom of the wide, white-painted slab of wood ended nearly a foot and a half above the linoleum, leaving our feet clearly visible to anyone who happened to enter the restroom.

As one unit, Hoagie and I scrambled up onto the tiny toilet tank above, hanging onto each other as we both teetered precariously on the rectangular lid, each with one butt cheek dangling over the edge. We had barely had time to stabilize ourselves when the door to the bathroom opened with a long, low creak.

We froze, arms wrapped around shoulders and hands gripping clothing in the world's most awkward position as we both held our breath and each other, hunching down so as not to be seen over the top of the short white door.

"Grrrmmmmuuhrmmm..." growled a deep, guttural, oddly familiar voice as the heavy, shuffling footsteps moved into the room. "Grrrmmmm....pooooooooop...."

I had to clap my hand over my mouth to quell an incredibly ill-timed fit of the giggles. Hoagie gripped me tight around the shoulders to balance me, compensating for the loss of my grabbing hand with his straining bicep.

"Poooooop...grrrrmmmmm...."

Even Hoagie was not immune to the absurdity of the situation, however. As the monster grumbled again, he quickly pressed his grinning lips into my neck to stifle a snort, half of which escaped to flutter a strand of my long hair and send a tingly, tickling sensation running down my back.

It wasn't so funny, though, when the creature's feet appeared below the stall door.

18

I RECOGNIZED those slippered feet instantly.

The faceless, feces-obsessed monster was none other than Big Momma, my very own gender-bending dinner date. Her brown, chunky cankles seemed to be straining to hold her up as she swayed, grabbing the handle on the outside of the door. With a dull moan, she gave it a yank.

Nothing happened.

She yanked again, harder.

I met Hoagie's wide eyes as she yanked once more, this time so hard that it shook the entire exterior of the stall structure. The door was locked, but the mechanism holding it shut was weak, poised and ready to break apart at any moment. All it would take was one good tug...

She yanked again and I called out shrilly, "Occupied!"

She stopped, bewildered by the presence of another life form on her planet. Then she grunted. "Mmmm..." she mumbled, "pooooooop..."

I was too relieved to laugh then, and too disgusted to laugh later as the creature that had once been Aunt Jemima's drag queen doppelganger slumped into the stall next to us and plopped down on the toilet with a loud, indecent-sounding sigh.

I tried not to listen as she proceeded to do her business, but I flinched with every splash, drip, and drizzle of water until finally, after what felt like a lifetime, Big Momma stood up and shuffled back out into the room.

"Mmmmm…" she moaned contentedly, sounding like a satisfied ogre, "goooood poooop."

Then she left, without either flushing the toilet or washing her hands.

The door had barely swung shut behind her when Hoagie leapt off the tank and told me, "That was officially the most disgusting thing I have ever witnessed."

"Tell me about it," I agreed, clambering gracelessly down from the toilet and rubbing my sore left butt cheek.

The air reeked with what smelled like an entire sewer's worth of human excrement and I crinkled up my nose as Hoagie held the stall door open for me.

"Geez," he said, using the inside of his elbow to cover his freckled nose, "what the heck are they feeding you guys here?"

"I wouldn't know," I said with a shrug, equally repulsed, "I didn't eat anything."

"Let's go get you some food then," he suggested, taking my hand and leading me toward the bathroom door.

"Anything to get us out of here," I replied, my eyes beginning to water with the sting of the rancid stench. "I can't take any more of this smelly 'pooooop…'"

Hoagie laughed so hard and so loud that it startled me, and I realized my sarcastic humor must have caught him off guard. After a few hours in the internment camp style mental institution, I had almost forgotten what genuine laughter sounded like.

"What?" I asked innocently.

"Nothing," he chuckled, reaching for the door handle.

"Nothing but 'poooooop'..." I groaned, doing my best Big Momma/Frankenstein impersonation.

"Stop it," he whispered, clearly enjoying this dorky exchange as much as I was. "Someone'll hear us!"

"Okay, I'll stop," I said solemnly, settling my face into a semi-serious frown.

"Good."

He reached out for the handle again, and I just couldn't resist. His laughter was like a drug to me, one that was surely more potent than any pill that The Institute could manage to slip me. I ran my fingers up his arm like a spider as I moaned, "Ggrrmmm...poooop..."

He slammed the door shut and whirled on me, grabbing me around the waist and putting his work-calloused hand over my mouth as he grinned, his eyes sparkling with barely repressed laughter. "I said quit it!"

I couldn't stop giggling as he dragged me away from the door, his palm pressed lightly against my lips as he pretended to get stern with me.

"Listen here, Charlie, you'd better cut it out right now. This is a serious mission we're on! If we get caught, it'll be all your fault."

I shrugged coyly, batting my eyelashes at him, and his grin spread wider.

"Now I'm gonna let you go, and you're gonna promise not to do it again, okay?"

I shrugged noncommittally, still giggling like a mischievous little kid.

"Charlie!"

I sighed, my breath moistening his palm as I rolled my eyes. Then I nodded.

"Okay, that's better."

He removed his hand from my face, but kept his other arm

locked snug around my white-robed waist. He stared at me expectantly for a moment, and I stared back, the picture of innocence.

"Okay," he said again, satisfied.

"Okay," I repeated, mimicking his deep, manly voice. "Let's get out of here and away from all this poo—"

He clamped his fingers over my mouth again, but this time I was ready. With a wide, wicked grin, I stuck out my tongue and licked his palm like a Golden Retriever. Immediately he jerked his hand away as I guffawed, but his eyes were still dancing with laughter.

"You're sick!" he said, trying to sound scandalized, as he wiped his big wet hand on his pant leg.

"Takes one to know one," I shot back, positively elated by our lame tête-à-tête. "That's your payback for covering me in slobber earlier!"

He looked impressed as he took my hand again, purposely using the one I had just spit on. "Alright." He grinned. "Well played. Now we're even. Can we please go?"

"Yes," I replied happily. Could it really have been just minutes ago that I was bawling my eyes out? "Let's get out of here."

He gave me one last humorously affectionate look, then he reached out for the door handle one more time. Before he could touch it, though, the door flew open and hit the wall with a bang and there, silhouetted in the doorway in all of his intimidating, authoritative glory, stood Dr. John Caleb.

19

THE DOCTOR'S eyes were wild as he stared around the room, taking in everything and nothing at the same time. Though still tall and strong and imposing, he appeared to have gone completely mad. Dark, painful-looking purple bags hung beneath his sunken amber eyes, and his stony face was lined with wrinkles and cracks that hadn't been there before. His short, graying hair was disheveled, and his big, powerful hands shook as he crashed into the restroom, just as unstable as Big Momma had been, maybe even more so.

I turned to Hoagie, poised to speak, but he shook his head to stop me. Though we were standing right in front of him, the doctor appeared to be oblivious to our presence, and to alert him to it would be suicidal.

Slowly, carefully, Hoagie and I inched toward the open door, hoping to slip out before Dr. Jekyll's transformation was complete. I had barely gotten a toe out into the hall when suddenly Dr. Caleb let out a blood-curdling shriek and fell to the floor, unconscious, clutching his stomach.

"Go, go, go," Hoagie muttered, pushing me out the door.

"But—" I started, my moral compass wavering at the

thought of leaving such a sick person behind, regardless of his evil affiliations.

"*Go!*" he hissed back, closing the matter to any further discussion.

Before I could make any more protests, he hustled me down that hall and another and another, leading me through a maze so complicated and convoluted that I would never be able to find my way back to the start. Wall after white-painted wall flew past in a blur as we half-walked, half-ran the full length of the building twice, coming to a stop in front of another narrow white door. Panting like a beached whale with asthma, I looked up at the big, black "109" printed across the top.

"My dorm!" I exclaimed, somewhat accusingly, as Hoagie wiped away the sweat that had sprung up across his furrowed brow.

I felt cheated. I had thought we were running away, escaping to somewhere safe (or at least not crazy-adjacent). But he had just led me right back to my white plaster jail cell, in which lay nothing but my zombified roommate and the sea of worry and self-doubt that I had been trying so hard to swim my way out of.

"Shhh," Hoagie hissed, removing a thick square of folded paper from his pants pocket. "No talking, remember?"

"But—"

"Charlie, please." His own eyes were a bit wild as they checked for guards or other escaped mental patients behind us. "You'll be safe in there. Someone dosed Caleb, and I don't want anyone thinking it was you."

I crossed my arms and gave him a look that said, "And what about you?"

"I'll be fine, I promise," he assured me.

I sulked. It was one thing to be unexpectedly thrust into danger with nothing but your wits and your guts to get you out of it, but it was much worse to be sidelined when the level of intrigue was skyrocketing and the adventure was just heating up! I felt like a stupid, useless damsel in distress, about to be locked away in her damp, dark tower while her prince went off to fight the battle she was perfectly capable of fighting herself.

"Don't look like that," Hoagie begged me, looking pained.

I shrugged dispassionately.

He grimaced, running a hand through his hair as he checked the hallway again. "Look, I don't have time to convince you right now. Someone will find Caleb any minute, then they'll start checking all the rooms and taking roll."

I nodded, putting my pouting on hold as I realized the precarious nature of our situation.

Then came the scream from the restroom down the hall.

Hoagie leaned over and opened the door, shoving me swiftly inside the dorm. Before I could regain my balance, he wrapped his right arm around my waist and shoved his wad of papers into my pocket with his free hand.

"Please be careful," he breathed into my ear, his chest pressed close against mine.

Then he kissed me on the forehead and hurried off down the hall.

20

I BARELY HAD time to process Hoagie's oddly intimate gesture before several of the doors along the hallway began to open. Within seconds, bleary-eyed, pillow-creased faces were poking out everywhere, all searching for the source of the commotion.

I snapped my door shut.

I had to get rid of those papers in my pocket—fast. I wasn't exactly sure what was on them, but I was positive that whatever Hoagie had written would be incriminating for the both of us. If the guards at The Institute were half as intelligent as Dr. Caleb, they wouldn't call off the manhunt for his poisoner after just a cursory bed check and a glance at a patient roster. They would check our pockets, check our beds, check each and every one of our bodily nooks and crannies, until they found the evidence they needed to lead them to their culprit.

I sprinted to the bed, toying with the idea of shoving the folded pages between the sheet and the mattress, but the fitted material was sewn to the bed itself, as well as to two and a half sides of the upper sheets (which explained why Sybil's bed was so neat). I moved to the desk, thinking I could stow my contraband in a drawer or under a lamp, but there were none of either.

The pillow had no case to conceal anything, and the floppy, gaping pocket on my raggedy robe would be the first place they'd look.

My throat tightened when I heard someone in the hall shout "BED CHECK!" like a warden in an army barracks. I skittered around the room like a cockroach, trying to find someplace, anyplace, to hide whatever information Hoagie had passed me.

I was just starting to consider trying to eat the short stack of papers like some sort of old-timey spy (hey, at least then I wouldn't be hungry anymore), when I heard a gravelly voice to my right.

"Here."

I jumped as Sybil pushed past me, her wispy hair brushing my shoulder as she knelt down and plucked one of the false wood slats from the floor. In the shadowy yellow light that crept in from the hall, I could see a deep cavity beneath the paneling about a foot long and three inches wide. Inside were a handful of assorted pictures and envelopes and ponytail holders, as well as a stash of hard candy and red licorice. That was not what caught my attention though.

It was the pills.

Scores and scores of little, white, diamond-shaped pills filled the small cavity, each of them identical to the ones I had just slipped to Hoagie. I looked down at Sybil in amazement, but we didn't have time for chitchat. She snatched the note from my hand and shoved it under a few of her well-worn letters in one smooth, fluid, perfectly coherent motion before snapping the board back in place.

"Now get in bed and act like you're stoned," she ordered, springing up from the floor like a jungle cat and leaping into the narrow gap between her own tightly sewn covers.

I didn't need telling twice.

My heart pounded as I got to my feet and dove into my own

bed. I was just getting situated beneath the ice cold sheets when the door swung open and a bright, harsh light filled the room.

I closed my eyes tightly, feigning sleep. I could hear heavy footsteps shuffle across the floor, and I felt my body stiffen with dread beneath the straightjacket sheets.

"Sybil Parker?" barked a dull male voice.

Sybil was silent.

"Sybil Parker?" the man repeated, just as dully as he had the first time.

She mumbled something unintelligible, her half-formed words muffled by her quilt.

"Screw it," groused the voice, and the feet shuffled some more, getting closer to my bed. "Jane Doe?"

I squeezed my eyes shut even tighter, faking unconsciousness with the skill level of a six-year-old.

The footsteps moved closer.

"Jane Doe."

I wasn't sure how to play it. Should I wake up with a gasp and pretend to be startled by his presence? Or should I continue to bluff my way to the championship round of the "Worst Fake Sleeper in America" contest?

I could sense the man's hand reaching out to poke me in the shoulder when another voice called from the doorway, "Forget it, we got 'im."

The tired-sounding stranger took a step back from me as he asked, "Who was it?"

"Some patient. One of the criminally insane ones," the other guy replied casually, as if he were discussing the weather or a semi-interesting news report on traffic.

"Which one?"

"I don't know," he sighed, exasperated, "the blonde one?"

My already-racing heart jumped to warp speed.

Chase.

The first man grunted, sounding satisfied. "I knew that one was trouble when they dragged him in here. They taze 'im?"

"Hell yeah, they did. They tazed the bejeezus out of 'im!"

"Sorry I missed it," chuckled the bed checker.

Then they left, so busy laughing at my brother's misfortune that they didn't even bother to close the door behind them.

21

OH CHASE, I thought miserably, *how could you be so stupid?*

How could he do this? How could he drug a doctor—*the* doctor, by the looks of it—when he was already the number one suspect in a murder investigation? Didn't he realize how much trouble he could get into? How badly they could hurt him? And where did he even get the drugs in the first place?

I froze, half-in, half-out of my straightjacket sheets.

"Sybil?" I hissed through the shadows, momentarily forgetting my vow of silence.

She didn't reply.

I rushed over and slammed the door shut, plunging us back into darkness. "Sybil, where did you get all those pills?"

For a few seconds, nothing happened. Then I saw a glint in the blackness, and Sybil's bright eyes glowed like a cat's as they refracted what little light filtered in under the door.

"Are you a cop?" she asked, her voice rough from disuse.

"No," I replied, without weighing the consequences of telling the truth, "are you?"

"No."

I waited for her to go on, but she just stared at me, her face two pinpricks of pale light in the inky darkness.

"Well?" I urged, impatient. The adrenaline coursing through my veins was making it very hard to stand still.

"Well, what?"

"Where did you get all those pills?"

She hesitated. "Are you sure you're not a cop?"

"Oh my God," I groaned, agonized by the ludicrous nature of our circular conversation.

Too antsy to keep still any longer, I knelt down on the floor and pried up the loose board to remove my handful of papers from the shallow abyss below. I was about to seal the makeshift safe shut again when I reached in and grabbed a fistful of red licorice to go with it.

"I'm eating your candy," I informed Sybil moodily, brandishing it at her before sprawling across the laminate on my belly to read my papers in the hallway light.

Fuming, I bit off a hunk of the stale, gummy rope and unfolded the note Hoagie had slipped me. Like last time, I spread the papers flat on the faux wood, smoothing out the creases as I squinted in the pale yellow glow, wondering if a person could go blind by a mixture of prolonged anxiety and eye squinching.

After a minute or two, my squinchy eyes had focused enough to read the handwritten words on the first page. It looked like a letter, written carefully and purposefully by a straight, steady hand. For a moment, I stopped to admire Hoagie's professional-looking penmanship, feeling a bit self-conscious about my own sad, second-grader's scrawl. Then I got down to business.

"*Charlie,*" he wrote, with his perfectly formed, black-inked letters, "*Here is all the information I found on your brother, in case I don't get to explain it to you in person. I don't want to get you down, but it doesn't look good. The police say he killed a man named Benjamin Hawkes, who just so happened to be a doctor here—and a professor at your brother's school."*

My stomach dropped. If the police could connect the two of them that easily, that would only make their case against Chase that much stronger.

I swallowed, then kept reading.

"That's not even the weirdest part though," Hoagie went on. *"Apparently the Hawkes family begged the police chief to send Chase here instead of to jail. Why would they do that? Seems fishy to me...*

"Anyway, the rest of the info is here. I made copies of all his files while you were getting checked in. Hopefully it'll all mean more to you than it did to me. And hopefully it's not as bad in here for you as it seems. Either way, any time you want to break out, just let me know. I love a good escape plan."

I grinned, biting my lip. He was even cute on paper.

"See you later (I hope). Good luck!" he wrote, before signing it as "Hoagie," which made my grin even wider.

I was just about to move on to the next sheet in the stack when I noticed a small arrow at the bottom of the page, indicating that there was more to the message on the other side. Curious, I flipped it over and read: *"P.S.: Seeing as I was an idiot and used both of our names in this note, it'd probably be best to destroy it after you're done reading it. I suggest tearing it up and trying to eat it like that guy on Get Smart. I hear paper is very good roughage."*

I stifled a giggle.

How was it that, no matter how scary and nerve-racking it got for me in The Institute, Hoagie could still find a way to make me laugh?

Smiling to myself, I reluctantly tore the loose leaf into dozens of tiny little blue-striped snowflakes, which I then shoved into the space beneath the floorboard. Just as I was about to drop in the last piece, however, I took a second to glance around the room. Then, grinning like an idiot, I placed the scrap of paper on the tip of my tongue. I could taste the ink and a hint of chemicals that reminded me a bit of communion wafers from a Catholic church as I rolled it around in my mouth. Almost immediately it got stuck to my tongue, then between my teeth, then against the inside of my cheek and the roof of my mouth before I finally just crammed another chuck of licorice into my mouth to help get it down.

I would have to work on my spy skills.

With my act of inappropriately timed jocularity complete, I turned my attention back to my small stack of documents. They all seemed to be official records, forms, and reports from varying sources, and all were smudged with the tell-tale smear of copy-machine toner. There were seven papers in all, most of which were covered from top to bottom with long, typewritten sentences, all of which contained words my half-completed college career had not yet prepared me for.

But I got the gist.

The first piece of paper was a police report, recounting the events at the movie theater in gruesome, excruciating detail. The candy churned in my stomach as I read about the shattered skull and the far-flung brain matter of the man they called "Doctor Benjamin R. Hawkes," who, "witnesses" say, was just innocently crossing in front of the screen to get to the restroom when Chase (whom they referred to as simply "the alleged murderer") approached with a metal baseball bat and proceeded to bludgeon him with it.

Already things didn't add up.

First of all, Chase had been going to the lobby to get napkins. Why would he go down and cut across the front of the theater for that? The exit door was at the end of our row (which was standard practice for us, due to my habit of drinking 64 oz. drinks during the movies and needing to rush to the restroom the second they were over), and our seats were at least fifteen rows up from the screen. Given his penchant for heroism, Chase must have run to the front (or been pushed or dragged there) after the scuffling started.

Secondly, who gets up to go to the bathroom as soon as they get into the theater? Benjamin Hawkes was supposedly a doctor and a professor (a pretty prestigious one, according to the accompanying documents). Shouldn't he have had enough sense to go before he came in, so as not to disrupt any of the other theater patrons or lose his seat?

Thirdly, lastly, and most importantly, the theater was pitch black at the time of the murder, I was there. I was cowering in my seat, but I was there, fully aware that, no matter how close these "witnesses" had been to the actual crime scene, they wouldn't have been able to see much more than a flash of limbs or a glint of the metal bat in the disorienting light of a cell phone screen.

Someone was lying. Possibly they were just mistaken, or had used guesswork to fill in the holes in their story, but I was beginning to doubt it. The next few pages came from The Institute's files and, though I was in desperate need of a dictionary to help sift through all the medical jargon and psychiatric mumbo-jumbo, I could still see that Hoagie was right. There was something extremely fishy about the hospital paperwork, starting with the fact that they had marked my brother as a "Permanent Resident."

Chief Hudson had told my father (and me, indirectly) that Chase was only being sent there for evaluation, which could take up to six weeks at the most. It was never supposed to have been permanent. It was becoming quite obvious that Benjamin

Hawkes' estate (and whoever might be controlling it) wanted Chase stuck in The Institute. But why?

My stomach turned to lead.

I knew why. I had seen Chase earlier, his face battered and bruised, his hands and feet shackled like a slave on an auction block in the 1800s. They wanted him there so they could punish him; they wanted him there so that they could exact their revenge, whoever "they" were. Prison would have been horrible, but it would have kept him safe from whatever crazy acts of vengeance and retaliation The Institute had in store for him. So, seeing this fact, the Hawkes family must have begged the governor (probably a family friend) to send him here, where he would be subjected to unspeakable acts of cruelty and torture, the signs of which the doctors could easily pass off as incidental injuries sustained during the course of his treatment.

For a few seconds, a blinding rage rose up in me, threatening to take over my body and send me up and out the door on my own poisoning spree, but I let it pass. Now, more than ever, Chase needed me, and my gut told me I was onto something.

The Hawkes family had to know someone at The Institute. Hawkes had worked there himself, but that wasn't enough of a reason for the other staff members to become accomplices in their revenge scheme. They had to know someone there, *really* know them, in order to convince them that Hawkes' death was worth avenging. Or, perhaps The Institute staff itself was responsible for the murder, and was planning to cover it up by getting rid of Chase, or at least keeping him under their control.

I flipped to the last paper in the pile. It was a letter, the one that had been forwarded to the police from the victim's family, begging for mercy on my brother's behalf.

"Dear Governor Marquez," it began, in thin, loopy, hand-written letters on expensive-looking, monogrammed stationary, *"Our family grieves for the loss of our treasured Benjamin, but it*

also grieves for his murderer. It takes a very disturbed young man to commit such a heinous, unspeakable act of violence as the one that was inflicted upon Benjamin, and we sincerely hope that he will receive psychological treatment instead of being sent to prison. Our Benjamin worked with men and women like this one over the course of his entire career, and it would be an insult to both his memory and his legacy if the Chapman boy was sentenced to a life of untreated mental illness in jail before at least being evaluated at Gray's Institute for Mental Health.

"Our best wishes go out to you and your staff, as well as to Mr. Chapman. We truly hope that he can be helped.

"Sincerely, The Benjamin Hawkes Estate."

"You've gotta be kidding me," I said aloud, rereading the obviously bogus letter of sympathy and commiseration.

"Okay, okay, I'll tell you where I got them!" croaked Sybil's voice from her bed.

I jumped. I had been so caught up in conspiracy that I had forgotten she was there.

"Got what?" I replied stupidly, still stuck on why a murder victim's family would be so opposed to sending his killer to jail.

"The pills."

I glanced over at the mound of pills stashed away under the floor, and curiosity won out.

"Okay, where'd you get them?"

She paused, thinking it over, wondering if it was wise to tell me or not. I wouldn't trust me if I were her, but I was so entangled in a web of lies and intrigue at the moment that I wouldn't even have trusted my own mother.

"Necie and I," she started, her brittle voice barely a whisper, "we stopped taking our pills about two months ago. We tricked Dr. Caleb into thinking we took them, but really we just hid them in our mouths where he couldn't see, then we brought them back here and put them in the floor."

"Who's Necie?"

"Necie was my roommate, the one before you. The one who couldn't speak. The one who died in your bed."

I felt a shudder go up my spine. "Oh," I said, "that one."

"She really did kill herself, I wasn't lying. See, we thought that if we stopped taking the pills, we'd get better, more alert and alive, like we were before we came here. Only...we didn't think it through."

I frowned, not sure I knew where this was going.

"It turns out, you can't just stop taking the pills once you get used to them. They're too strong. You have to sort of wean yourself off them slowly, or else it screws with your brain. It makes you crazy and depressed and—"

"Suicidal," I finished grimly.

"Yeah," she whispered. "Once I figured it out, I started taking small doses again so that I could gradually get used to being without them, but Necie was too far gone. One night, she just gobbled up two big handfuls of the pills we had saved and she swallowed them all before I could stop her."

Her voice was breaking with unshed tears, but I couldn't stop the detective in me from asking, "What did it look like... when she overdosed? What did she do?"

"After a few seconds, she got really weird, stumbling around and moaning with these crazy eyes. Then she screamed really loud and grabbed her stomach, then she just fell onto the bed."

That sounded familiar.

"I tried to get someone to help her, but all the doctors and nurses did was stand around and watch while she died. It was horrible."

"Sybil?" I said after a moment, my voice much gentler this time.

"What?" She sniffed.

"I'm going to get you out of this place. You and everybody else."

"Okay," she replied, her voice thick.

Then I lay back down on the floor to begin mapping out my strategy. My reconnaissance mission had just turned into a prison break, and there was no time to lose.

22

APPARENTLY THERE WAS a little time to lose.

Somewhere between drawing a diagram of the rooms I had seen thus far and making a list of everything I knew about Chase, the pills, and The Institute with a stubby little golf pencil I had found in the floor, I must have fallen asleep. I awoke roughly at seven a.m. (or what I assumed to be seven a.m., based on the hustle and bustle of the people clambering down the hall for breakfast) to the sound of bare padding feet and the pain of the dorm room door smacking me in the face as Sybil left for the cafeteria.

"Sorry!" she squeaked, looking embarrassed.

I gave her a grumpy wave and sent her on her way, stowing my files and escape plans beneath the loose floorboard. Rubbing my aching forehead, I swept the room for leftover evidence of my deviance, but found it clean. Satisfied but stiff, I followed Sybil down the hall to the front of the building.

The cafeteria was about half full with patients chatting happily amongst themselves as they waited in line to get their morning dose of zombie pills. There was a pleasant sort of excitement in the air as they all chirped like birds, and I felt my already strong resolve harden.

These people were not crazy. Most of them might have had legitimate mental issues, yes, but that wasn't all they had. They also had lives and hopes and dreams and personalities, all of which would be obliterated once again the moment they swallowed those meds.

I scanned the room for Big Momma and found her at a table near the front window, gossiping with a waifish blonde, who was smiling shyly and chuckling at every word she said. I spotted Sybil in line, separated from me by three sleepy-looking male patients. She, too, seemed aglow with liveliness, and as she turned back to smile at me, I was struck by the realization that I was the one responsible for her high spirits. By promising her a way out of that hellhole, I had given her something to hope for, something to believe in.

I really hoped I wouldn't let her down.

The line moved much more quickly than it had the night before, and in no time I had reached the front. I physically jumped when I caught sight of Dr. Caleb. Like before, he stood at the head of the line, passing out pills followed by mushy food. This time, though, he was gaunt and haggard, with a thick, graying five o'clock shadow on his hollowed cheeks and deep, dark lines beneath his bleary amber eyes. His broad shoulders slumped beneath his lab coat, which hung haphazardly over his seemingly emaciated frame, and his voice was low and cracked as he croaked, "Here."

My hands fumbled as I took the cup of pills. I watched him, afraid to take my wide eyes off his face as I tipped the cup back and spilled the contents into my sleeve. He handed me a cup of water and I downed it in one gulp, pretending to swallow the medicine. He grunted wordlessly (only adding to the illusion that he, too, had joined the legion of the undead), and shoved a tray of pureed garbage into my hands.

A bit robotically, I walked my tray over to a table in the back so I could be alone to evaluate this new development. The overdose obviously hadn't killed Caleb, but it must have been close. He seemed to have kept himself alive out of pure spite, but for what? So he could continue to regulate the patients' drug intake? Or to maintain his position at the head of whatever sort of evil organization he had going on here? And what had happened to Chase when the doctor regained consciousness and found out what he had done? Nothing good, that's for sure.

My dark, worried thoughts were interrupted when someone elbowed my tray, sending it and its repulsive contents crashing to the floor with a loud, squishy sounding "bang!"

Startled (but not entirely ungrateful), I turned to catch Hoagie out of the corner of my eye as he crouched down on the floor, his baby blue scrubs spattered with mutated mashed potatoes.

"Sorry," he muttered, scooping finger-fulls of the goopy paste back onto the tray with impossible slowness, "I'm all elbows."

I resisted the urge to smile as relief washed over me. I scanned the room, searching for spying eyes. When I found only two dozen half-converted zombies, I knelt down beside him to help clean up the mess.

"Anyone listening?" he mumbled, focusing much too intently on a speck of gruel on the clean white floor.

I shook my head.

"Good. You read the papers?"

I nodded.

"Helpful?"

I nodded again.

"Wanna talk about it?"

His bright blue eyes flicked up to my face for a moment. I nodded vigorously.

He grinned, making my bent knees a bit weak as I remembered those lips on my forehead the night before.

"You have a meeting with a therapist in an hour. I'm not sure which one. Meet me in the supply room on the second floor right after that."

I nodded once more, trying to hide my eagerness as he scooped up the last pile of mush and slapped it on the plate. I started to wipe my grimy hands on my robe, but he stopped me.

"Here," he said quietly, glancing around the room. Surely we didn't have much time before we became suspicious. "Let me."

Then, with soft, gentle hands, he used a wad of his own shirt to wipe the mess from my palms, making sure to clean out every crease and crevice, and taking extra time to wipe away the gunk from between my fingers. By the time he was finished, I was blushing spectacularly and was, for once, grateful for my vow of silence.

"There," he said, with a satisfied smile, as he gave me back my now-sweaty hands, "that's better!"

I grinned bashfully in reply and his eyes sparkled with delight.

"See you later," he whispered, grabbing my ruined tray with one hand and my elbow with the other as he helped me to my feet. It sounded more like a promise than a plan, and I wished I could just skip the therapist and leave with him right then.

He gave my arm a squeeze as he walked away, and I had to put my fist in my pocket to keep from giving him a sappy, girlish, goodbye wave.

I guess my movie had room for a love interest after all.

23

I TURNED out to be very good at therapy.

All I had to do was sit quietly in a chair and pretend to listen as the on-site psychologist, Dr. Jill Friedman, explained to me the origins of my mental illness and the probable causes of my "mutism." She went on and on about traumatic events and feelings of powerless I never knew I had while I nodded every now and then, making sure to look lost and confused and drug-addled. I am sure that her information would have been helpful if I were truly in need of help, but mostly it just bored me and gave me an opportunity to go over my plan again as I tuned her out.

First of all, I would have to ask Hoagie for more information about The Institute and the people who worked in it. Someone on the grounds was a party to whatever revenge plot or cover-up scheme the Hawkes family was enacting, and I needed to know who it was (possibly for my own revenge plot or cover-up scheme).

Next, I needed to find out what exactly was in those little white pills, and how many someone would have to take in order to have a reaction like Dr. Caleb had the night before. If Chase had really drugged him (and my gut told me he did), he would have needed to accumulate much more than a few days' worth of medication to do it, I would think.

Which led to the third, most crucial part of the plan, the part the whole thing hinged upon: I needed to talk to Chase.

I needed to see him, to speak to him, to find out what had really happened both at the theater and at the hospital. It had been my goal all along, but now, more than ever, I found that Chase was the key to solving the case and clearing his name...as well as to saving all the other patients while simultaneously taking down The Institute from the inside.

I had a lot of work to do.

I sighed heavily and Dr. Friedman stopped mid-affirmation. She pulled her big, coke-bottle glasses down on her sharp, narrow nose and surveyed me with quizzical, grass-green eyes. I could feel my entire body tense up as I realized that I had broken character.

"This *is* getting a bit dull, isn't it?" she asked, settling back in her much larger, much more comfortable-looking desk chair and raking and handful of her straight-cropped brown hair out of her face.

I shrugged guiltily.

"Let's talk about something else then," she started, leaning forward as she placed a hand on her big mahogany desk.

I shrugged again, running out of noncommittal response options.

"Let's talk about your medication."

I felt myself go pale.

"Have you been taking your pills at every meal, Jane?"

It took me a minute to remember who Jane was, then I nodded quickly. Too quickly.

"I thought so..." she murmured, with a strange glint in her eye that implied that she knew everything, not just about the pills, but *everything*: everything I had ever done wrong in my entire life, up to and including the time I had stolen little Lucy Hance's crayon box in the third grade.

I could feel the uneaten pills fermenting in the now-sweaty pocket of my robe at that very moment, sinking lower and lower as it became more and more obvious that I hadn't taken them.

Stop it, Charlie, I warned myself, working hard to keep my nervous hands from twitching and my too-wide eyes from glancing down at my robe. I hadn't had time to go back to my room after breakfast to deposit the meds in the floor safe with Sybil's. Immediately after breakfast, one of the giant hunky orderlies had taken my arm and led me into the maze of blank white hallways, getting us lost twice before finally passing me off to a second, more experienced orderly with a scar on his left cheek and calf muscles the size of an elephant's. I had barely made it to my appointment on time, and I had had no other choice but to keep concealing the pills on my person until I could find a garbage can to dump them in. I had almost forgotten about them altogether until that moment, but suddenly they were all I could think about.

"I know you are new here, but I must stress the importance of those pills," Friedman told me, her voice icy for reasons I had to pretend not to understand. "They not only help regulate your moods and keep you healthy, but they also allow you to interact with the patients and the staff here in a safe, controlled manner."

I raised an eyebrow.

Screw playacting. This woman was crazier than I could ever pretend to be. She had no clue what was wrong with me, yet she had prescribed pills to "control" me and "make me safe."

Before she could speak again, a buzzer sounded to end my session, saving me from any more Hitler-esque pill propaganda.

"Oh, Jane," she called just as I reached the closed, locked door.

I hesitated. My body told me to ignore her and get the hell out of there while I still could, but my brain was still urging me to play along, at least for another minute.

I turned toward her as she approached me. She was much taller than I had realized, and she towered over me with an odd, sinister sort of triumph that I couldn't quite explain.

I unlocked the door.

"Here," she said, reaching deftly into my front pocket and extracting the two not-yet-discarded capsules, "don't forget your medicine!"

Her thin red lips curved up into a wicked, witchy smile as she leaned closer to me. I made to take the pills from her claw-like fingers, but she was too quick. With reflexes like Jet Li, her hand shot out and caught me by the throat, causing me to part my lips in an involuntary gasp.

Before I could stop her, she had hurled the pills into my mouth and slammed it shut, pinning my lips together with her sharp, red-polished nails. I wanted to scream, to shake her off, to break away, but I forced myself to stay calm. I couldn't risk accidentally inhaling those pills.

I could already feel their chalky poison infecting my tongue as I held them in my mouth, glaring defiantly at the doctor.

To my surprise (and horror), this only made her laugh.

"Do you really think that you're the first patient to ever refuse her meds?" She cackled, grinning viciously. "Trust me, in the end, everyone does what I want, whether they like it or not."

Then she took the claw from my throat and pinched my nose shut with it. I sputtered, unable to breathe in or breathe out, unable to gain control, unable to prevent the inevitable.

With a ragged, choking, gulp, I swallowed the pills.

24

Already the white walls were growing dim and wavy as I raced down the hall, stumbling over my own feet and tripping over things that weren't there. I was tired, so tired, and my arms and legs seemed to be slowly filling with sand, weighing me down while my head threatened to lift up and float away.

I needed to find Chase. I needed him to help me, to tell me what to do. I needed him to pick me up in his big strong arms and carry me home like he used to do when we were kids and I fell off the swings at the park. I needed him to get me out of there; he was the only one who could help me.

Except maybe Hoagie.

I stopped, just managing to keep my balance as I turned to run back the other way. Hoagie! Hoagie could help me!

But where was he? He had told me to meet him somewhere, somewhere private, somewhere janitorial...but where? I could barely remember my own name, let alone whatever instructions my confederate had given me two hours ago!

"You alright there, honey?"

I whirled around. For a few seconds, the world just kept

spinning. Then I saw a skinny, bearded man holding a broom—the supply closet!

I slapped him gratefully on the arm as I ran past him and down the hall to the elevator.

"Second floor, second floor, second floor..." I whispered to myself as the shiny metal doors closed and my brain threatened to slide down my neck and out my belly button.

After what seemed like an hour of wavy lines and oddly-bright, surely unreal color changes, the silver doors opened again and I fell out onto a cold, tile floor.

I felt bad, really bad. My stomach was wriggling with worms (when did I eat worms?) and my head was spinning like a top as someone draped a thick, heavy blanket of drowsiness over me. For a moment, I considered just closing my eyes and going to sleep right there on the floor, half-in, half-out of the elevator shaft.

*It would only be a quick nap...*I assured myself, as my weighty eyelids came together.

No! There was no time for napping! I was going some-where! I was doing something!

But what?

I could no longer remember where I was going or why, how I had gotten there or where I had been.

"Oh my God."

I lifted my concrete head, turning my face toward the sound.

"Oh my God, Charlie!"

Someone knew my name! *How nice,* I thought dazedly, resting my cheek back against the cold floor.

"No, no, no, Charlie, don't do that. Stay with me!"

I shooed the sound away with my floppy hand, but it wouldn't go. I squeezed my eyes shut tighter, willing it to leave me alone.

"Charlie, did you take the pills?" The sound sounded strangely warped and distorted, as if it were coming through an old, worn-out guitar amp. "Did someone make you take the pills?"

Pills? What pills?

"Charlie!"

I jumped, banging my forehead on the tile.

"Yes…" I groaned. Maybe that would make the sound go away.

"Dangit!" It growled back, crossing three different octaves with each syllable. "How long ago did you swallow them?"

"Swallow what?"

"The pills!"

Pills? What pills? What was a pill?

"Charlie, concentrate!"

That time the sound was clearer, more distinct somehow. It reminded me of something. Or someone…

"Hoagie?" I murmured, wishing I could reopen my eyes.

"Yes! Yeah, it's Hoagie!" said the sound as it rippled like a sparkling shadow across my brain. "Now did you take the pills just now, or a long time ago?"

Pills? What—

Then I remembered. I could feel the eagle's talons on my nose as a goblin sewed my mouth shut, forcing me to swallow two tiny poisoned rocks.

"Soon," I told the sound, "just soon. Not long."

"Okay." It sounded relieved. "Now just hold still a minute, this is gonna be weird."

"Weird?" Was that even a word?

Then, while I tried and failed to open my eyes again and the dark, sticky blackness threatened to swallow me up, someone pried apart my stitched-up lips and shoved something big and wiggly into my mouth. I wanted to spit it out, but I couldn't move my tongue. I couldn't stop the wiggly thing from tickling the little hangy ball at the back of my throat. At first it was kind of funny. I almost laughed. Then it started to hurt, and I started to choke, to gag, to retch, until finally my stomach exploded and my belly full of worms spewed out of my mouth and all over the floor, making a much louder, much more disgusting sound for my staticky ears to hear.

25

Before I had even stopped vomiting, Hoagie was helping me up and ushering me back into the elevator cab, murmuring things like "That's good," and "You got it," while he patted my back reassuringly. He jabbed a button on the wall and the doors banged shut so loud that it felt like a bomb had just gone off in my head. The elevator gave a lurch and rose up, up, up, while I slid down, down, down the cold steel wall to sit on the floor.

"It's okay, Charlie, you'll feel better in a few minutes."

"I'm really trippin' out here, man," I told him, leaning over to lie down on the even colder metal floor.

He let out a relieved-sounding little chuckle and said, "I know, dude."

"Are my eyes open?" I asked, still watching a strange, filmy sort of colored light show swirling around me.

"No, they're closed. Why don't you open them?"

"I forgot how," I grunted truthfully, bending my useless fingers as I rubbed them across my nose.

"Do you want me to help you?"

"You would do that for me?" I squeaked, suddenly overcome with emotion and touched beyond belief.

I could tell that he was trying hard not to laugh. "Of course I would do that for you. What are accomplices for?"

"That is *so* nice," I warbled tearfully, surely sounding like a complete idiot. "You are such a nice person, Hoagie."

"I know," he chuckled as he knelt down beside me on the floor.

I could feel the heat from his hand as he put it across my nose, his palm rough to the touch, but gentle as he ran it up my forehead, slowly pulling up the two-ton lids to expose my watery green eyes.

"Better?" he asked, cocking his head and grinning down at me as if I were an adorable little kitten instead of a drunk girl most likely covered in her own vomit.

"Better," I replied dreamily, trying to count his freckles as they chased each other across his face like little brown ants.

The elevator stopped and the doors slid open. The world still tilted at an unnatural angle, but I could see from the open air and the absence of blank white walls that we were on the roof, probably at the top of one of the three ominous towers I had seen from the highway.

"You wanna get out?" Hoagie asked, placing his foot in the track of the door so it wouldn't close.

I nodded, sending the sky and the wispy white clouds in front of me adrift on a sea of psychedelic waves. I thought about puking again, but decided against it.

"Do you think you can get up?"

"You sure ask a lot of questions," I grumbled, suddenly grouchy. Maybe I should have taken that nap after all.

"Does that bother you?"

Even in my unstable mental state, I still caught the joke. I grinned wryly as he helped me to my feet once more. "Very funny," I told him, as we stepped out onto the unfinished grey concrete slab that covered the rooftop.

"I thought so," he teased, putting his arm around my waist as he guided me over to the ledge.

"Are you gonna make me jump off?" I asked stupidly, trying to keep my eyes from rolling around so much in my skull.

"Why would I do that?"

"I don't know, for fun?"

"That doesn't sound like much fun to me." He laughed, taking my hands and placing them both on the top of the four-foot retaining wall so that I could brace myself and stand up of my own accord.

"Me neither," I added lamely, closing my eyes for a moment to enjoy the feel of the light, feathery breeze as it caressed my cheeks and ruffled my hair. "Oh man, I forgot how much I love air."

Hoagie's laugh sounded a bit forced that time, as if it were covering up some deeper emotion that I was still too whacked-out to interpret. I flinched a little when I felt his arms encircle me from behind, wrapping themselves around my stomach and my surely soiled shirt. It felt nice: warm and safe and comfortable, and I opened my eyes a bit as I leaned back against him, laying my throbbing head on his right shoulder.

"I'm sorry, Charlie," he told me, sounding pained. "I should have been watching you closer. I shouldn't have let them slip you those pills."

"It's not your fault." If there was one thing I remembered, it was that Hoagie was not the one to blame.

"Feels like my fault," he returned, sounding morose. "If I had just—"

At that moment, my foggy head cleared and I recalled a real story—one that didn't involve eagle talons or goblins or tiny poisoned rocks.

"Hoagie, the therapist grabbed me by the neck and shoved the pills down my throat. How was that your fault?"

I felt his arms tense up and he was silent for a long time.

"What are you thinking?" I asked finally, my voice quiet as my wits and wariness slowly returned.

"I'm thinking that I kind of want to kill your therapist," he replied, his voice like rough, jagged ice.

"I don't think that would be helpful." I decided to wait until later to tell him the part about her clamping my nose and mouth shut.

"Maybe not, but it'd sure make me feel better."

"Not me." I shrugged, nestling my head more securely into the crook of his neck as I looked out at the tops of the tall green trees, watching them sway back and forth in the same slight breeze that was still playing across my face like weary fingers across piano keys. "I have something better in mind."

"Count me in."

I laughed. "You don't even know what it is yet!"

"I don't care. I think I'd do just about anything you asked me to at this point."

I felt a flutter in my achy, empty stomach as he leaned his head down to rest his cheek against my messy hair. I decided to try a joke to hide my flattered embarrassment. "I bet you say that to all the patients."

"No," he answered, the smile returning to his voice, "only the crazy-cute ones."

I bit my lip to keep from grinning outright. I could feel a blush coloring my cheeks, and I wondered if he could feel it through my hair.

"You know," I told him, with just a hint of my former sassiness, "I would have a great comeback to that if I wasn't so crazy-stoned right now."

I could feel the laughter rumbling up through his chest as he said, "I'm sure you would."

I was feeling a bit more stable, so I decided to risk taking one of my palms off the wall. I wobbled a bit, but I was still able to put my hand over Hoagie's, folding my fingers into his as they rested against my bellybutton.

"Are you feeling any better?" he asked quietly, his breath warm in my ear.

"A little," I answered, closing my eyes for a second. "The fresh air is helping."

"I was hoping it would. That's why I brought you up here instead of to that tiny old broom closet."

"You mean it wasn't just for the view?"

"Well, there's that, too," he admitted. "But what do you know about the view? You won't keep your eyes open long enough to see it!"

I smiled, feeling much better as my sense of humor returned. "I can't. I forgot how."

"Again?"

I nodded, trying to look helpless and pouty.

"Well, we'll just have to fix that, won't we?"

I shrugged coyly, keeping my eyes closed tight as he turned me around to face him. My cheeks burned as I leaned back against the ledge and he placed his fingers over my eyelids and tried to slide them upward.

I clamped them shut.

"Hey! Cut that out!"

"Cut what out?" I teased mischievously, scrunching up my nose to squish my eyes shut even tighter.

"Don't you make me pry them open!" he warned, tightening his hold around my waist and reminding me of our play fight in the bathroom the night before.

"Okay, okay," I placated, "I'll be good. Try again."

"Alright, now relax. I can't help you if you're all tensed up."

"Fine." I sighed, shaking the fake tension from my shoulders and decreasing the pressure on my eyelids. "Go ahead."

"Okay," he said, satisfied. "Here goes nothing!"

I grinned in anticipation, toying with the idea of covering my eyes with my hands as I prepared myself for the feel of his fingers on my skin again.

It didn't come. Instead, I felt a pair of warm, soft, lightly-stubbled lips press against mine for the briefest of seconds.

My eyes flew open in surprise to find Hoagie standing in front of me, smiling bashfully as his freckled face burned bright red.

"Hey, look," he said, "it worked!"

"Well, that's one way to do it," I returned shakily, my face probably just as red as his was. I felt a ticklish sensation in my stomach as the worms from before were resurrected as butterflies.

"Are you hungry?"

My mouth opened and shut twice before my still-groggy brain could process the quick subject change. "Uh...yeah...I guess I could eat."

"Good," Hoagie said, nodding as he took my elbow and led me over to a sunny spot on the roof just to the right of the tall, blocky concrete chute that housed the elevator. "I'm pretty sure your brother would kill me if he found out how little food you've been getting. I'm pretty sure he might kill me anyway, actually..."

That triggered something in my dopey brain, and just like that it was firing on all pistons again.

"Did you talk to Chase?" I asked, as I sat cross-legged on a patch of sun-bleached stone.

"Not really, but I saw him today," he replied, sitting down across from me, "and he does *not* look like a guy I wanna piss off."

As he began to pull what looked like dozens of little pack-ages of crumpled Little Debbies and smashed sandwich crackers out of his apparently bottomless pants pockets, I noticed that his pale blue scrubs were filthy. I felt a bit guilty as I studied all the stains on his shirt, knowing that I had been responsible for each and every one of them.

Except for one.

"Hoagie, is that blood on your shirt?" I felt a prickle of dread tickle my spine as the butterflies in my stomach all died.

There, beside the greenish-orange-brownish mess of dried breakfast food wiped from my fingers that morning, just above the streak of still-shiny yellow vomit on the hem (I cringed at the realization that the big wiggly thing in my throat before had been Hoagie's hand), was a splash of semi-dry, maroonish-red blood.

He looked down slowly, as if caught off-guard, obviously trying to buy himself some time to think of the best way to answer that. "Uh...yeah. I mean yes, that's blood."

"Whose?"

He squirmed, laying out twelve beat-up packages on the ground between us, straightening them into three perfect little rows of four. "Well...it *might* be Chase's—"

I clutched at the neck of my hospital gown.

"—or it might be one of the guards'!" he finished quickly, with a hurried gesture of reassurance.

"What happened?" I asked, unable to breathe, as the blue sky began to pulse behind his head (due to lingering effects of the medication or an oncoming heart attack, I wasn't sure).

"Maybe we should eat lunch first..."

"Hoagie!"

"There was a fight," he confessed, his face a bit grey as he finally stopped fidgeting with his snack crackers.

"A fight?" I repeated. "Over what?"

He looked conflicted. His blue eyes darkened with misgiving, then he lowered them to his lap. "Over you."

Before I knew it, I was standing up, my legs straight and stiff again as all traces of medication left my body for good.

"No one knew it was over you, though," Hoagie added, jumping up to grab for my wrists, which I crossed over my chest out of his reach. I needed to process this without him distracting me with his damn cuteness again. "No one but Chase and I knew what it was really about. The guards just thought he was being crazy."

"He *is* crazy!" I shouted, throwing up my hands. "Why does he keep doing all this stuff?"

"I don't—"

"It's bad enough that he's been framed for murder, but he's only making it worse by drugging doctors and fighting with orderlies! How am I supposed to clear his name after that?!"

"You know he's the one who drugged Dr. Caleb?" Hoagie asked, sounding a bit impressed.

"I think it's pretty obvious," I snapped back, fuming.

"Yeah...especially after he admitted it this morning during the fight."

I smacked myself on the forehead. "Why is he being so stupid?" I demanded of the sky, of the trees, of Hoagie and his sweet, freckled face. "Why can't he at least *pretend* to be safe and sane until I can get him out?"

"Well that's even more obvious, isn't it?"

"What? What's so obvious?"

Hoagie dropped his arms to his sides and let out a heavy, world-weary sigh. "Charlie, *he's* trying to get *you* out."

26

"Great!" I snarled, pacing back and forth across the wide-open rooftop. "This is just great!"

"Charlie, calm down," said Hoagie, obviously wanting to reach out for me again, but not wanting to risk getting his hand bitten off.

"No! I can't calm down! Don't you see what's happening here?"

"I'm not sure..."

"We're both trying to save each other!" I shouted the words, as if yelling would make me feel less helpless and afraid. "Like always! Only this time, our rescue plans are canceling each other out!"

"What do you mean?" He frowned, looking a bit less nervous now, as if the threat of me randomly punching him had passed.

"Just think about it." I stopped to hold up a finger as I counted off the detrimental criss-crossings of our respective strategies. "First, Chase gets arrested and I sneak in here, thinking it'll help clear his name. But instead," I held up a finger on the other hand, "he sees me in the cafeteria and thinks that I cracked up and got sent here too. So, understandably, he launches his own plan to get *me* out. Then—"

"I get it, I get it," Hoagie interrupted, running a hand through his shaggy hair in a gesture of complete consternation as I mashed my two fingers together in metaphor. "Everything you do to help him gets undone when he gets the wrong idea and tries to help you back."

"Exactly."

"So, what do we do?"

"We need to find a way to talk to Chase." My voice was grim as I began to lose steam. "It's the whole reason I came here in the first place."

"Okay..." Hoagie said slowly, thoughtfully, as I plopped back down to rest beside the smashed snacks he had laid out earlier, "let me think about it for a minute."

I nodded as I grabbed a package of bright orange crackers stuffed with peanut butter. I was getting tired of thinking anyway. It was almost a relief to let Hoagie do it for me for a while. The drugs, for the most part, seemed to have worn off, but they had left behind a residual feeling of achy tiredness that sank deep down into my bones, as if it were settling in to stay with me forever.

"Did you find anything out about those pills?" I asked as he sat down across from me, his brow furrowed in concentration.

"Not much," he replied, as he selected a mushy chocolate cupcake from the array of vending machine fare, "just that they're some sort of super-strong depressant."

"Wait, did you say 'depressant?' Don't psychiatrists usually prescribe *anti*depressants?"

"Usually, yeah," he said through a mouthful of cupcake as I shoved a whole cracker into my mouth, suddenly ravenous as I remembered that all I had eaten in the past twenty-four hours were a few strands of stale licorice and half of Hoagie's hand. "That's why it's weird. It supports my theory, though, that the doctors are using them to control the patients for some reason."

I gulped down my bite, nodding in wholehearted agreement. "And the scariest part is that they start to affect you so fast! I hadn't even swallowed mine before I started feeling like I was on some sort of acid trip."

"That's probably because you were freaking out," said Hoagie knowledgeably, munching on a round, white cracker now. "Your anxiety and your running increased your heart rate and blood pressure, which pumped the drug through your system more quickly than it would for other people."

"Thanks, Dr. Oz," I snarked, opening a giant oatmeal pie. "Next time they drug me, I'll just stand really still and breathe like a yoga instructor."

"Oh, they're not drugging you again," he assured me, as he licked the leftover chocolate off his fingers, "I won't let them."

"How are you going to stop them?"

"I'll think of something." He winked, handing me a cupcake as I finished off the pie.

I was quiet for a minute as I opened the cellophane wrapper and removed the oozy brown snack cake inside. "Hoagie?" I said finally, before any more seeds of self-doubt could take root in my weary brain.

"What?"

"Do you...do you think any of this will really work?" My voice was small as I looked down at my smashed snack, turning it around and around in my grubby hand. "Do you think we'll actually be able to save Chase and the other patients? Or are we just kidding ourselves?" My eyes flicked to his face on the last syllable, and I found him staring intently at my lips, as if he had been hanging on my every word...or thinking of kissing me again. "Well?" I urged, when he didn't respond.

His blue eyes found mine then, and I saw nothing but sincerity in them when he said, "I think it'll work. I think that, with all your brains and your heart and your courage, you can do anything you want."

I blushed. "Who are you now, the *Wizard* of Oz?"

"Maybe." He shrugged, smiling slightly. "All I know is that I've been trying to get something done about this place for years, and nothing changed. But as soon as you show up, things immediately start turning around."

"But I didn't do anything yet!" I protested, putting down my half-eaten cupcake.

"Yes, you did," he returned, his face somber and his expression earnest, "you helped me get those pills and send them out for inspection—for evidence."

"That was nothing..."

"And you gave me hope," he said quietly, honestly, "you gave me a reason to keep trying. You gave me back a spark of life when mine had burned out."

"Oh geez, now he's a poet..." I groaned, attempting to hide how truly touched I was by his words.

"I'm serious," he insisted, reaching over to take hold of my sticky fingers, "I'm going to help you because you helped me. In more ways than you know."

As I met his bright, crystalline gaze, I was reminded of how much he had at stake— and of the fact that he had already lost someone at the hands of The Institute, just as I would if we weren't careful. At the beginning, I had thought only of Chase, and had placed Hoagie's purpose on the backburner, using it only as a stepping stone as I reached toward my own goal. Right then, though, I realized how alike we were, Hoagie and I, and how important it was for both of us—not just me—that we succeed.

I squeezed his hand in a gesture of unity and solidarity, and he squeezed right back. "We can do this, Charlie," he told me, his voice strong and determined.

"I know." I smiled, my confidence restored. "But first we're gonna eat the rest of these Little Debbies."

27

As we ate our way through a fat man's food fantasy, I told Hoagie about the falsity of the eyewitness reports and the bogus nature of the letter from the Hawkes Estate. He, in turn, told me about the fight that had broken out in the prisoners' wing a few hours earlier.

Apparently Chase hadn't been taking his pills either. That morning, he had woken up, bright-eyed and bushy-tailed—and filled with a wild, insatiable thirst for vengeance. The first thing he had done was call one of the guards over to his cell under the pretense of asking him for a drink of water. Hoagie (who had been doing some recon on Chase and the doctors who were treating him), showed up just in time to see Chase's huge, already-bloody fist jut out from between the metal bars that contained him and grab the guard by the shirt collar. In one swift, impossibly quick motion, Chase had pulled his thick arm back, slamming the guard's face against the steel, knocking him out cold.

Immediately, two other guards had appeared on the scene, armed with tazer guns and hypodermic syringes. By that point, though, Chase had ripped the keys to his cell from the unconscious guard's belt loop (along with a large portion of his pants, according to Hoagie) and had set himself free.

He had then roared like the beast in an old Disney movie (Hoagie's words, not mine) and had run straight at the two armed men. As he slammed into them, he shouted, *"WHAT DID YOU DO TO MY SISTER?,"* to which both men were unable to reply, seeing as he had just flung them to the ground and trampled over them like a psychotic steamroller.

More guards had come running, but not before Chase had reached Hoagie, who had been standing, paralyzed, at the entrance to the staircase.

"WHERE IS MY SISTER?" he had screamed, this time into Hoagie's face, as he grabbed a fistful of his scrubs with his big, bloodied hands.

Three more guards were running up to them, tazers drawn, and Hoagie had been conflicted. If he helped Chase escape or helped him to find me, he would blow my cover, not to mention his own. If he *didn't* tell him where I was, though, he ran the risk of turning Chase into even more of a monster.

In the end, Hoagie hadn't been able to bear the look of pure, crazed agony in my big brother's eyes, and he had done the only thing he could think of to do. In a fit of insane courage (or "suicidal stupidity," as he put it) Hoagie had jumped up and grabbed Chase around the neck, pulling him down to his level as he pretended to try to apprehend him on his own. "Charlie's safe," he had said into his ear, just as the guards arrived.

Chase's head had flown back and, for a moment, his eyes had registered nothing but disbelief. Then, the guards had tazed him and that's all Hoagie would tell me.

"So he knows I'm alright now?" I asked, barely noticing that I was gripping my own leg so hard that I was leaving little moon-shaped marks on my bare skin.

"Yeah, if he believed me," Hoagie replied, reaching over to

gently pry my fingernails out of my flesh. "But, to be honest, I'm not too sure he did."

I disregarded that negative thought. There was no time to be pessimistic. "Where did they take him after the fight was over? Back to his cell?"

"I think they were taking him to the infirmary when I left. Why?"

"Because that's where we're going to go," I answered decisively, getting to my feet. I took a moment to enjoy the crystal clarity of my now sober brain, then I reached down to help Hoagie up.

"Okay..." he said, seemingly reluctant to release my hand once he had regained his footing, "I hope you have more of a plan than that."

"What do you think I am, an amateur?"

"You're going to get me in so much trouble one of these days," he sighed, shaking his head as a smile spread across his freckled face.

"I'm looking forward to it," I said with a wink, then I dragged him into the elevator.

28

"Alright, you got it?"

Hoagie ran a hand through his hair, as if that would help him focus. "Maybe we should go over it one more time, just to be sure..."

"Hoagie, we've ridden this elevator up and down three times already!" I exclaimed, getting impatient. "It's time."

He sighed. "Okay, then I guess I'm ready."

"You guess?"

"Charlie, this plan is insane!"

"Good thing we're in a mental institution then."

"Come on," he begged, grabbing a hold of my finger before I could jab the silver number "5" button on the wall, "what if something goes wrong? What if something happens to you and I'm not there to help?"

I closed my eyes, praying for patience. "I told you already, I'll be fine. You've got the dangerous part of the plan anyway!"

"Yeah, well, I disagree," he said, crossing his arms over his chest like a stubborn four-year-old.

"Are you seriously doing this right now?" I snapped, my

worry over Chase (and Hoagie and the patients and me...) shortening my already-short fuse.

"Doing what?"

"Being *that* guy!"

"What guy?"

"The guy that thinks he has to protect girls from everything all the time! Believe it or not, I'm not as fragile as I look."

"I didn't mean it like—"

"And anyway, that's beside the point!" I went on, getting more and more irked the more I thought about it. "Chase is *my* brother, so if anyone has to get hurt saving him, it's gonna be me!"

I stabbed the elevator button then, hoping to close the matter to any further discussion. No dice.

"I'm not '*that* guy,'" Hoagie said quietly, using lopsided air quotes, "I'm just trying to look out for you, that's all."

"Well, that's not really your job, is it?" I shot back, crossing my own arms.

"It could be." He shrugged. "Are you hiring?"

I bit back a smile. "No."

The elevator pinged as it passed the second floor on its way up.

"That's a shame," Hoagie replied, shaking his head. He was obviously enjoying our not-so-witty banter again, now that the tension had ebbed. "I'm a very hard worker."

The elevator pinged again on the third floor.

"Just shut up and get into position." I laughed, moving toward the doors.

"Yes ma'am."

I made to lie down on the floor as we had discussed, but before I had even bent my knees, Hoagie moved over and swept me up into his arms.

I squeaked involuntarily and grabbed a hold of his neck,

clinging to him like a startled cat. "What are you doing?" I gasped, "This isn't the plan!"

"You're not my boss, remember?" he returned, with an air of smug defiance. "I can do whatever I want."

I wanted to argue, but my heart seemed to have gotten lodged in my throat somehow. His face was so close to mine, and I could smell the warm scent of aftershave lotion on his chin and neck as he grinned down at me, his lips mere inches away from kissing me again.

Some heroine I was.

"Alright, alright," I said finally, waving a hand to clear away the heat between us as we passed the fourth floor, "have it your way."

His boyish grin widened.

"But the rest of the plan stays the same," I warned, my heart speeding up as we neared our destination.

"You got it, boss."

A bell dinged and the doors opened on the fifth floor. A long, empty hallway lay before us, painted white with red trim —the only real color I had seen there in days.

"Okay, now act like you're stoned," Hoagie whispered, his arms tensing up beneath my knees and behind my back.

"Boy, if I had a nickel for every time somebody told me that..." I muttered, loosening my grip on his neck as we stepped out of the elevator.

"Who else told you that?"

I heard the faint ticking and whirring of machinery coming from somewhere close by, and I decided that it wasn't the best time for a chat.

"I'll tell you later," I whispered, preparing to fall into a swoon, as our plan required.

"Alright," Hoagie replied, sounding nervous but steadfast. "Ready?"

"Ready." I closed my eyes and let my arms go limp as I feigned unconsciousness. Then I changed my mind.

In a quick, awkward, hurried motion, I scooched my way back up Hoagie's chest and put my arms around his sweaty neck again. He looked a bit startled, but I ignored him. Summoning all the brazen courage I could muster, I leaned up and planted a kiss on his stubbly cheek, allowing myself only a few milliseconds to enjoy the feel of his rough, scratchy beard against my lips and to wonder why he smelled like aftershave when he obviously hadn't shaved in days.

His blue eyes widened.

"For luck," I explained, feeling my own cheeks redden as my overworked heart pumped even more excess blood to my face, "and...and in case I don't see you again."

"Oh, you'll see me again," he swore, as if he were pledging an oath.

I gave him one last grin, then I closed my eyes and fell backwards, trusting him to hold me as I let my body go limp in his arms.

Hoagie waited a few seconds, most likely second-guessing our plan again, then he shouted, "Hey! Hey, I need a nurse out here!"

Blood rushed to my head as I dangled (hopefully lifelessly) from Hoagie's arms. He grunted, straining under my weight (I was only slightly offended by this) as he took a few tentative steps down the cold, narrow hallway.

"Coming!" someone called, and I was a bit alarmed to find that, once again, I was enjoying myself too much. The thrill that tickled its way up and down my curved spine alternated between pure terror and pure excitement, and it was all I could do to keep from squeezing Hoagie's hand to see if he felt it too.

I think he did. I could feel his heart thudding against my ribcage as he cradled me like he was Count Dracula and I was the defenseless damsel that he would be feasting on that evening.

That thought made me a bit uncomfortable, so I decided to focus on my own heart, which pounded out a loud, erratic drumbeat against my palm as my right hand rested on my chest. My other hand hung loose at my side, and banged dully against Hoagie's pant leg as he staggered closer to the voice that had just called to him.

I heard the patter of a pair of quick, tiny feet scurry toward us, and I forced myself to breathe deeply and slowly, as if I were sleeping instead of pulsating with the spirit of adventure.

"What's going on?" demanded a high-pitched female voice from a few feet away.

"It's this Jane Doe." Hoagie panted, lifting me up as if he were showing her a selection of meats at a deli counter. "She must have eaten something weird, then she passed out."

"What did she eat?" the woman asked, sounding suspicious.

My heart sped up. She was already onto us!

"I have no idea," he replied, sounding much more believable than he had when he had lied to the receptionist in the lobby, "but I found her on the roof. There were food wrappers every-where. Do you think she could be allergic to something?"

"We need to go check out those wrappers," the nurse said, seemingly taking our bait after all. "Come put her in the infir-mary and then show me where you found her."

"Yes, ma'am."

Hoagie had told me in the elevator that the hospital, being understaffed, could only afford to keep one nurse on duty in the hospital wing at any given time. Since the patients she saw were always stoned out of their skulls, he or she could often be persuaded to leave his or her post if something more pressing came up, such as a manufactured medical emergency like ours.

Hoagie huffed and puffed his way down the main hall and

down a second one to his left, where we entered a room full of clicking, ticking, buzzing machine sounds.

"Just toss her over there," the nurse instructed, as if caution wasn't necessary when dealing with sick people.

"Okay," Hoagie groaned.

I could feel the sweat beginning to trickle down his chest and seep through his thin shirt as he shuffled further into the room. For a second, I was fairly convinced that he was just going to fling me onto a bed or a table or the floor, as the nurse had suggested, but I relaxed as he lifted me up and lowered me gently, carefully, down onto a hard, flat surface.

"Come on, let's go," snapped the nurse, apparently not feeling a need to examine me for signs of anaphylactic shock. Hoagie ignored her. Instead of rushing off as per her instructions (and our previous discussion), he lingered for a moment to straighten out my robe and adjust the hem of my gown so that it lay flat against my knees and protected my modesty. Then, as if that weren't sweet and unnecessary enough, he reached down and brushed a few strands of my tangled hair out of my face, the tips of his rough fingers as light as a leathery feather as they grazed my lips and cheek.

I hoped that blushing wouldn't give me away.

Just go, I begged him with my mind and, finally, he did.

"Who are you again?" I heard the callous nurse ask as their voices moved out into the hallway.

I could hear the heavy sigh in Hoagie's voice as he answered her, and I had to fight back a smile.

Once they had been gone for about thirty seconds, I opened my eyes. There wasn't much time. Hoagie would take the nurse to the roof, where they would try to interpret the contents of the cellophane wrappers he and I had left behind earlier, as well as any and all possible allergens in the remaining crumbs and/or surrounding air. When they made their way back, Hoagie would fake an elevator malfunction, buying me a few more precious minutes to find out what Chase knew about Hawkes. Even then, though, our time was limited. Very limited.

I sat up and swung my legs over the side of the sterile-looking hospital bed, taking in the room. There were several large, silver boxes along the perimeter that squeaked and buzzed mechanically, but they didn't seem to be attached to anything, not even the blank white walls behind them. There were several rows of beds that matched mine, but all of them were empty. There was not another soul in sight, and a chill slid down the back of my neck.

I felt like I had just entered the Twilight Zone. Everything seemed odd and eerily empty, as if the room were an unused set on a Hollywood soundstage, just waiting for a Sci-Fi director to come and rent it out. Nothing moved but the lights on the phony machines, which flashed red and gold and green as they tatted out a strange, techno music melody.

I hopped off the bed and onto the floor, making a sticky slapping sound with my bare feet. That's when I heard it: a long, low-pitched moan that rolled across the floor in waves strong enough to jostle my nerves and threaten to knock me off balance.

I knew that moan.

"Chase?" I whispered though the stillness, through the empty, buzzing air, "Chase, are you here?"

I had heard that moan before, but only once. That was the sound my brother had made when his best friend, Billy Burkheart, had been hit by a car in front of our house when they were ten years old. It was the only time I had ever heard Chase cry.

"Chase!" I called again, more urgently this time, as the memory of that day threatened to choke me. "Chase, where are you?"

The moan changed to an odd, garbled shout and I ran to the back of the room, where a straight, flat white curtain hung, blending in perfectly with the surrounding plaster walls. Without hesitation, I ripped it aside and felt my heart contract with horror.

29

"OH MY GOD," I choked, as I took in the nightmarish scene before me. There, strapped to a cold, sharp-edged steel table in the center of a small alcove was Chase. His arms and legs were bound with thick, metallic cuffs that were secured to the table by a series of nuts and bolts, and his bare chest was covered in muck and blood and round, rubbery blue disks that fed information into the tall, rectangular, completely functional machine to his right. There was an I.V. in his left arm, causing the veins around it to bulge grotesquely, and his head appeared to have been shaved by a drunken sheep shearer, who had left clumps and patches of short blond hair scattered across his scalp. His lips were cut and bloody as they jutted out around a red-stained towel that someone had tied around his head as a gag, and the rest of his face seemed to be comprised of one big, brownish-blue bruise.

It was his eyes again, though, that scared me the most.

His wide, unblinking brown eyes (well, the unswollen one, at least) stared wildly around the room, unable to focus, unable to settle on any one thing as they searched relentlessly for a way out. He looked trapped, scared—nothing at all like the kind, soft-hearted big brother I knew, and my chest ached as I realized what was really happening. The Institute was trying to turn him into the very thing that the police had accused him of being all along:

A monster.

"Chase," I said again, my voice ragged and broken as I rushed over to try to free him. My fingers fumbled over the knot in the towel behind his half-bald head, and his vacant, crazy stare flicked to me as I fought back tears. "It's me, Charlie," I told him as I removed the rank-smelling towel and threw it across the room.

"Charlie?" he repeated, his voice strangely hollow, as he frowned.

"Yes, Charlie," I said, as the first of my tears spilled out and dripped down onto his right arm. "Your sister. Remember?"

My hands shook as I turned the tight thumbscrews on the steel restraint. I couldn't look at him anymore, I couldn't bear it. They had done something to him; they had taken my brother away and left me with a scary, broken, shell of a person I wasn't so sure I could fix.

After two full minutes of my precious time had ticked away, I pulled out the last screw, releasing Chase's right arm.

"There." I hiccupped, finally looking back up at his pale, bruised face. "That's bett—"

Before I could finish my sentence, Chase reached out and grabbed me, pulling me into a fierce, painfully tight, one-armed embrace as he sobbed into my hair, "Oh, Charlie, Oh, Charlie, thank God!"

Relief and a desperate, aching rush of gratefulness washed over me as I stopped trying to free him and threw my arms around his naked neck, sobbing even harder and louder than he was.

"I'm so sorry!' I told him, barely able to breathe as he

crushed me to him, his chest heaving as the monitor beside him went crazy.

"I thought you were dead." He swallowed. "They told me you were dead."

"Who told you that?" I asked, trying to pull back, but he just held on even tighter.

"The doctors. The nurses. That stuck-up receptionist. Everyone! They said you snuck in here to save me, and you had a reaction to the pills."

That time I managed to get free. "They know I snuck in here?"

His face was red and blotchy now, and his eyes still streamed as I used the sleeve of my robe to wipe the snot from beneath his nose. "Yeah," he grunted, "they said someone told them last night."

"Who?"

"I don't know, Charlie! Who cares?" he shouted, with a peal of insane-sounding laughter. "You're alive!"

"Not for long," I said with a grim-sounding sniffle as I slid off him to start working on the other restraints.

"What are you saying?"

"That we don't have much time," I replied, loosening the screws near his thick ankles. "Can you undo your other arm?"

"I'll try," he said, without questioning my foreboding statement.

Someone had found out about me and my connection to Chase. Then that person—whoever they were—had used that information, not to capture me, but to torture Chase even further. But who? Who else knew about Chase and me? I hadn't told a single other soul in that building who I really was...

Except Hoagie.

A cold, sick feeling of dread twisted my stomach as I realized that I *had* been sleeping with the enemy all along. I had told Hoagie everything—I had held nothing back. And what I hadn't told him about Chase, he had found out for himself when he had copied his files. He had gotten close to me, had gained my trust so completely that it was embarrassing. Then he had double-crossed me.

The last bolt fell to the floor just as Benedict Hoagie himself came rushing into the room, pulling back the curtain so hard that he ripped it right off the rod. "Charlie, we've been made!" he panted, in his outdated t.v. spy lingo, barely noticing Chase as his blue eyes bored into mine. "The nurse, she—"

That's when I punched him.

30

PAIN FLOODED my knuckles as blood spewed from Hoagie's nose, but I didn't care. I slid my arm under Chase's shoulder and helped him off the table.

"Why did you just punch that kid?" he asked, sounding a little concerned as Hoagie fell to his knees, uttering a stream of his patented almost-obscenities.

"Forget it," I said, plucking the sticky blue disks from his massive, bruised chest and taking a better look at him. "Where are your pants?"

Chase's big hands moved quickly downward in an attempt to conceal his only remaining article of clothing—a skin-tight pair of Catdog boxer briefs I had gotten him for Christmas six years ago.

"They took all my clothes when I got here," he said with a shrug, "and I don't know what they did with my gown when they hooked me up to that machine."

Before he had even finished speaking, I had whipped off my robe and flung it over his shoulders. "Here," I said, fussing over his shaky wrists as he tried to shove them through the too-tight sleeves, "just put this on. We don't want to blind anybody on the way out."

"Charlie, listen," Hoagie grunted, struggling to get to his feet, "they're onto us. The nurse knows—"

"Oh, I bet she does," I snarled, taking Chase's hand and leading him out into the main infirmary area, shoving Hoagie aside as I went.

"What does that mean?"

I snapped.

"It means that you screwed me over!" I shouted, whirling around so that my face was inches from his. This time, though, the only heat between us was generated by the fire of my irrepressible rage. "You told them everything!"

"I didn't tell anyone anything! Charlie—"

"Whatever," I interrupted, turning away before I decided to hit him again.

"But I didn't! I didn't tell anyone anything, honest!"

"Charlie, maybe he's telling the truth," Chase mused, pulling me up short as I tried to drag him toward the exit.

"Are you kidding me?"

"I saw him earlier," Chase explained, frowning thoughtfully as he mulled things over much more calmly and rationally than I had. He had always been the reasonable one. While I was driven by recklessness and passion, his thoughts were rooted in solid, rational, well-reasoned logic. It was really quite annoying, actually. "He was the one person who told me that you were okay. Everyone else kept telling me you were dead."

"So?"

"*So*, why would he do that if he was looking to screw you over?"

"I..." I found this infuriatingly concrete logic hard to swallow, "I...well, I don't know! But what I *do* know is that he's the only person here who knows about both of us besides me!"

Everyone was silent as my accusation hung heavy in the buzzing air. Then came a loud, pulsating screech from the hallway as some sort of alarm went off.

"Crap!" Hoagie semi-swore, clutching his nose as dark red blood oozed out between his fingers. "They're locking the place down!"

"What does that mean?" Chase asked warily, his palm growing slick in my death grip.

"It means that we're all gonna be trapped in this room in a minute unless you guys come with me."

"Yeah, right!" I exclaimed.

"I don't think so, buddy," Chase added gruffly, deciding to take my side after all.

Hoagie's eyes widened. He was clearly panicking now. "But Charlie—"

"We don't need any more of your help, *Hogarth*," I spat, as if it were an insult instead of a name, "for all we know, you'll lead us right to them!"

He looked as if I had slapped him.

He hadn't looked nearly as hurt when I punched him as he did at that moment—the moment he realized that I had lost my faith in him. His bright, ocean blue eyes seemed to be fading to gray as he stared at me, searching my face to see if there was any way to change my mind about him.

There wasn't.

I had trusted him, I had relied on him, I had cried on his shoulder while my world fell apart, and he had betrayed me. He had helped to torture and maim my brother, the only person in the world I just couldn't live without, and he had made me look like a fool for falling for him and his unassuming, boy-next-door charm. Still, though, I almost regretted my harsh words, the ones that seemed to have shattered his traitor's heart.

Almost.

I had to get out of there. I pushed past him again, plunging into whatever sort of ambush might be awaiting us in the hallway. Any attack by the guards or the doctors or the mad scientists that ran the place would have been better than being trapped in that room with Hoagie and the sweet, freckled face that still showed no hint of his true nature.

"Charlie, wait!" he called, but I kept going. Chase squeezed my hand as if to show his solidarity as he limped along behind me, weakened by whatever punishment or experiment they had been subjecting him to before I showed up. "Charlie, please!"

A door swung open along the claustrophobic corridor behind us and we ducked into the stairwell beside the elevator shaft. Hoagie barely made it in before a small, heavily made-up nurse burst out into the hall, searching for the source of all the commotion. As we all flattened ourselves against the wall, sucking in our guts as we cowered behind the 6-inch doorframe that hid us from her view, a vicious, vengeful part of me wanted to shove Hoagie back out, but I just couldn't do it.

"Stop following us!" I hissed at him instead, while Chase slumped against the concrete wall, panting much too heavily.

"No!" he hissed back. "Not until you let me help you!"

"No!"

"Yes!"

"Hoagie—"

"Come on, guys," Chase moaned, either annoyed by our childish bickering or itching to move on.

"Charlie, listen to me," Hoagie said, grabbing the fingers that were not busy holding up Chase, "I know this place like the back of my hand. I'm the only one who can get us out of here safely."

"I. Don't. Want. Your. Help!" I growled, through gritted teeth.

He looked away for a second, obviously trying to come up

with a way to convince me. "Do you remember what I said to you when we first met?" he asked finally, his eyes finding mine again as blood continued to gush from his rapidly swelling nose.

"You said a lot of things," I replied, shrugging noncommittally. I knew what he had said. I just didn't know if I could believe it anymore.

"I said that I wouldn't let anything happen to you. I swore it."

"Oh, yeah..." I said, pretending to remember as I looked down at my bare feet, "that's right."

"Charlie, I meant it. If you don't let me help you now, I'm just going to find some other way to do it without your permission."

My eyes snapped back to his face. In my peripheral vision, I could see Chase as he looked back and forth between us like someone watching the last round of a ping-pong tournament.

"Why?" I frowned, even more suspicious than before.

He didn't seem to have an answer to that. Not one he wanted to share, anyway. "Look, you trusted me once before, I know you did. Would it really be so hard to do it just one more time? Just until we get out of this jam?"

I could feel my resolve weakening and cursed my stupid girlish heart. No, it wouldn't be so hard. It wouldn't be hard at all, that was the problem. Why did he have to be so nice all the time? Why did he always seem so sincere? Why did he always find a way to endear himself to me when that was always the last thing I needed at the time?

I glanced up at Chase, who was wearing an odd expression of mingled fascination and what looked like amusement as he watched me squirm with indecision.

"Don't look at me," he said, waving a hand between Hoagie and me. "You seem to be the one running this thing."

I looked back to Hoagie one more time, biting my lip. I

could feel the guards and the nurses getting closer every second, but I couldn't make up my mind. He was right; he did know more about the layout of the hospital than I did. He also knew the people who worked in it, and the methods they would most likely be using to track us down. In that aspect, he would be invaluable.

But what if it was a trick? What if he had been conning me, lying to me, setting me up to fail the entire time?

I searched his eyes again, then I trailed the blood as it dripped down from his nose onto his lips. Suddenly, I could feel the scratch of them on my forehead, then on my own lips as he coaxed me into opening my eyes to see the view from the rooftop. I could feel the gentleness with which he had fixed my hair and smoothed out my gown in the infirmary, even after the brusque nurse had told him to just toss me aside like a sack of potting soil. I could feel the way he'd hugged me so tightly before we'd even entered the building, the way his laughter had tickled my neck in the bathroom the night before, and the way he had saved me from Dr. Caleb's crazy pills in the grossest, most disgusting, most selfless way possible, and I knew then that, for better or for worse, I trusted Hoagie James.

"Okay," I told him, my jaw tight, "lead the way."

There was a flash of relief and triumph in his eyes as he nodded.

Then they found us.

31

Chaos erupted in the confined space as two big, beefy orderlies tried to grab Chase. The infirmary nurse stood in the doorway, shouting encouragement as they grappled with my already-weakened big brother, and I heard Hoagie sputter what sounded like a swearword.

Without missing a beat, I leapt up and straddled the biggest guard from behind, wrapping my bare legs around his taut (probably perfectly sculpted) abs as I tried to put him in a sleeper hold like good ol' Arn Anderson, squeezing his throat tighter and tighter in my vice-like grip. He stumbled backwards, surprised, and slammed me into the opposing wall, knocking the wind out of me.

As I tried to get an even tighter grip around his thick neck, Hoagie kicked the other guard in the back of the knee, sending him lurching forward as he lost balance and fell into an awkward, hunchbacked crouch. Chase then punched him in the face so hard that I heard bones crack, and the nurse screamed for help and ran back down the hall the way she had come.

My orderly rammed me into the wall again, and that time I saw stars. The orderly must have seen them too, because his

Adam's apple jerked up and down a few times against the crook of my elbow, then he slumped over, landing facedown on the concrete floor as I finally released the pressure from his windpipe.

I leapt to my feet, dizzy but ready for action, but it was all over. The boys must have already taken out their guy when mine fell, because they were both standing there gaping at me, with almost identical expressions of completely warranted awe on their faces.

"What?" I panted, adrenaline coursing through my veins like some sort of absurdly potent heroin.

"That was awesome!" Hoagie exclaimed, as Chase broke into a proud, slightly chagrinned smile.

"I know, right?" I shouted back, resisting the urge to slap them both a high-five.

As we raced down the stairs toward the lower floors, I had to reign in my excitement. I had never felt more alive in my life! Not only had I just broken my brother out of a mad scientist's lair, but I had just choked out a guy three times my size without even breaking a sweat! Colonel Hogan and his heroes would have been proud.

We skidded to a stop on the second floor landing and Hoagie threw open the heavy door that led to another maze of hallways. After doing a quick visual sweep of the area, we went with the assumption that the coast was clear and rushed in, tiptoeing across the shiny white tile until we reached a door marked "Employees Only."

Hoagie held a finger to his blood-slick lips and gestured for us to follow him. Quiet as three little field mice infiltrating the inner sanctum of a wild mountain lioness, we crept into the small, darkened break room. We passed several blue-cushioned chairs, a skinny brown card table, and a lightly humming mini-fridge (most of which were barely visible in the gloom) before we reached a blank, white plaster wall.

Hoagie took another glance around the empty room as my adrenaline threatened to morph into anxiety. What was he doing?

Chase and I watched, dumbfounded, as he stared fixedly at the wall and we waited for him to realize that we had reached a dead end. Instead, though, he tapped the wall a few times, his fingers barely making a sound as they knocked against the plaster, then he flattened out his palm and slid it across the surface, leaving a smear of blood that even a blind detective couldn't miss.

"Hoagie," I whispered, "what—"

Then he found it. He let out a sigh of relief as his fingers slid into a small, almost invisible indentation on the right side of the wall panel, and he slid the whole thing aside, revealing a dark, dungeon-esque passageway that looked like it would have been less out of place in a crypt.

Chase locked his fingers around my wrist, obviously wanting me to think long and hard before entering the Temple of Doom. Thick, stringy spiderwebs dangled from the low, tiled ceiling and draped across Hoagie's shoulders as he took a slow, careful step inside. We all jumped as a mouse or a rat or a spider the size of a squirrel skittered across his path, but we really had no choice but to move forward. We had already wasted too much time there to turn around and, if my ears were not deceiving me, I could already hear a cacophony of angry voices beneath the blaring of the alarm that was still ringing in the hall.

Moving like reluctant, overly cautious tortoises, Chase and I followed Hoagie into Harry Potter's lost Chamber of Secrets and he moved around to close the door behind us. A click echoed through the now pitch black darkness as he locked it, and my previous exhilaration was replaced by an awful, anxious, gut-wrenching fear that exceeded even the one I had felt when the lights had gone out at the theater on the night of Hawkes' murder.

I could feel myself start to tremble as Chase moved his sweaty fingers from my wrist to my hand, clutching it tight as he silently offered to let me do the same to his. I had to stifle a scream as Hoagie brushed back past me and took the lead and my other hand (how he found it in the blackness, I will never know), and began to edge us forward, deeper into the tunnel.

My eyes bulged as they searched desperately for even the tiniest, most useless little pinprick of light to focus on, and my heart was beating so hard and so loud that I was sure that it was going to explode out of my chest like dynamite at any moment. This was it, my greatest fear: being lost, trapped, smothered in a darkness that I couldn't escape from by something that I couldn't see. It was silly to be afraid of the dark, I knew that, I had read all the children's books about it fifty times. But it wasn't the external darkness I feared, not really. It was the darkness within the darkness—the darkness that lived in the souls of whatever and whoever else was around me.

Something crawled across the top of my bare right foot and I took that opportunity to let out the frightened, girlish whimper that had been building in my throat since we had first entered the secret passageway.

As if they were one unit, both of the boys dropped my hands and closed in around me, feeling for me in the blackness as their worried voices whispered simultaneously, "What's wrong? What happened? Are you alright?"

Someone's hand was on my hip and the other's was on the back of my head, and suddenly I was stricken by an insane urge to laugh. Perhaps the situation wasn't as dark as it seemed.

"It's okay." I exhaled, expelling a bit of my pent-up panic as

I remembered that I wasn't nearly as alone, lost, or helpless as I felt. "I think it was just a mouse."

"Oh, okay," Hoagie answered, sounding just as tense as I did.

"Dude, get your hand off my ass," Chase demanded, and I really did laugh that time as I felt Hoagie jump back, releasing his grip on my waist.

"Sorry," he muttered, "I thought it was Charlie's. No! I didn't mean that! I meant—"

I laughed even harder as he tried to take back his ill-chosen words and climb back out of the hole he had dug for himself.

"Just keep your hands to yourself," Chase growled, the threat in his voice implicit to Hoagie, but sounding perfectly empty to me. In spite of his intimidating stature, my brother was really just a big teddy bear at heart...well, he was to me, anyway.

"Yes, sir, Hoagie replied hastily. "No, wait, I mean—"

"Just go, Hoagie," I sighed, still laughing as I pushed him forward.

32

THE REST of the tunnel went much more smoothly. A couple more things brushed against our legs and scurried over our feet, but now that the tension had broken, I found it more entertaining than scary. As we traversed the seemingly endless narrow passage, Hoagie informed us that it had once been used as a "body chute" of sorts.

"Back in the early 1900s, the mental hospital was decommissioned and converted into a sanitarium for people who had tuberculosis," he said, wheezing like a tuberculosis patient himself as he tried to talk and breathe through his mouth at the same time. "That happened with a lot of these places back then. Anyway, hundreds of sick people stayed here, and they were all so depressed and downhearted already that the staff didn't think they could handle seeing them cart out the dead bodies of the ones who didn't make it, so they built this tunnel. It connects one side of the building to the other—the side that used to hold all the patients to the one where the doctors and nurses lived... which was also the place where they cremated the bodies."

"So, which side are we going to?" I asked, trying to ignore

the imaginary moans of the dead as ghostly hands caressed my cheek and stroked my hair.

"The old patients' side. Most of it's been shut down for years, ever since they remodeled the other half we were in before."

"Just most of it?"

"Yeah. There are still a few of the more...interesting... patients living over here now, but that shouldn't be a problem for us."

I was just about to ask him what he meant by "interesting" when he stopped and I ran right into him, causing a three-car pile-up as Chase sandwiched me between them.

"Sorry!" Hoagie grunted, trying to push me off of him without actually touching me (as per Chase's orders). As I was trying to extricate myself from Chase and his big hairy legs, there was a click and a snap and a low, spine-tingling creak as Hoagie slid open a door and filled the passageway with light.

"Windows," I said stupidly, marveling at the open area before us. The rest of The Institute had been blank and lifeless and confining, but this new area (or old area, according to Hoagie) was so spacious and unrestricted with its walls and walls of big, screened-in windows and light, comfortingly warm breezes that it made me feel as if we were free already.

"Nice, isn't it?" Hoagie said, watching a bird fly past the biggest window at the end of the hallway with a sad, nostalgic little smile on his face. "They used to think that open air was a curative for T.B. back in the day, and they designed this area so that it would let in as much fresh, clean air as possible."

I was still stupefied by the breeze and the feel of the sun as it streamed in and blanketed the floor with soft, shadow-dappled light, so I didn't respond. Chase, however, let out a quiet, breathy choking sound that he quickly tried to muffle with his hand. Startled, I turned to see tears trickling down his bruised, pallid face.

"Chase?" I asked worriedly, putting my hand on his arm as I reverted back to the same mother hen persona I had adopted in the infirmary.

"No, no, it's alright," he said, waving his hand as he gently tried to shoo me off of him, "it's just..." He glanced at Hoagie, who suddenly became fascinated by a tall tree swaying in the wind outside. "It's just... I was starting to think that I'd never get to see the sun again."

If hearts could really break, mine would have been shattered to pieces by the sad, haunted look in my brother's big, wet brown eyes. I knew it had been bad for me in The Institute, but surely that had been nothing compared to what he had been going through since his arrest and his subsequent admission to the hellish hospital.

"Chase, what did they do to you?" I whispered, searching his eyes for an answer I didn't really want to hear. I needed to know that had happened, and what type of physical and psychological torture Dr. Caleb and his sadistic staff had been subjecting him to, but I wasn't sure I could bear the thought of him being in any more pain than he was at that moment.

He must have sensed this, because he replied, "I'll tell you later," with a sad, watery smile and a brotherly pat on the shoulder. "For now, we should probably keep moving."

I stared at him for a moment longer, wondering if he would ever really, truly tell me what had happened to him, but he was right. We needed to move on before someone else picked up the poorly-hidden trail of blood and bodies we had left behind us.

I turned my stinging eyes to Hoagie, who seemed to be looking to me for permission to move forward. I gave him a nod, which he returned, his expression grim.

Slowly, we set off down the hall, passing several multicolored doors and a myriad of cheery open windows, but we didn't stop to admire the view. Instead, we entered another concrete stairwell identical to the one in which we had scuffled with the giant orderlies, and we made our way up to the fifth floor.

"They'll be guarding all the entrances and exits pretty heavily right now," Hoagie whispered, his nasally voice still deafening in the empty hall, "so I think we ought to find a place to hole up for a while and wait them out, just to be safe."

Chase and I exchanged a worried glance. He, like me, seemed reluctant to spend even one more second within the confines of the asylum. However, he, like me, also knew that we didn't have much of a choice at that point.

Hoagie led us all the way down to the last door on the right, where he stopped and began fidgeting with a small, silver lock hanging from the door handle.

"You guys don't happen to know how to pick locks, by any chance, do you?" he asked, letting out a nervous chuckle.

"We're not into that kinda stuff, man," Chase replied staunchly, as if he had just offered us a hit off his bong.

"Wait a minute..." I said slowly, recalling another one of Grandpa Max's hokey—but surprisingly useful—tricks. "I could probably do it if you had a bobby pin or something."

"Why would I have a bobby pin?" Hoagie replied, sounding exasperated.

"And where did you learn to pick locks?" Chase demanded, as if I were in for a lecture (unfortunately he hadn't been with me the day Grandpa Max had had to break into his own house to keep his pan of Ramen noodles from boiling over and ruining the stove).

"What about a paperclip?" I suggested to Hoagie, ignoring Chase and his "judgy" face for the time being.

He dug around in his bottomless pit pants pockets and came up with six crumpled one dollar bills, a ticket stub, part of a paper plate, twelve unwrapped Fig Newtons, a dart board dart, a library card, the leg from a Buzz Lightyear doll, and half of a smashed, wilted-looking cheeseburger, but no paperclip.

As I gaped at him, trying to decide how best to go about mocking him and his hoarding tendencies, Chase smirked. "Is that all?"

"I think so..." Hoagie frowned, sticking his tongue out as he jockied his pile of miscellany around so he could reach into his left pocket one more time. "Oh! And this ink pen."

"That'll work." I grinned, snatching the Bic from him and unscrewing the bottom to release the tube of ink inside.

"Charlie, you are really starting to worry me..." Chase sighed, shaking his head like he no longer knew what to do with me.

"Relax," I replied, rolling my eyes at him, "this is the last weapon in my arsenal of criminal skills, I swear."

While the boys watched, bemused, I crouched down in front of the door and guided the silver tip of the ink tube into the keyhole. I closed my eyes, feeling the scrape of metal on metal as I listened for the telltale click of contact between the pen and the tumblers, but it didn't seem to be working.

"Hand me that dart," I instructed Hoagie, who fished it back out of his pocket and passed it to me like a nurse assisting a surgeon.

Biting my tongue between my teeth, I stuck the sharp, pointed end of the throwing dart up into the mechanism until I felt it scrape against the pins. Relieved that there was still a chance to avoid looking like an overconfident jackass, I pushed the ink pen back up there as well, sliding it into the space I had just created and pushing back the remainder of the lock's tumblers.

There was a clank as the Masterlock broke open, and a loud, dull clunk as it slipped out of its holster and fell to the floor, but that was all muffled by the sound of Hoagie's inappropriately loud crow of victory.

"Amazing!" he exclaimed, slapping my hand enthusiastically as I stood back up. "Incredible! Wow! Just, wow!"

"Shhhhh!!!" Chase and I hissed back, but I couldn't help but grin as Chase pushed past us to open the door, shaking his head. After he went inside, I gave Hoagie a bow and mouthed *"Thank you, thank you,"* and he, embarrassed but elated, gave me a silent round of applause.

33

I couldn't seem to stop smiling as Hoagie and I followed Chase into the musty-smelling dormitory. It was astounding how quickly my doubts and fears had given way to jubilation and confidence with just the simple (but also incredibly impressive) picking of a lock. This was going to work, I could feel it. With Chase's focus and determination, Hoagie's in-depth knowledge of the grounds, and my apparent penchant for criminality, we would have no trouble coming up with a new escape plan.

Chase, however, did not seem to be sharing in my excitement. As Hoagie locked the door behind us from the inside (obviously a bit too confident in my lock-picking ability), he crossed the room and plopped down on one of the two twin-sized mattresses, sending up a cloud of dust particles that glittered in the afternoon sunlight streaming in through the small, square window behind him,

"You okay?" I asked, wading through the dirty air to join him.

"Getting tazed three times in two days takes a lot outta ya," he muttered, rubbing his bruised head with his hands, as if he were trying to keep himself awake.

"Do you want to lie down for a little while?" I asked him, tutting over his gray-flushed face and the way his shoulders slumped forward beneath his robe. It was as if he were in the process of collapsing in on himself. "Hoagie and I can keep watch while you get some sleep."

He looked at me for a moment, his good eye bleary and tired, as if it had seen a thousand years' worth of troubles in just the past twenty-four hours. Then he let out a sad, melancholy chuckle. "I should be asking you that, you know?"

"What do you mean?"

"I mean, I'm the big brother here. *I'm* supposed to be protecting *you*, not the other way around."

He looked old then; old and defeated and world-weary, and I couldn't, for the life of me, understand why.

"We can't protect each other?"

"We *can*," he said heavily, "but I wish we couldn't. You shouldn't have had to come here, Charlie. You shouldn't be doing all this for me. It's too dangerous."

"But you're my brother!" I exclaimed, offended by the insinuation that my life was more important than his. "You would have done it for me!"

"Yeah, because it's my job to look out for you!" he shouted back, a spark of frustrated anger in his weary brown eye. "That's how it's always been!"

"So, now I'm just returning the favor." I said with a shrug.

He growled wordlessly in reply, as if he just couldn't tolerate my naïveté any longer.

"Chase, don't you get it?" I insisted, perching on the edge of the bed now. "It's always been you and me against the world! It's always been Chase and Charlie, Charlie and Chase; never one without the other, right? No matter what happens, no matter how scary or crazy or stupid or sad things get, we always stick together! We're always a team! I can't do this without you. *That's* why I had to try to save you. Why can't you see that?"

The darkness in his eyes melted away as I finished my clumsy but heartfelt speech. Instantly, the Chase from before was back; the Chase who smiled, the Chase who always knew what to say to bring you up when you were feeling down, the Chase who was strong and brave and quick to laugh—the Chase who was everything I wished I could be, but probably never would.

"So... even though I'm a psychotic murderer and a whiny sad sack that holds up all your escape plans, you still need me?"

"*Alleged* whiny sad sack," I corrected. "And yes, of course I still need you! I always will."

"Right back atcha," he replied with a grin, pulling me in for one of his trademark bear hugs as he tousled my hair affection-ately. "There's just one problem though," he said then, frowning with faux solemnity as he gave me a noogie and I pretended to be embarrassed.

"What's that?"

"It doesn't seem to be just 'Chase and Charlie' anymore. Now it's turning into 'Chase and Charlie and this other guy.'"

I had almost forgotten about our apparent third wheel until Chase pointed at him. "That's Hoagie," I laughed, as our perpetually polite companion continued to rifle through a pile of old sheets on the other bed, feigning deafness.

"What kind of a name is 'Hoagie'?" Chase scoffed.

"It's short for Hogarth."

"Oh my God," he groaned, running his hands down his face.

"It's a family name." Hoagie sniffled defensively, proving that he had been listening the whole time.

"Yeah, it's a family name," I repeated, trying hard to stifle another laugh as the man in question gave us a long-suffering sigh and an eye roll as he broke into a grin.

After having been reassured of his usefulness and brotherly value (and after making a few more good-natured jokes at poor Hoagie's expense), Chase was more than happy to comply with my earlier suggestion that he take a well-deserved nap. His head hadn't even hit the pillow before he was out, snoring like a rhino with a deviated septum. I carefully covered him with a light, moldy-smelling blanket and left him in dreamland, where I hoped he would avoid some of the horrors that came with being awake.

"Man, he must have really been beat," Hoagie observed. He was sitting in a rickety wooden chair in front of a small, roll-top desk stuffed between the two beds, dabbing at his broken nose with the corner of a sheet. He flinched every time the fabric made contact with his skin, and my guilt over having punched him returned—with interest. He looked like a sad, sweet little cocker spaniel that had been smacked on the snout with a newspaper for the first time, and was wondering what it had done to deserve such cruel, heartless treatment.

"Here, let me help you," I offered, taking the sheet from his hand and slipping into the space between him and the desk.

"You don't have to..." He snuffled, but he didn't stop me as I folded the corner down and gently swept it across his chin, scrubbing away the sticky, half-dried blood as I slowly cleaned my way up his face.

"I shouldn't have done that," I told him, pointing at his swollen schnoz.

"Don't worry about it," he replied, waving a hand in dismissal as he tried to talk over Chase's obnoxiously loud snoring. "I would've done the same thing if I was in your shoes."

"No, you wouldn't have," I said, wrinkling up my own nose

as I began to wipe the blood from the scruffy line of his lower lip.

"No," he shrugged, smiling ruefully, "no, I probably wouldn't have."

"Chase got his nose busted like this once," I murmured, concentrating hard as I wet the corner of the blanket with my tongue and tried to get rid of the rusty red stain below his stubbly pseudo-mustache. "He got into a fight at school with this big kid who shoved me in the lunch line. I fell down and scraped my knee, so Chase gave the guy a black eye. Needless to say, the guy did *not* appreciate that."

"Now I see why you couldn't hire me as your bodyguard." Hoagie grinned, his lips curving up beneath my rag. "The position has already been filled."

I laughed. "Looks like it." By that point, all that was left to clean was the vertical crease above his lip line and the oozing nostrils themselves. I rotated the sheet to find some fresh fabric and bit my own lip as I leaned in to dab at his face. As expected, he winced.

"Sorry," I hissed, wincing back and almost wishing I hadn't volunteered for the gruesome task in the first place. But I had done the crime, so I was thusly obligated to do the time. "I'm almost done."

"It's okay," he said, patting me on the leg reassuringly. "It still feels much better than what I was doing."

"Yeah, right."

"Tell me more about Chase's big fight," he suggested, leaning back into the creaky chair, as if he were relaxing in front of the television instead of being subjected to a new form of cruel and unusual nose torture.

"Well, that was the only time Chase had ever gotten into a fight with anyone before he came here," I went on, still soaking up the congealing blood as it continued to dribble out of his nose. "I was so afraid that he was going to get in trouble that I rushed him into the girl's bathroom to try to clean him up before anyone else saw him. I must have gone through two rolls of that crappy public restroom toilet paper before I finally came up with a solution."

"What was it?"

I took a step back to admire my work on his round, boyish face... and to build the suspense. Then, with a mischievous grin, I said, "Tampons."

"*What?!*"

"Tampons," I repeated cheerfully, wiping away the spurt of blood that had shot out of his nose when he snorted in disbelief. "I bought two tampons from a little machine they had in there, and I shoved them up his nose, one in each nostril. I thought it was quite ingenious, myself."

"And what did Chase think?"

"Not that." I laughed. "He was completely disgusted by the whole idea. Apparently men have some sort of built-in aversion to feminine hygiene products."

"Shocking," Hoagie smirked, clearly enjoying my endearing anecdote.

"It didn't really matter anyway, though." I shrugged, leaning back against the desk. "All the tampons in the world couldn't keep his nose from swelling up like a balloon...or keep the other kid from telling the principal what happened. When my dad found out, Chase and I were both grounded for a month."

"Why did *you* get grounded? You didn't do anything!"

My mischievous grin widened. "Sure I did. Why do you think that kid shoved me in the first place?"

Hoagie laughed out loud, brushing my gown as he slapped his knee. "You're hopeless, you know that?"

"It's all part of my charm," I said with a wink, making him laugh even more. "Hey, stop that," I scolded, still giggling, as more blood trickled out of his nose. "I can't stand here and clean your face all day long!"

"I wouldn't mind it," he replied, sounding much too earnest.

I paused for a moment, taking in the freckles hiding in the shadowy bruises beneath his eyes as I remembered that I shouldn't like him so much, I shouldn't trust him so completely. In a way, trusting him was the most reckless thing I had done since I had infiltrated The Institute. The only person I knew for sure that I could count on was Chase, not Hoagie. Hoagie could still be lying, could still be plotting against me.

So why didn't I care?

"I'm sorry about your nose," I said softly, running a remorseful finger down the bridge of it as I tried to ignore the doubt that still nagged at me.

"I'm sorry you feel like you can't trust me anymore," he replied, taking my finger and holding it in his loose fist as he stared down at it, all traces of laughter gone.

"Someone told the staff about Chase and me," I whispered, feeling more guilty and conflicted than ever as he opened my hand and brushed his thumb across my sweaty palm. "No one knew about that but you."

"I know."

"What was I supposed to think?" I asked, my voice rising as some intense form of dismay started to choke me. "I mean, we just met, right?"

"Right—"

"And we barely know each other!" His eyes found my face as I continued to get more and more distressed. All of the sudden, I couldn't keep it in. Everything that I had been bottling up since I found Chase in the lab was threatening to come spilling out of me, and I was powerless to stop it. "And you work here! You work here, with all these...these crazy doctors who tortured my brother! Why *wouldn't* you sell me out? You don't owe me anything! You don't even know me!"

Hoagie stood up then, a strange light in his ocean blue eyes that only made me talk faster.

"I *shouldn't* trust you, right? And *you* shouldn't trust *me!* It's stupid, really. Idiotic! It's not even your fault either. I'm the one who assumed you were on my side! But why would you be? Why would someone like you—"

Then he was kissing me.

His coarse, copper-flavored lips pressed against mine as he pulled me to him, wrapping me up in his arms as I closed my eyes, sighing as all the tension and fear and regret left my body, leaving behind a warm, safe feeling of contentment I had never felt before.

After a long, dizzyingly beautiful moment, he pulled back and I opened my eyes. His were still closed as he continued to savor the moment, his face flushed. He wore a sweet, adorably dopey smile beneath his still-oozing nose as he told me, "*That's why.*"

34

A LITTLE WHILE LATER, while he and I sat across from each other on the empty bed playing makeshift Jenga with the crumbly Fig Newtons from his pocket and taking turns blushing at each other, Hoagie asked the question I had been pondering for the past two hours.

"So...if *I* didn't rat us out, who did?"

"As far as I'm concerned, it could still be you," I said casually, biting a chunk out of a cookie before placing it atop the wobbly stack between us.

He pretended to be hurt. "Really? After what just happened between us?"

"Sure." I shrugged as he toppled the Newton tower for the fourth time in a row. "One kiss doesn't prove that you're innocent."

"Oh no?" he returned, wiggling his eyebrows and giving me the goofiest come-hither look I had ever seen. "What about two?"

I snorted, trying to stifle my giggles with my hands as Chase grunted restlessly in his sleep. "Nice try," I whispered, "but I'm not kissing you again until your nose clots. Do you think I wanna ruin this outfit?"

It was his turn to laugh as I waved at my thin gown like Vanna White revealing the solution to a word puzzle. "I must say, that look *is* working for you."

"I bet," I scoffed, doling out the cookies again so we could start a new tower.

"No, really," he insisted, "the green really brings out your eyes. And that clingy fabric really shows off your—"

"Hoagie!" I gasped, crossing my arms over my chest.

"Legs!" he shouted, blushing redder than a ham under a heat lamp, "I was gonna say legs!"

"Sure you were..."

"'Sure he was' what?" came Chase's groggy voice from across the room.

Hoagie's panicked eyes widened as he blinked at me, surely remembering my earlier anecdote about the fighting and the tampons. I grinned as I realized that he was silently begging me for mercy.

Lucky for him, he was cute.

"Nothing," I replied, watching with amusement as Hoagie let out the breath he'd been holding. "Go back to sleep."

"Nah, I'm up." He yawned, sitting up to look out the window. "Somebody's got to keep an eye on you two."

"Why's that?" I asked innocently. Hoagie blanched.

"Well, this guy could still be a narc, right?" he pointed out, shuffling over to the bed so he could sit down, uncomfortably close to poor, pre-faint Hoagie. "Or he could just be looking through your shirt."

That time, I really was embarrassed. It was nothing compared to Hoagie, though, who made a strange, choking sound somewhere between a cough and a retch as he tried to scoot away from Chase, who tossed me a blanket to cover up with. "I...I wasn't—"

"So, did you guys figure out who the mole is yet?" Chase interrupted, swiping one of the Fig Newtons from Hoagie's pile.

"Not yet," I admitted, pulling the blanket up to my chin to preserve whatever modestly I had left. "Do you have any ideas?"

"I told you, I've got no clue. All I know is that after I saw you at dinner, they locked me in this tiny little cell that I hadn't been in before. Then, later, a woman came and told me that my sister was dead."

My stomach sank.

"Which woman?" Hoagie asked, but I was stuck on another point.

"Chase..." I said slowly, not quite sure how to say it without upsetting him, "I don't think there is a mole."

"What? How can that be? Someone had to tell them about you!"

I saw the answer dawn on Hoagie before I spoke again. "I think...I think maybe *you* told them."

"No. No way, I..." He trailed off, his face turning white as his shoulders sank. "Oh my God, I did, didn't I? Or I might as well have, seeing as I was standing there screaming at you like an idiot for ten minutes!"

I felt a stab of pain as I replayed the scene in my mind.

"They couldn't have known she was your sister just based on that," Hoagie chimed in, playing the role of Group Optimist. "If I hadn't known you guys, my first thought would have been that she reminded you of a friend or a girlfriend or something, or she was just someone you thought you knew from a long time ago. People do that kind of thing in here all the time, and in most cases they don't even know the person they're screaming at. Somebody must have gotten more information from somewhere else."

"Like my file?" Chase snarled, as if mocking his naïveté. "Or from you?"

"Take it easy," I interjected, not liking the murderous look he was giving our well-meaning third wheel. "That's not really important."

"Oh, yeah, because putting you in danger isn't important."

"Cut it out, Chase!" I snapped, growing tired of his newly adopted self-loathing technique. "It would have happened sooner or later anyway."

"Yeah, and I picked sooner."

I rubbed a hand across my forehead in frustration as I stood up, abandoning my white veil of modesty to pace the room. "That's not important," I repeated, irritated by the irrelevance of our line of thinking. "We're asking the wrong questions. We're sitting here going around and around, blaming each other for stuff that doesn't even matter when we should be trying to figure out who framed you in the first place!"

The room was silent.

"Well?" I urged, stopping to stare at Chase, who shrank away from the intensity of my expression.

"You mean, who killed Hawkes?" he asked, looking a bit sick.

"Of course that's what I mean! That's why we're all here! Someone killed Benjamin Hawkes, and we're paying for it. Now who did it? Who did you see at the front of the theater that night?"

"No one."

My legs felt weak, so I sat down on the dirty floor, running my hands across my face again before burying it in my palms. That was it, then. If Chase couldn't identify the real killer, no one could. If he hadn't seen the crime committed, then he would take the blame for it, and there was nothing I could do to clear his name, no matter how many insane asylums I infiltrated.

"Ben Hawkes was my old psychology professor," he said, as if he were excavating each word from a pile of memories he had buried in his mind. "I hadn't seen him in two years, so when he bumped into me in the aisle of the movie theater, I didn't think he'd remember me. But when he looked up at my face, he got this weird look in his eye and he said, 'Chase Chapman, you've got to help me.'"

I felt a chill as I removed my head from my hands to listen, riveted by his story and his haggard, hollow voice.

"So, of course, I said I would, and when I asked him what was wrong, he dragged me up to the front of the theater, toward the emergency exit right next to the screen. I tried to tell him I couldn't leave, that you were waiting on me to bring you some napkins, but he just wouldn't listen. Then the lights went out."

I closed my eyes, remembering the thick, inky darkness as it wrapped itself around me.

"My first thought was to get back to you, Charlie, since I knew how scared you must have been. But then Hawkes grabbed my arm so hard that his fingernails broke the skin, and he whispered, 'You've got to help me!' And I tried to, I really did! But before I could even figure out what he wanted me to do, someone ripped Hawkes off me and started beating him. I tried to stop it, I tried to grab him or whoever was hitting him, but then someone else came up and grabbed me around the neck from behind, squeezing my throat with these big, disgusting, hairy arms. He was strong, really strong. Way stronger than me, and no one could hear me yelling for help.

"Then, after the first guy had hit Hawkes twenty or thirty times, he shoved a bat into my hands and they both disappeared, leaving me standing there over the professor's dead body when the lights came back up."

I gaped at him, clutching at the neck of my gown, as if to root myself in reality. I'd never been more horrified in my life. I couldn't think of a single word to say that would make my brother feel safer or better or less like a person who had failed to stop a killer from running free, and I couldn't imagine the powerlessness he must have felt as his former professor died at his feet.

I was stricken, absolutely paralyzed by the thought of our combined helplessness. I had been plunged into a new kind of darkness now, a kind that couldn't be erased by the flip of a light switch or the lighting of a candle. A kind that was more terrifying than any I had ever encountered, a kind that was powerful enough to render even the bravest, strongest, and most heroic amongst us completely useless.

This harrowing new realization must have shown on my face, because Chase immediately reached out for me. "Come here," he said gently, his eyes losing their scorching flame of pain and misery as he beckoned me over.

Obediently, I stood up and padded over to him, feeling like a little girl looking for solace after waking from a nightmare. I could feel tears tickling my eyes again, but I still couldn't seem to form any words. There weren't any, really. My big brother's innocence had been lost forever, and so had mine. And there was nothing anyone could ever say that would bring it back.

I felt a bit silly as Chase pulled me into a hug, patting me on the back as I wrapped my shaky arms around his middle, just as I had a lifetime ago, when I really had been a scared little girl waking from a bad dream. This time, though, it felt wrong. Chase was the one who had been hurt, not me. Chase was the one with the demons to fight, the cross to bear, the memories to live with. Yet, still, he was the one comforting me as I rode an emotional rollercoaster that would have given even a hormonal pregnant woman motion sickness.

"It's okay," Chase murmured, and I hoped that Hoagie had found something else to feign interest in again as I fell apart for what seemed like the twelfth time in two days. "Hey, I'm okay! We both are. It's going to be alright."

"I shouldn't have sent you for those napkins," I said into his shoulder, suddenly convinced that the whole thing could have been prevented if I hadn't been such a klutz.

"Now you're just being ridiculous," he chuckled, holding me out at arm's length to wipe the hot tears out from beneath my eyes. "If I hadn't have gone for napkins, you'd have just spent the whole movie wiping your buttery hands all over my nice clean t-shirt!"

I let out a hiccupping laugh and leaned in to give him one more hug.

"Okay." I exhaled, rubbing my sodden cheeks. "So now what?"

"Well, now we know there were two killers, not just one," Hoagie supplied, his eye strangely soft and misty as he looked at us.

"Right, and they were strong." I sniffled, sitting down on the other side of Chase, who put his heavy arm around my shaky shoulders.

"And they were guys," Chase added. "Well, at least one of them was. I heard him grunting when he was swinging the bat."

"Good, so now we've narrowed it down to about fifty percent of the world's population," I said sarcastically.

"Hey, that's fifty percent closer than we were!" Hoagie pointed out, astounding us both with his perpetual optimism.

"Well, actually, we *do* know something else." I frowned, thinking back to the pile of papers Hoagie had slipped me the night before. "I'm pretty sure that the murders have a connection with The Institute."

"Oh, definitely," Chase agreed, nodding vehemently. "That must be why they sent me here in the first place. My theory is that they didn't intend to frame me at first, but since I had been there at the scene of the crime, they couldn't risk me telling the cops what I had seen, on the off-chance that they'd believe my story. So they pinned the whole thing on me..."

"...and brought you here to find out what you know..." Hoagie said slowly.

"...and to keep you away from anyone else who might be able to help you," I finished, not surprised that our theories matched up almost perfectly.

"Exactly."

"So, did you tell them?" asked Hoagie, frowning. "What you know, I mean?"

"No, I didn't tell anybody anything. The police wouldn't listen, and the doctors here are psychopaths who just keep shoving pills at me, so I figured there was no point in talking. Unless it was to you, of course." He shrugged, giving my shoulder a squeeze.

"And they were okay with that?" Hoagie pressed, his frown deepening.

Chase glanced sideways at me, apprehension written all over his bruised face. "No..." he said slowly, looking away, "that's kind of why they put me in that room in the infirmary. Well, that, and the fact that I broke out of my cell and tried to kill Dr. Caleb."

I wasn't sure which question to ask first, so I went with the one that seemed less painful to answer. "Why did you try to kill Caleb?"

"Because he was the one doling out all those pills," he growled, anger darkening his brown eyes again. "They told me you had died from a reaction to the pills, and I knew he was the one who gave them to you."

"But she didn't take the pills," said Hoagie, unnecessarily. "She only pretended to. Well...until the therapist shoved them down her throat later."

"WHAT?!" Chase exploded, leaping to his feet in a whirl of fury. Hoagie and I both moved away instinctively. "Why didn't you tell me that?"

"It didn't come up!" I yelled, in my defense. "Calm down, Hoagie fished them back out anyway."

"He *what?* What does that even mean?"

His livid glare zeroed in on Hoagie, who seemed to be trying to blend in with the faded white wallpaper behind him.

"I...uh...I found her in the hallway and I figured out what happened. So then I stuck my finger down her throat to make her throw up."

"Thus, getting rid of the pills," I finished for him.

Chase continued to stand there for a moment, simmering in his rage.

Then he surprised me.

With a gruff, wordless sound, he pushed past me and grabbed Hoagie, who yelped like a frightened Dachshund before he realized that my giant brother was trying to hug him, not murder him.

"Thanks," Chase muttered, trying to sound manly as he let go of him and cuffed him on the shoulder, "I owe you one."

"No, you don't," Hoagie replied, still looking a bit shell-shocked. "I'd do it again in a heartbeat."

Chase regarded him for a minute as I raised my eyebrows, feeling like we had all been sucked into some cheesy, over-emotional soap opera that just wouldn't end. "You're alright, Hogarth," he announced, slapping him on the shoulder again. "Any guy who looks out for my sister is alright in my book."

"Thank you, sir," Hoagie replied gratefully. Then he blushed. "No! I meant—"

"We know what you meant," Chase and I replied in unison, with identical sighs and eye-rolls.

"So, wait," Chase said turning to me now, "he said you

pretended to take the pills. How did you do that with Caleb standing there watching you?"

I felt my mischievous grin return. "Take a guess," I told him, pinching the sleeve of the robe he was wearing.

A huge smile spread across his face as he caught on instantly. "Grandpa Max would be proud," he declared, looking pretty impressed himself.

"Of what?" Hoagie asked, confused. "Who's Grandpa Max?"

"He's the guy who taught our resident magician all of her tricks," Chase informed him, giving me a wink.

"Oooohhhh..." Hoagie replied, looking as if he had just been given the key to solving a riddle he'd been working on all day. "But you never said how exactly you did it!"

"A magician never reveals her secrets," Chase and I reminded him.

"You guys are getting really annoying with that stuff, you know that?" Hoagie informed us, unable to hide his amusement.

"We know," we said in unison.

35

AFTER A FEW MORE MINUTES OF teasing Hoagie (he made it so easy!), I decided that it was time to steer our conversational train back onto its tracks. There was still a lot of information to go over, and I wasn't sure how much time we had left.

"Chase, what did they do to you...to try to get you to talk?"

The leftover smile slid off his face and his wizened, weary old man expression returned. "Charlie, I don't really want to tell you this."

"Come on, I won't get upset this time, I promise!"

He sighed. "It's not that. It's just...I don't really want to think about it anymore. Or make you think about it."

I mulled that over for a moment, but I couldn't really see a way to avoid the topic. It seemed crucial to our case (or to the future case we would file after we made our harrowing escape), and we needed all the facts we could get. "Well, do you think you could just give me the gist?"

He gave me a long, pitiful-looking grimace, but he complied. "Alright. Well, at first they tried to beat it out of me. They got some big orderlies to do that. When that didn't work, they tried drugging me, but you aren't the only one who took a page out of Grandpa Max's book."

I flashed him an encouraging smile, still amazed by how in sync we had always been.

"Then, after I broke out and slipped my four days' worth of unswallowed pills into Caleb's coffee, they tazed me like fifty times and I woke up in my cell, strapped to my bed. So they asked me again, 'What did you see?' And I kept telling them 'nothing,' so they injected me with something that felt like it set my veins on fire."

I felt sick again, but I tried to stay focused.

"They just keep asking me that same question: 'What did you see? What did you see?' and promising to give me some sort of antidote if I told them the truth, but I wouldn't. Then they left me alone for a while and I fell into some sort of sleep full of all these crazy dreams, and when I woke up, the drugs had worn off, so I broke the restraints, tricked a guard, and busted out of the cell. That's when I first met our buddy Hogarth here."

Hoagie nodded in confirmation, his face pale.

"Then they tazed me again and shot me up with a bunch more stuff, and I woke up in the infirmary, strapped to that machine you saw."

"What did the machine do?" I asked, trying to keep my voice steady.

"Shocked the shit out of me," he replied bluntly. "Every time I didn't give her the answer she wanted, this woman turned a dial and lit me up like a friggin' Christmas tree, shooting all these volts of electricity into my chest, all the while reminding me over and over again that you were dead, so there was no point in being strong or brave or whatever anymore. If she hadn't have heard you guys calling for help in the hallway, I'd have been fried to a crisp by now."

"Wait a minute..." I said slowly, "You mean that little blonde nurse from the infirmary?"

"No, the tall, skinny-looking lady with the brown hair and the glasses. She ran out a door in the back when you guys came in."

"The one with the pointy nose?"

"Yeah, and the fingernails that looked like—"

"Claws," I finished, feeling more spooked than ever. "Chase, that's the therapist who shoved the pills down my throat. She must have known about us the whole time."

"Oh, boy." Hoagie looked as if he'd just seen a ghost. "That's Doctor Friedman. She's even worse than Doctor Caleb."

"Great..."

"Yeah, it is great!" I argued, getting up to pace again, this time with a burning sense of impending accomplishment. "Don't you see? Now we know who's in on it! Now we know who to get our answers from!"

"Hold on just a second." Chase stood up, grabbing my wrist to stop me from pacing. "What do you mean? I thought we were just talking about escaping!"

"We *were*," I conceded, with an off-handed shrug. "But, assuming we could make it out of here in the first place, they'd just find you and catch you again. The only way to stop that from happening is to find enough evidence to prove that this whole place is some sort of torture factory and that you were framed! It's the only way to get the police to help us."

Hoagie appeared to be thinking it over, but Chase said flatly, "No."

"But—"

"No. No way. We're not doing that. It's too dangerous."

"And escaping isn't?"

"Charlie, I said no."

"Chase!"

"Hogarth, help me out here, would ya?' Chase implored.

I knew then I was sunk. If Hoagie hadn't been willing to help me break into the hospital wing to talk to Chase, he sure as hell wasn't going to let me capture and interrogate the scariest, most powerfully evil woman at The Institute.

"I...I think she has a point," Hoagie responded weakly, shrinking under Chase's intimidating stare. "If we can crack Friedman, we can take the whole Institute down from the inside."

"Then we wouldn't just be saving *your* life," I said, poking a finger at Chase's barrel chest, "we'd be saving all the other patients' too."

Chase glared at Hoagie, who, for once, held his gaze. This was what he had wanted all along—this was his part of our deal. He had almost compromised it for me, but now he didn't have to. At least, he wouldn't, if we could get my fiercely overprotective brother to see our side.

Chase turned his eyes back to me, his brows furrowed in frustration. When he saw that I wouldn't back down, though, he lowered them. "Charlie, I'm not losing you. I can't. Not again."

"You won't," I promised, hoping my faith in myself was not misplaced.

"You swear?"

I stepped under his chin to meet his big, somber brown eyes. "I swear."

"Alright," he said, defeated. "What's the plan?"

36

THE PLAN WAS SIMPLE: sneak back into the main section of The Institute and break into Dr. Friedman's office, where we would hopefully find either the woman herself or some concrete evidence of her crimes. It was a bold plan, a daring plan, a gutsy plan.

It was a stupid plan.

Chase led the way as we slipped out the door of our temporary safe house and into the rapidly darkening hallway. The early evening sunlight was barely able to filter through the dust and the gloom in the air, but I didn't need to watch where I was going anyway. Chase, garbed in an odd, makeshift toga he had crafted out of a pair of mildew-infested hospital blankets (he had insisted that I wear the robe in case anyone else developed a wandering eye), had his fingers locked tightly around my wrist, encircling it like some sort of warm, sweaty handcuff. He had agreed to everything we had suggested, had approved of every single crazy idea we (okay, I) had come up with—on one condition.

"Chase, this is silly," I whined, feeling like a toddler

strapped to one of those obnoxious baby leashes as we started down the stairs.

"I told you," he whispered back, leaving Big Foot-sized tracks in the layers of dirt on the floor, "we are *not* getting separated again. That's the rule. You agreed to it."

"Yeah, but I didn't think you meant it so literally!"

"I think it's a good idea," Hoagie chimed in, as he tiptoed along behind us, occasionally brushing his hand against mine in a gesture that I was fairly certain could be classified as "accidentally-on-purpose."

"Suck up." I stuck my tongue out at him as he grinned, feigning innocence as we stepped into the second floor hallway.

"Shhhh!" Chase hissed, stopping abruptly just in front of the door to the secret passageway. "I think I heard something."

My entire body tensed up as I froze, listening with every pore in my body. I didn't hear anything.

"Now it stopped." He frowned, cocking his head as he squinted at the window down the hall.

"What did it sound like?" I asked him, my nerves still on full-alert. I had seen enough television to know that no sound was worse than a loud sound anytime.

"Voices," Chase replied, his frown deepening as silence continued to buffet our over-tuned ears.

"It could be the patients upstairs," Hoagie posited, his breath warm on my neck as he stood close behind me. "They still keep five or six of the major cases on the top floor of this section."

"Major cases?" I repeated, getting a bit of a chill as he continued to breathe down my collar.

Chase had to have been distracted to overlook that.

"Yeah, like the patients that are dangerous to themselves or others, like violent schizophrenics or people that stay up all night screaming, no matter how many pills they give them."

"That must have been it," I told Chase, but I wasn't so sure. The walls were made of thick, solid concrete. There was little to no chance of hearing another person talking ten or fifteen floors above us.

"Yeah, must've been..." I could tell he wasn't convinced, but being still was becoming much harder than moving on, so he let it go. "Everybody ready?" he asked, giving us one last look as he placed his big fingers into the indentation on the door.

We nodded.

Chase gave my wrist a squeeze and slid the door open. He looked like a Grecian soldier, leading his troops into battle as he gave us a grim nod and plunged into the darkness of the tunnel.

"See you on the other side," I whispered to Hoagie, who left the door ajar behind us, just in case we needed to backtrack quickly. He didn't seem to like my joke, however, because his hand shook as he slipped it into mine, gluing our palms together with our mingling sweat.

For a few minutes, we trudged silently through the passage, which got blacker and blacker with every step we took. As before, rats and spiders and other foul beasts brushed against our legs and over my naked toes, all surely heading for the open door to make a mass exodus from their claustrophobic tomb.

Then I heard the voices: whispers, hisses, a quiet groan of frustration, all gliding through the dank air and bouncing against the walls of the tiny space, slithering into my ears and down my spine like gossamer snakes. The boys must have heard them too, for we all stopped, frozen like statues as we listened to the ghostly conversation that seemed to be happening all around us.

"...in there..." one voice said, sounding excited.

"Not like that!" barked another.

"Slide...this way—"

All of a sudden, it clicked. As if we were of one mind,

Chase, Hoagie, and I turned and shot back down the passage, not bothering to muffle our footfalls as we ran, full-out, back toward the door we had left open.

They had found us. They must have seen the smear of blood Hoagie had left on the false wall, they must have figured out what was behind it. They must have been tracking us for hours, or lying in wait like the predators they were, counting on us to slip up and make a dumb, stupid, ridiculously irrational move like the one we had just made.

I heard a crash as several large, angry orderlies ripped the plaster door from its frame and flooded the tunnel with a blinding, dazzling light that illuminated everything about us, from our exact location to the frightened, helpless looks on our faces.

Hoagie made it. He slid through the open door and leapt out into the well-windowed hall. I could hear the angry shouts and the heavy pounding of the orderlies' feet behind us, but we were clear! We were free!

We were idiots.

Just as Chase and I were stepping out into the free, fresher-smelling air, a particularly fat rat ran under my heel and I tripped, sending us both crashing to the dirty, web-strewn, feces-covered ground. The rat screeched in terror as it scrambled across my face, making tiny little scratches in my forehead as it tried to get away. Chase, in an attempt to keep himself from squashing me like one of the bugs that were currently crawling up my hospital gown, somehow somersaulted over me, slamming his head into the doorjamb.

Hoagie rushed back in to help, but it was too late. Already, hands were grabbing at my arms, my legs, my neck. I thrashed and clawed and wriggled my way into the open hall, but they followed me. They were like an army of bodybuilders: five huge, strong, well-muscled men, filing into the dusty space, whipping out tazers and needles and their fists, all fully prepared to take us in—dead or alive.

Then I realized something.

The men, though handsy, did not seem to be interested in Hoagie and me and all. They only had eyes for Chase, who was still struggling to get to his feet as a large, swollen red lump sprouted out of his furrowed forehead.

"Hoagie!" I shouted, as one of the men—a large, angry looking black guy whose upper body rivaled that of the Incredible Hulk—plucked him up by his collar and tossed him aside like a pesky dog, "Hoagie! They're after Chase! *Just* Chase!"

Hoagie looked confused for a moment. Then I saw him turn to my brother, who was rapidly getting dog-piled by the blue-clad orderlies, and he got it.

Chase was the key. He always had been, for me and for whoever had framed him. They couldn't let him escape, especially not without finding out how much he knew about Hawkes and his murder. Hoagie and I were just nuisances to be dealt with later, when they had a little more time on their hands.

Without wasting another second, I hurled myself into battle, screaming like Xena the Warrior Princess. My horror movie had morphed into an action film, and just like that I was Bruce Willis, I was Sylvester Stallone, I was one of those chicks from that awful *Charlie's Angels* remake. I could—and would—do anything to protect the people I cared about, and I had no doubt that I could do it. With a gut full of confidence, I punched The Hulk in the eye and kneed another orderly in the nose, while Chase struggled to shove them all off his chest. Hoagie yelped as one of the men kicked him in the ear when he tried to muscle his way into the fray, and I cursed as someone grabbed a chunk of my hair and ripped it backwards, sending me sprawling across the tile floor.

We had to distract them. We had to find a way to divert their attention so that Chase could escape. There was no more plan, there was no more mission, there was no more time for gathering evidence, there was only the burning, blistering need to get Chase out of there alive.

Hoagie fell to the floor beside me with a horrible, graceless slapping sound. He made to jump right back into the action, but I grabbed his arm.

"Don't let them get Chase," I told him, my eyes begging him to focus on me instead of the fight for just one second. "Whatever happens, we have to get Chase out."

"I know," he panted, as if I were wasting his time telling him something he already knew.

"No, you don't understand," I insisted, tightening my fingers around his bicep. "Whatever happens, you get *him* out. No matter what."

"Charlie, what—"

One of the men howled as Chase jabbed him in the eyeball with his thumb and bellowed, "I could use a little help over here!"

Hoagie tried to get up again, but I yanked him back down.

"No matter what," I repeated. Then I kissed him full on the mouth, enjoying one last moment of over-dramatic bliss before I allowed my recklessness to consume me.

He swayed slightly as I shoved him away and dove back into the tussle, where I deftly slid one of the guards' tazers from its holster. The guard shouted in anger and alarm, but immediately crumpled to the floor when I shot him with it, watching with a sick sort of satisfaction as he writhed and twitched like a dying cockroach.

That got their attention.

Two more of the orderlies broke free from the pack and

lunged for me, but I danced out of their reach, luring them down the hall and away from my accomplices. They growled wordlessly as they followed me like enormous gorillas, bent on capturing me for their next meal.

I turned and saw a second orderly fall in the distance, and felt a rush of relief. Chase and Hoagie could take on one henchman without my help, no matter how burly and ripped he was!

Unfortunately, that millisecond of relief cost me.

Sensing my distraction, both gorillas reached out for me at the same time, each getting a chunk of my flimsy robe as they closed in on me, pinning me to the wall. Panic filled my body as I tried to override my brain's instructions to surrender immediately and save myself from the brutal brand of torture that was surely in store for me now. My legs felt weak as the bigger ape laughed in my face.

I couldn't seem to hold myself up. Fear and shock were making my already sore legs weak and wobbly, and I didn't seem to be able to support my own weight.

That's when it hit me: the perfect defense.

Like a hysterical woman in a silent film, I swooned dramatically and went limp, sliding down onto the floor like a pile of wet noodles. Nonplussed, the orderlies let go of me and leaned down to get a better look, giving me just the opening I needed.

With already bloodied fists, I punched one man in the throat and the other in the gut as I rolled out from under them and back onto my feet. Only one of them followed as I raced back down the hall to the pile of broken and/or unconscious bodies lying at the other end.

Hoagie seemed to be holding Chase upright as The Hulk staggered away from them and fell to the floor, a huge, empty syringe sticking out of his back like a traitor's sword.

We did it! Already I could feel the prideful palpitations of victory swelling up inside me as I reached the boys. I rushed right into Chase's arms as Hoagie let go of him, whipping out a bright yellow tazer, which he aimed at the remaining orderly. I didn't even have to look to know that the voltage to his massive chest took him down right away, and I didn't have to tell anyone how grateful I was that my plan of self-sacrifice had left me both alive and relatively unharmed.

Silence fell over the corridor then, broken only by a few grunts and groans from our fallen adversaries. Chase, wobbly but lucid, squashed me into another bear hug as Hoagie flung himself around us both, enclosing us in a tight embrace that made me feel like the cream filling in the center of an Oreo cookie. I realized that I was laughing, quite hysterically, it seemed, but I wasn't the only one. Hoagie was giggling like a psychotic preschooler between whoops of triumph and remarks about how "freakin' awesome!" we all were, and Chase's chuckles rattled through my bones as he refused to let go of me.

Finally, after the light-headed giddiness of unexpected victory had passed, we all broke apart. Hoagie, familiar with the layout of the entire building, recommended that we take the fire escape instead of the creepy deathtrap tunnel, and Chase agreed wholeheartedly. As we all limped down the hallway together, he put the kibosh on any further spy missions, and Hoagie and I had no choice but to comply. I wanted to clear Chase's name, but not at the expense of his life. Or Hoagie's.

"Hey, wait," I said, as Hoagie opened an unlocked door at the end of the hall, "I want to go back and get one of those tazers, just in case."

"No," Chase said firmly, but I was already halfway there.

"I'll be quick!" I promised.

Maybe the victory-fueled exhilaration had filled me with a sense of immunity and immortality that left me impervious to any further fear for my life, or maybe the thrill of adventure had finally just driven me insane. Either way, I saw nothing wrong with going back to the site of our greatest battle to pillage the weapons of our fallen adversaries.

As if shopping for fruit at a supermarket, I rifled through the pile of guys and guns in front of the death tunnel and pulled out the only un-deployed stun gun I could find. "See?" I said brightly, holding it up for Hoagie as he closed in on me, worry written all over his freckled face, "no big—"

Suddenly a pair of sharp, curved talons dug into my chest and ripped me out of the hall and into the mouth of the tunnel. I screamed, dropping the tazer as Hoagie grabbed my outstretched arms.

"Let go, Mr. James," drawled the low, stern voice of Dr. Friedman from behind me.

"You let go!" he shouted back, panic in his beautiful blue eyes as he tried desperately to hang on to me.

She slipped her claws out of my skin and wrapped her thin, lithe arms around my shoulders, squeezing the air out of me like a boa constrictor. I struggled and fought against the pressure, but that only made her tighten her grip. She was slender and frail-looking, but she seemed to be stronger than all five of the orderlies put together.

Hoagie's grip was loosening, I could tell. I could feel his slick fingers slipping down my arms, his nails dragging long, jagged white tracks down my wrists, and I knew it was over. I heard Chase thundering towards us, but I knew what I had to do.

I made a desperate lunge forward with the last of my strength and I grabbed Hoagie's collar. "Get. Chase. Out." I told him, through gritted teeth, as the doctor pressed the air from my lungs.

His eyes bulged with fear and anguish, but he nodded.

Then I let go, allowing the devil woman to drag me to Hell as Chase screamed my name and Hoagie slammed the door shut behind me.

37

CHASE AND CHARLIE...CHASE *and* *Charlie...Chase and Charlie...*

The words swirled around and around in the darkness of my brain as I floated somewhere between consciousness and unconsciousness, grasping uselessly at rafts of thought that sank before I could reach them.

The wicked witch had drugged me, and she had drugged me good. I couldn't tell up from down, reality from unreality, sleep from wakefulness. All I knew were those three words: *Chase and Charlie. Chase and Charlie.*

And darkness. I knew the darkness. Thicker, more cloying, more velvety than any darkness I had ever felt before, it wrapped itself around me like a cocoon, swaddling me in inky blackness that stole the breath from my lungs.

I couldn't seem to open my eyes.

My lids were made of iron and my fingers seemed to belong on someone else's hands as I willed myself to wake up. I was no action hero now. I was Snow White or Sleeping Beauty—some sad, defenseless pseudo-princess who had to rely on some guy to come save her.

In a way, that was the worst part. I had always thought of myself as a strong-willed, competent, independent young woman, fully capable of taking care of herself (well, when her big brother wasn't around, at least). I shouldn't have needed some Prince Charming to rescue me! I was too much of a feminist for that! I should have been able to open my own eyes without having to wait for some dude to come along with a fetish for kissing dead chicks.

Wait, was I dead?

I seemed to be doing a lot of thinking for a dead person. The thinking was neither coherent nor constructive, but any thinking at all indicated brain activity, didn't it? And a person with brain activity can't be dead.

Right?

I tried to calm down and put my thoughts into some kind of order.

Chase and Charlie...Chase and Charlie...

What did it mean?

Chase and Charlie...Chase and...Chase and...

Suddenly the darkness cleared.

———

"Say goodbye to Chase," the wicked witch had said with a cackle, as she dragged me down the endless narrow passage back into the heart of The Institute.

"Screw you," I had spat back, my fury fueled by nothing but adrenaline and pure terror.

"You're scrappy," she noted approvingly, "I can see why Young Hogarth likes you."

"*Young Hogarth?*" I chuffed, trying to slow our descent into the catacombs by digging my bare heels into the solid concrete. "Where are you from, a Jane Austen novel?"

I could feel my skin beginning to rub off against the webby, scat-laden floor, so I let up. Friedman's grip on my chest had loosened, but her arms were as solid and unyielding as ever as she forced me forward, shoving me through the broken door and into the disused break room where the boys and I had embarked upon our suicide mission.

"No, I'm from New York, actually," she returned snootily. "But you misunderstood me. I was not referring to him as 'Young Hogarth, heir to a British throne or master of a sprawling estate in Connecticut.' I was referring to him as the younger of the two Hogarths in residence here."

"What the hell are you talking about?"

"You'll find out soon enough."

I could hear the satisfied smile in her voice as she shoved me down the hall and into an elevator. My heart was pounding in my ears as she stabbed a large, green button at the top of the wall panel with one of her red-painted talons.

I jerked involuntarily as the elevator began to shudder upward. I tried to slow my racing thoughts long enough to think of a defense or an escape strategy, but all I seemed to be able to do was watch the red numbers flick by on the small, black digital readout above the reflective metal doors.

We rose higher and higher, passing floor after floor after floor until I was sure that I was misreading the numbers on the panel. Then, the screen went blank. The black, empty background was replaced by an eerie green glow and the cab slowed to a stop.

I held my breath as the heavy door slid open, revealing a large, empty white room. For a moment, I thought I was being put into some bizarre form of solitary confinement. Then I heard a click in the distance and a thin, unmarked door opened in the blank wall opposite us. An odd, electric blue light spilled out onto the slick, shiny tile floor, and I felt my boiling blood run cold.

"He's ready for you," Friedman whispered in my ear, her saccharine voice laced with venom and an odd, almost seductive quality that was surely the last sound chipmunks hear before they are eaten by a poisonous viper.

"I...I don't think I have an appointment," I said, trying hard to stop the full-body tremble that was starting in my spinning stomach.

She laughed. "That's okay. Dr. James prefers walk-ins."

With that, she shoved me forward and I fell to my knees on the cold, white floor. Panicking, I turned to scramble back into the elevator cab, but it was too late. The door was closing quickly, impossibly quickly, as the witch laughed her wicked laugh and grinned her wicked grin, leaving me all alone in the lair of a beast that was surely even more deadly than she was.

———

The black, satiny darkness threatened to swallow me up again as I struggled to recall what happened next. My half-conscious brain was like a broken charm bracelet, spilling beads from its endless chain faster than I could catch them. For a few minutes (or hours, who could tell?), panic impeded my thought process even further as every single memory I had seemed to fall away, leaving me with nothing but a vast, awful, hollow emptiness.

An emptiness like the one in Hogarth's eyes.

———

I was back in the white room with the blue light, crouched on the floor as I searched for more hidden doors in the perfect walls with my wide, unblinking eyes.

There had to be a way out. There had to be a door or a window or a fire escape to climb out of. This was not how movie heroines met their end.

But this wasn't a movie.

"Come in," called a warm, inviting male voice from inside the blue room, "I won't bite."

I felt the blood drain from my face.

By that point, the man on the other side of that doorway had become bigger than life. He had become so powerful, so evil, so violently intimidating that he may as well have been a dragon, curled up and lying in wait for me at the mouth of a mystical cave in a storybook. He was bigger than Caleb, badder than Friedman, and if those two were capable of such terrible acts, then I could only imagine what sort of horrible atrocities their boss had committed, and what sort of torturous end he had in store for me.

Well, there was only one way to find out.

With legs like a jellyfish, I stood up and gathered whatever remained of my courage. Then I set my jaw and tried not to think about how badly it would hurt to die as I strode forward into the eerie blue light.

"Ah, I knew you would come!" the man purred in a deep, sultry-sounding voice as I crossed the threshold.

For a moment, I was stricken by how normal he looked. I had been expecting a dragon, but instead I had been greeted by a handsome knight who looked as if he had no place in such a nightmarish kingdom. His short, auburn hair was slicked down and shiny, swooping down low over his forehead and hiding the true age implied by the streaks and specks of grey along his scalp and hairline. Although he was seated behind a large, ornate mahogany desk, I could tell he was tall, with square, solid shoulders and an easy smile that didn't reach the rest of his perfectly-chiseled features. His dark, midnight blue eyes seemed to have been spun from the same silk as his well-tailored suit, but there was a malice in them that was so deep and intense that I was forced to look away.

"Charlotte Chapman," he drawled, as if he were savoring every syllable, "you are one troublesome lady, you know that?"

"I have heard that, yes," I said stiffly, taking in the floor-to-ceiling bookshelves that covered every wall, leaving no room for a conveniently placed escape hatch.

"And clever, too," he went on, leaning back in his black leather chair to regard me with what looked like respect. "I would be lying if I said I wasn't impressed."

I shot him a look of disbelief and he laughed. It was a familiar sort of laugh, though. It was as if I had heard the sound before, but I couldn't quite place it...

"What you did for your brother was...quite admirable. And what you tried to do for my dear little nephew—"

I resisted the urge to clap my hands over my mouth as it all clicked into place.

I remembered my last conversation with Hoagie before we had infiltrated the asylum. He had told me that he would be looking out for me, day and night. He had told me it was because he lived on site.

Because his uncle owned the place.

How could I have forgotten about that?

"Oh, you finally figured it out, did you?" the silken snake grinned, bearing a set of perfectly straight, blindingly white teeth that put the walls outside to shame. "Yes, I am the original Hogarth James. Well, the third, to be precise, the eldest living, but you get the idea."

I wasn't sure what to say to that, so I decided to just glare at him instead, trying hard to disguise my shock and disappointment that I hadn't put the pieces together myself. "Dr. James," Friedman had said, and "Young Hogarth," "the younger of the two Hogarths in residence here." Then there was their hair, their laugh, their easy, charming smiles and their youthful, boyish faces...they looked more like brothers than uncle and nephew! I couldn't believe I hadn't worked it out sooner.

"Don't look like that." He pouted, his furrowed brow and his folksy idioms so eerily similar to my Hogarth's. "There's no reason to be upset. No one has betrayed you. Young Hogarth has no idea what goes on in this office. Though he *is* suspicious."

"Would you get to the point?" I snapped, secretly grateful for the confirmation that my faith in Hoagie had not been misplaced.

A flicker of anger crossed his face, but his smile never wavered. His eyes, on the other hand, his dark, empty eyes, seemed to turn black in the light from the blue-shaded lamp on his desk. "Well, if you want to get down to business, we'll get down to business," he said with a shrug, steepling his long, slender fingers beneath his dimpled chin.

I felt like I was having an interview with the Devil.

"I'd like to make you a deal," he told me, playing right into the mental image I had just conjured up.

"No thanks." I had seen enough movies to know that making a pact with a man like him was suicide.

"The deal is this," he went on, his jaw tightening. "I know that you have been helping Young Hogarth investigate my doctors and their...'methods,' and I know that you believe that The Institute is behind the death of Dr. Benjamin Hawkes."

My expression remained stony.

"If you agree to keep that, shall we say...'sensitive'... information between us, then I will let your brother go free. No jail, no psych evaluation, no questions asked."

I felt a rush of cockiness as I realized that I didn't need his deal anyway. "Chase is already free," I said haughtily. "'Young Hogarth' got him out."

"Do you really believe that?" the Devil asked, with a sad, condescending little smile. "Do you *really* think that either of those boys would run off and abandon you in a place like this?"

My stomach fell.

He was right. I knew those two (well, Chase, anyway), better than I knew myself. And neither of them would ever leave me behind, whether I asked them to or not.

"So, what'll it be?"

I pretended to think it over. I couldn't take the deal, I knew that. And even if I did, he would find a way to screw me out of whatever he had promised me. I was sure of it.

"What if I say no?" I replied, trying to appear cold and uncaring while all my hopes of any of us escaping were dwindling down to nothing.

"Then I will use you to lure your brother back here, and I will kill him. Just like I had always planned to do."

His straightforwardness caught me off-guard. His fake smile was gone now, and his sinister eyes seemed to be staring straight into my soul as he waited for my answer.

"Why?" I asked.

"Why will I kill Chase? The same reason I'll kill you, too, eventually. He knows too much."

"But he doesn't!" I argued taking a step forward, "He has no clue who killed Hawkes or why! Hawkes is the only one who knows that."

"Is he?" A vicious grin spread across his all-too-handsome face. "Come on, Miss Chapman. You're a smart girl. You should know by now who killed my illustrious former colleague."

His indigo eyes sparkled with pride, and I knew exactly who the murderer was.

"You..." I said slowly.

"Who else?"

"But *why?*" I insisted, "Why did you kill him? And why did you frame Chase for it?"

"First of all, *I* didn't do the killing," he said smoothly, "I only orchestrated it. And I framed your brother because he just happened to be in the wrong place at the wrong time. That was Hawkes' fault, really."

"But why kill Hawkes at all?"

"Because he knew too much," he replied, his simple words heavy with meaning again.

"About what?"

"About a lot of things," he said, shrugging it off as if he didn't care. "About me. About The Institute. About her."

"'Her' who?"

His eyes widened briefly as his glance flicked to a small, square picture frame on his desk.

"No one," he replied cryptically. "So, what will it be? Deal? Or no deal?"

I heard a footstep and whirled around to see Doctors Friedman and Caleb behind me, the former of whom was holding a large, hypodermic needle full of a crystalline, yellowish liquid that glimmered in the dim lighting. I glanced back behind them and saw that the elevator doors had been propped open by a small, square plank of wood, surely to facilitate the speedy removal of my lifeless body after they injected me.

"Well?" The elder Hogarth urged, tensing beneath his exquisite suit jacket.

"No deal," I said.

Then, throwing forethought to the wind, I shoved past the mad doctors and flew into the wide white room, trying to keep my sweaty feet from slipping as I raced across the slick tile floor.

I was almost there. I could smell the metal of the doors, I could feel the light in the top of the elevator reaching out to embrace me, and I could hear the low hum of the straining cables as they held the car aloft, waiting for me to make my escape.

That's when it hit me.

Something hard, something hot, something painful, collided with the small of my back and I crashed to the ground. I couldn't feel my legs. I couldn't feel my toes. I couldn't feel my ankles or my bare feet as they sprawled across the shiny white floor.

A strange, paralyzing numbness was creeping up my spine, through my thighs, past my hips, into my chest and arms as someone turned me over.

It was her, the wicked witch, the she-devil, the demoness from Hell, who wanted nothing more than to see me suffer. Her evil grin was wider than ever as she pinned down my weakly flailing arms with her well-toned legs.

"Any last words?" she asked me, her bespectacled eyes dancing with murderous glee.

"See you on the other side," I grunted. Then, with the last bit of strength left in my body, I spat in her face.

With a ragged growl, she plunged a second needle into my throat.

38

FINALLY, the darkness receded as my memories fell back into place. My mind stopped swirling, my beads of thought stopped falling, and my iron eyelids slowly wrenched themselves apart.

I was lying on my back, staring up at a white stucco ceiling. Immediately I knew I was still inside The Institute, but I couldn't be sure of my exact location. I wanted to sit up to take in my surroundings, but a strange, paranoid fear kept me immobilized. What if I was strapped to a machine like Chase? Or tied down to a mattress, awaiting some other, more invasive, form of torture? What if I was still paralyzed, completely and permanently immobilized by whatever kind of tranquilizer dart Friedman had shot me with?

I closed my eyes again and took a deep, calming breath. *First things first,* I thought. Then, fully expecting to find them gone, I slowly twitched the first two fingers of my right hand.

Relief flooded my body as they wiggled, free from both paralysis and shackles as I raised my arm up to touch my stomach, my shoulder, my face—all of which appeared to be in perfect working order. Gingerly, I sat up, taking in the tight green sheets that bound me and the neat, impersonal little desk to my right.

I felt my relief drain away. "No," I said.

At least, I thought I said it.

Panic clawed at my chest as I tried again. "No," I mouthed, but I heard nothing. My lips kept speaking the word over and over, "no, no, no, no, no," but my throat wouldn't say it. My hands scratched at my neck, feeling for the voice box buried deep beneath my skin. I winced as my fingernails dragged across a large, angry bruise in the hollow of my throat, and I knew then what she had done.

I flew out of the bed, tripping gracelessly as I tried to disentangle myself from the straightjacket sheets again. She had done to me what she had tried to do to Chase. She had tried to turn him into the monster Evil Hogarth had needed, and she had turned me into the mute I had claimed to be two days before.

I reached for the door handle, but stopped.

I needed proof. I needed evidence. I needed something, anything to back up my story when I finally made it to the police. If I didn't have a voice, I would just have to find another way to make them listen.

I dropped to my knees on the laminate floor, dragging my nails across the slats until I found the loose board. I yanked it up and tossed it aside, creating a loud, banging clatter that seemed to explode against my eardrums like a grenade in the silent room.

Empty.

I plunged my hand into the narrow depths of the cavity, scraping the sides and the bottom and even just beneath the rim of the floorboard, but found nothing but wood-paneled emptiness. Where had they gone? All those papers, all that evidence, all that information couldn't have just disappeared into thin air!

And Sybil's pills! Where were they? What the hell was going on?

"You're the new Jane Doe, right?"

I felt a chill go up my spine as I froze, thrust back into the past by the slow, languid voice that called to me across the tiny room. Slowly, I turned to see Sybil, lying atop her mattress, staring up at the ceiling tiles with a sick, wasted look on her pale face as her wispy brown hair fanned out all around her.

"My last roommate couldn't talk either," she went on, her words frightening me even more than they had the first time because this time it was real. I could tell by the blankness in her eyes and the jagged edge to her voice that this time she really had taken the pills. This time she really was a zombie. "She died last night. And tonight, you'll die too."

Her head rolled to the side with her last words and she pierced me with a brown-eyed stare so terrifyingly otherworldly that I almost believed that she was a prophet, channeling her chilling message from a higher, darker power.

But she wasn't a prophet. She was just a girl; lost and sick and scared and alone, trapped in a palace of pain and torture and misery that she couldn't free herself from.

Just like me.

I ripped the door open and charged out into the hall. This time my pace was steady, controlled, charged with an eerie stillness that seemed to come from the solidity of my purpose.

Screw the mind games. Screw the torture. Screw the crimes and the cover-ups and the lies. I was getting out of that place, and no one was going to stop me.

"Where's the fire, honey?"

I glanced over as Big Momma fell into step beside me, her fat cheekbones like big red apples perched on either side of her pudgy black nose. Her dark eyes were kind but curious, wide beneath her heavily shadowed blue lids.

"Oh, I bet you're just hungry," she simpered, her voice deep and masculine as she attempted to sound more like a woman. "It *is* almost suppertime."

I stopped. What was this? Why were they all acting like they had never seen me before? Why were they all acting as if nothing had happened? As if no secrets had been revealed? As if no voices had been stolen and no one had been hurt in the pursuit of some half-assed cover-up scheme?

It was as if I were watching a rerun of my life, reenacting scenes that had been over days ago. The words were slightly different, but the acting was the same: Sybil, creepy and cryptic; Big Momma, sweet but ridiculous with her outfits and her mannerisms and her reassurances, and me; supposedly mute and obviously being toyed with by the big bad boss man.

I marched on, fury joining the terrified horror growing in my gut. They were screwing with me. Friedman and Dr. James were trying to make me think I was crazy so that I would play better into their twisted scheme.

Fat chance.

The mirrored glass door of the cafeteria flew open with a bang as I shoved it aside, and all eyes were on me. Like a fly to honey on a VHS tape on rewind, Wolfman Norman was stuck to me like glue, undressing me with his hungry old man eyes again. This time, though, there was no Hoagie there to save me.

So I slapped him.

He stumbled backwards as my backhand collided with his grisled gray cheek. He gaped at me in shock as the tiny old addict with the white hair froze on her way over to tell me about her checkered past.

The room was silent as I took my place in line, relishing the thought of what I would do when I got to the front. First, I would kick Caleb square in the cojones. Then I would hit him in the face, before grabbing a hold of his long, pointy nose and twisting it until he screamed for mercy, after which I would tell him he could go to Hell.

Clearly, I truly was becoming a bit unhinged as I inched forward, itching to get my hands around the neck of the mad doctor. I should have been concentrating on my next great escape, but my thoughts had strayed far too close to revenge to leave now.

Then I heard it: the thick, scraping jangle of chains as they slid heavily across the tile floor.

No, I thought, not even trying to say it aloud that time. *No, please, not again.*

I didn't look, but I knew Chase was there. I could feel it in my bones. That bastard had lured him back in just like he said he would. He had tricked him into obeying him, using me as a bargaining chip at a table that Chase could never walk away from.

My resolution gone, my spirit shattered, I turned to see my brother shackled between two other inmates, his shoulders slumped and his face bruised and battered, with eyes as blank and lifeless as the white paint on the walls of our inescapable prison.

I wanted to yell, to scream, to shout his name across the crowded room, but I knew it would be no use. Even if I had had a voice, he wouldn't have heard me. He had taken the pills, that was obvious. There was no getting through to him now. Though he was just at the other end of the line, he may as well have been a thousand miles away from me.

My eyes burned with tears, but I would not shed them. I clenched my fists to fight off the pain and the fear and the throbbing, aching realization that I had failed Chase, utterly and completely, the one time he had ever really needed my help. No matter what else the doctors had done or might still do to me, I would never give them the satisfaction of seeing me cry.

The line moved forward but I had lost momentum. I no longer wanted to strangle Caleb, I wanted to run away, right then and there, to a place where no one was crazy and I wasn't scared or alone, but I knew it was pointless. They had used me to trap Chase, but the opposite was just as effective. As always, it was Chase and Charlie—one unit, one team, one life. Just like he knew Chase wouldn't leave without me, Hogarth knew I wouldn't leave without my brother, I couldn't.

There was only one person left in front of me, and still I had no plan. I was considering taking my pills and shoving them down Caleb's throat out of pure frustration, but then the last person standing between us moved, and I gasped.

"Hoagie," I mouthed, afraid to believe what I saw. I felt faint as I took in the bloody scrubs, the shaggy hair, and the scruffy, gore-matted beard stubble of my would-be Prince Charming, all of which was exactly the same as the last time I laid eyes on him in the death tunnel. His nose was still swollen and dark, and deep bags now lined his vivid, electric blue eyes as he stared at me with an expression I couldn't even begin to read.

"Here are your pills," he said, his voice hoarse and ragged, as if he had been yelling for hours.

Disconcerted, I looked down at the cup in his hand and saw two small, white, diamond-shaped pills, the ones he had warned me never to take. My eyes flicked back to his face, but he looked away, pain and shame sparkling in his beautiful, blue gaze.

I grabbed his shirt and leaned in close, forcing him to look at me, silently begging to know what was going on and why he was doing this to Chase. To me. It had to be part of a plan! It had to be an act, a piece of a clever ruse we were enacting to trick the hospital staff and eventually overthrow them!

But it wasn't.

"Take the pills," he said softly, his voice thick and strained.

I shook my head vehemently and he closed his eyes, swallowing hard as a quiver shook his lower lip.

"Charlie, please, just take them," he pleaded, whispering now.

I let go of him and stepped back, still shaking my head. No. This was not happening. He was not betraying me. He couldn't be! Not after all we had been through! We were partners, we were a team! We were supposed to save Chase and expose The Institute and fall madly, deeply in love with each other! (Well... that last part was negotiable.) We were not supposed to switch sides right when we needed each other the most. We were not supposed to let my brother get drugged and tortured and killed for something he didn't even do!

Most of all, though, we were not supposed to break my heart.

"Charlie—"

I slapped the paper cup out of his hand. We both watched as it spun up into the air for a moment, then clattered to the ground.

"Charlie, please don't," he begged as a tear rolled down his ashen face. "Please don't."

But I did.

I threw him one last look of hurt and disgust and pure, gut-wrenching contempt, then I turned on my heel and ran for the locked front door. I could hear someone shouting as my bare feet pounded against the reflective tiles, and I heard those shouts change to screams as I threw my arms over my face and hurled myself through the cold, clear glass.

Well *THAT* wasn't a repeat performance.

Nothing I had ever felt in my life could have possibly prepared me for the sharp, excruciatingly painful, full-body sensation of being shredded by hundreds of thousands of shards of glass slicing into my skin like razor blades as I rolled onto the concrete sidewalk outside.

It was lucky that I had become a mute. Otherwise, I would have wasted too much of my precious time and energy screaming in agony and filling the late summer air with obscenities as I writhed on the prickly ground, covered in my own hot, sticky blood. Instead, I was free to skip that step and move on to the next one:

Running.

I shot off across the parking lot, pounding the pavement and shoving thick slivers of glass even deeper into the soles of my tender feet. I shook my head, trying to shake out the tiny little crystalline snowflakes that dusted my scalp as I clumsily rid myself of my bristled robe.

I had to find a cop, and I had to do it fast. Without me as a bargaining tool, Chase was useless to them. It was only a matter of time before they realized that I wasn't coming back (not alone, anyway), and when they did, they would quickly remove any and all threats to The Institute's security and secrecy—starting with my brother.

I started limping when I got to the road. The rage that had been acting as a painkiller was quickly losing its potency. It felt like dozens of tiny knives were tearing into my flesh as I hobbled down the shoulder of the empty, two-lane highway, wondering where all the traffic was.

What would I do even if I could find a cop? I couldn't speak to him, I couldn't tell him about Dr. James' den of atrocities! And even if I could, why would he believe me? With my green gown and rumpled wristband, I looked like a stereotypical escaped mental patient (which, in a way, I guess I was) as I wandered aimlessly down the road, frazzled and disoriented and wired with a crazy, desperate energy that I couldn't seem to dispel. At that point, not even my own mother would have believed me.

A different kind of pain pierced me as I thought of my mother, of the look on her sad, fragile, porcelain face when I (or someone with a functioning larynx) told her that Chase was gone, and that I had failed to save him when I had the chance.

I stopped.

What was I doing?

Running away from a fight was not my style (just ask the kid from the lunch line in fifth grade). Charlie Chapman was not one to flee at the first sign of trouble (even if she was, theoretically, going to try to find a policeman). Charlie Chapman was reckless and stubborn and pigheaded, and she refused to give up on anything, especially not the only person who had ever appreciated those qualities in her!

No, Charlie Chapman was a fighter, and she wasn't leaving that godforsaken loony bin without her brother.

40

As I CREPT through the thin strip of woods that hid Gray's Institute from the desolate highway, I could hear orderlies and guards shouting for Jane Doe, still pretending that they didn't know who I was. I skirted the edge of the parking lot, making sure to keep all of the men in sight so as not to accidentally bump into one of them. As I passed from tree to skinny, dehydrated tree, I counted fifteen guards in all, way too many for me to take out even if I hadn't just been turned into the world's first human porcupine. At the moment, they all seemed to be concentrated in and around the shattered glass entryway, perhaps in an attempt to keep the other patients inside while they scanned the area for me.

I would have to find another way in.

As silently as I could manage, I slunk through the underbrush to the back of the enormous gray building. There, the last of the evening sunshine seemed to darkle instead of shine as it played across the scaly bricks, throwing shadows at me as I snuck over to press my back against the stone facade. There was no search party here, but I still couldn't shake the feeling that I was being watched as I slid over to stand beneath the fire escape on the far right corner.

The metal ladder ended three feet above me, and my stifled lungs cried out in torturous agony as I jumped up to grab it, landing hard on my glass-prickled feet when I missed. Squeezing my eyes shut to block in the tears, I took a deep breath and jumped again. That time, I was able to wrap my right hand around the lowest rung on the ladder, but as soon as it made contact, a sharp, stabbing pain shot through my palm and I let go.

Cursing inwardly, I dug a nasty shard of long, jagged glass out of my hand and leapt up to try again. That time I caught the bar with both hands, but the blood on my fingers acted like grease and I just slid right back off. Frustrated, I balled up my fist and punched the concrete wall, lighting up my brain with even more excruciating pain that I didn't need.

Eyes watering, hand throbbing, cursing my own idiocy, I gathered my last bit of strength and determination and gave it one more try. That time, as my wet hands clamped down on the cold steel, I gave it a yank. The rusty, disused ladder clanked loudly in protest, but eventually slid down to my level.

I pumped my sore fist in victory before mounting the ladder, ascending the rungs like a skillful squirrel scurrying up a tree trunk. Once I got to the second floor landing, I pulled the ladder back up as quietly as I could to cover my tracks, and to make it harder for someone else to follow me. Then, without wasting time waiting to see if anyone had heard me, I raced up the next set of stairs and the next, barely pausing on the landings to catch my breath between floors.

I must have scaled twenty flights of rusty metal steps before I ran out of fire escape. I knelt down hard on the scaffolding, the criss-crossing pattern of the iron making deep, wicker-esque imprints on my skinned knees. I wasn't quite sure where to go from there. I knew that I was on the old side of the building, the one that housed the "interesting cases" and the ghosts of long-dead tuberculosis patients, but that was all I knew. I had no clue whatsoever what lay on the other side of the wall, and I had no clue how to confront it.

There was a square, blocky window to my left, but I couldn't make out any shapes, human or otherwise, beyond the dust-caked screen from the angle in which I was crouching. There was a stone ledge about fifteen feet above me that could, theoretically, have been a decorative ledge jutting out from the roof of one of the asylum's three towers, but I couldn't be sure.

Tentatively, I crawled over to the window. I held my breath as I peeked inside, pressing my nose to the netting.

I gasped (well, I opened my mouth, anyway). Inside the small room were dozens of large, full-color paintings, all of men and women in pastel-colored hospital gowns. Some were screaming, some were crying, some were eating mounds of goopy green mush, but they were all clearly former or current residents of The Institute. The huge blocks of canvas were leaned against walls and atop tall brown cardboard boxes and spindly chairs, as if they were on exhibit in a tiny art gallery.

There was one piece, though, that stood out from all the others. It was a beautiful, incredibly lifelike portrait of a woman in her thirties with brown eyes and long, wavy brown hair. There was a yellow flower tucked behind her right ear (a lily, I thought), and she was smiling sorrowfully down at a toddler who was playing with a set of wooden blocks at her feet. The toddler, a young boy with matching brown hair and bright, ocean blue eyes, was wearing a cherry red jumper over an orange-striped shirt, and looked a bit like a minuscule train conductor in a kid's cartoon. The mother, though, was garbed in a pale, mint-green gown and a thin, white robe that gaped open as the robe's belt snaked up to curl around her thin, graceful neck.

I had never seen anything like it. The woman was so elegant and beautiful, but still somehow so sad as she looked down at the little boy, smiling as if to hide the fear and doubt in her angelic face.

But this, though, was not was struck me about the painting.

My eyes trailed from the canvas and up the long, wraithlike arms of a withered old man sitting atop a lumpy, paint-spattered mattress, weeping quietly as he stared at his own work.

Again, I was disconcerted. Hoagie had told me that the only patients in that wing of the building were on the upper floors, but this man didn't seem like a patient. He was dressed in a paper-thin gown like me, but his room, unlike mine, was full of color and light and homemade art that made it seem more like an artist's studio than a suite in an insane asylum. He seemed to be separate from the rest of the patients, above them somehow, yet he had obviously come into contact with them at some point in order to paint such realistic portraits in their likenesses.

A part of me was aching to turn around and keep going, to find another way in that didn't involve drawing the attention of a potentially violent schizophrenic painter. Another bigger, gutsier part, though, told me to tap on the screen.

41

"Well, hello there!" The old man blinked, widening his weepy eyes in surprise.

I waggled my fingers at him.

"What are you doing all the way up here? Are you lost?"

I shrugged. In a way, I *was* lost, but not as lost as him. His hair was white and his skin was weathered and wrinkly, but his voice and mannerisms were that of a three year old—of a child who had forgotten to grow up. His rust-gray eyes were round and innocent, and he seemed to be completely oblivious to the river or white-yellow snot dripping down onto his leathery, calloused hands.

He moved to the window, holding his arms out as if I were a little bird perched on the sill and he was trying not to scare me away. "You wanna come in?" he asked in a loud, childish whisper. "I've got candy!"

I hesitated. It seemed stupid to trust someone so odd so easily, but there was just something so endearing about his big, hopeful eyes and his wide, goofy, mostly toothless grin that I couldn't resist. The promise of candy didn't hurt either. It was the oldest trick in the kidnappers' handbook, but I fell for it.

I was a worried mother's worst nightmare.

I nodded and he clapped his hands, startling me. He covered his mouth in distress when I flinched, surely believing that his little blonde bird was about to take flight.

I gave him a weak smile and he relaxed. Wiping his streaming nose on the sleeve of his gown, he shoved the dusty wire screen open and held out a hand to me. "Come on," he said invitingly, trying to coax his new pet inside, "I won't hurt ya."

I had already wasted too much time exposed on the shaky scaffolding, so I gingerly placed my bloody hand in his and let him help me over the sill and inside the dorm. I winced as my glass-gouged feet hit the floor, swearing like a sailor on shore leave at a silent film festival.

"Oh no, you're hurt!" the old man exclaimed, getting upset once again. "Here, sit down on my bed."

I nodded, still grimacing as I ignored yet another "stranger-danger" warning signal and hobbled over to perch on the edge of his multi-colored mattress. As I lifted my feet off the floor, I took a moment to try to relax and quiet the screaming in my head. I took a deep, steadying breath, then I put my left knee up on the bedspread and took a good look at my prickly foot.

For a second, I thought I might faint. There was almost as much glass as there was blood covering my skin. I felt like a grotesque version of Cinderella, whose pretty little glass slippers had shattered the moment she stepped onto the dance floor. Wondering if I looked as green as I felt, I swallowed hard and began to pick out the loosest shards, placing them all in a small, manageable pile on the bed next to the old man's painting.

"Can I help?"

I glanced up at the geriatric toddler and saw that he was wearing a worried frown that seemed to double the depth of the baggy creases under his eyes. He had his hands folded against his chest and was restlessly wringing them as he waited for the opportunity to assist his newfound friend.

Against my better judgment, I nodded again.

He sat down on the bed to my right, beside himself with excitement over what he seemed to think that a great privilege, and I scooted back across the sheets to plonk my right foot in his lap.

"Wow, this is bad..."

I gave him a "tell me about it" look and went back to picking crystalline steak knives out of my heel.

I jerked and punched myself in the thigh as the old man ripped a chunk of glass from the ball of my other foot, making sure to wiggle it around roughly before he yanked it out and held it up for me, beaming.

"Got one!" he declared proudly.

My brain seemed to be on fire, so I didn't respond. I spent a minute or so writhing atop the comforter, squeezing my watering eyes shut and reminding myself over and over that it was not nice to hit old people, then we both got back down to business again.

Thirty mind-numbingly bloody, excruciatingly painful minutes later, all the glass was out, including a few stray shards that had gotten lodged in my hands, arms, and shoulder blades. Aside from my feet, my flimsy robe seemed to have protected me from the worst of the damage and, despite the fact that my severed flesh was peeling off me like an onion skin, my injuries could have been much worse.

After that, the old man helped me to clumsily wrap my feet and right hand in strips of his torn sheets, and the bleeding seemed to have slowed enough for me to get back to the task at hand...after I got my candy, of course.

"Here, two Snickerses for you, and two Snickerses for me,"

the man said happily, slapping two king-sized candy bars into my sore right palm.

I gave him a grateful grimace, and he sat down next to me on the bed again.

"Do you like my paintings?" he asked, pointing at one of a large, hairy man who appeared to be screaming at his own slippers. "I did some of them myself."

I nodded enthusiastically. I *did* like the paintings, very much. They were even more amazing than I had originally thought, with intricate designs and color combinations that made them come to life. The nearly invisible brushstrokes on the canvas made me feel as if I were looking through a window at a real, flesh-and-blood person, and I just didn't get it. How could such a genius live within the mind of such an otherwise simple man?

"I've always been a good painter," he went on, puffing out his chest as he talked with his mouth full, spitting nougat all over himself (and myself). "Momma always told me that I'd be an artist. She said I was good because I could paint from my memory."

That thought brought something to the forefront of my own memory, and I pointed at the painting of the little boy and his mother, asking the question with my eyes instead of my lips as I looked up at him.

"Oh," he said, his cherubic face falling, "That's her. The boss's lady."

Stunned, I looked again at the portrait, then back at him.

"He loved her," he sniffled, snot oozing out of his wide, whiskery nostrils again. "Everybody loved her. Especially him. And me. And her baby, Little Hogarth. We were neighbors."

My eyes snapped back to the painting. Why hadn't I seen it before? The eyes, the hair, the round, boyish face—it was Hoagie playing with the blocks. Hoagie wearing the tiny little train conductor's outfit, Hoagie, captured in that moment forever with his mother, who had apparently been a patient at that very hospital at least twenty years ago. Just like in Hogarth's office, I had missed the obvious evidence of his link to the asylum as it stared out at me from everywhere, just waiting for me to see it and finally put two and two together.

I pointed at the canvas, more urgently this time.

"Well don't hurt her," the old man huffed, disgruntled, as he pulled the taut square of canvas onto his lap and away from my jabbing finger.

I mouthed, "Who?"

He seemed confused. "'Who?' 'Who' what?"

I tried to point at the woman in the painting, but he moved it out of my reach.

"She doesn't like that!"

I got up and tripped through a pile of paintings as I moved over to the small, cluttered work desk near the door.

"Hey! Stop that!"

I rustled through his things (mostly scraps of old canvas and sticky candy bar wrappers) until I found a small, square piece of paper and a little can of red paint. I grabbed a thin brush from a caddy on the corner of the table and I dipped it into the paint before hastily scrawling, in all caps, "WHAT'S HER NAME?"

"Why do you wanna know?" he returned, suddenly suspicious. He clutched the picture to his chest, as if he were afraid I was going to take it from him.

I gave him an exasperated, silent, sigh.

"Alright, alright," he grumbled back, easily persuaded. "Her name was Virginia James. She lived here a long time, until she died."

"HOW?" I wrote.

"I don't wanna say..."

I glowered at him and he gave in again.

"She got choked to death. Like in the picture. See?"

He turned the canvas around and ran his paint-speckled finger along the belt that encircled her neck.

I hesitated, realizing that I might have finally figured out why Hoagie wanted so badly to destroy The Institute and save the patients inside. "ACCIDENT?" I wrote finally, my hand sweaty on the brush handle.

The man shook his head.

"SUICIDE?"

He looked away, his expression unclear.

I waited a moment, then I scribbled one last word on the back of the paper. "MURDER?"

He dropped his eyes to the floor.

I had found it: the final key to solving the mystery, the last crucial piece of the puzzle that would allow everything else to fall into place. *That's* what Bad Hogarth had been talking about. She was the "her" he had mentioned in his office, as well as the reason Hoagie had spent the last four years working at The Institute, wasting his life away as he tried to discover an answer that I had just stumbled upon by accident.

She was the answer to everything.

I needed to find Hoagie. He had to know more about what happened than the old man did, and he needed to know who had killed his mother, if he didn't already.

I was halfway to the door when I stopped.

There was one more thing I needed to know before I left, one more question that needed to be answered. With the still-loaded brush, I spelled out one last word across the white bandaged palm of my left hand:

"WHY?"

The letters dripped like blood, sliding down the makeshift tourniquet as I held it up for the old man to see.

A tear slipped down his cheek. "Because he loved her too

much," he replied, his childish voice much older now, "and she didn't love him back."

I crossed the room and pulled him into a hug. He squeezed me back, squishing the painting into my spine. I didn't know his name or his illness or why he felt so connected to the James family's drama, but I would always be grateful for the help he had given me.

I kissed him on the cheek and mouthed "thank you," as I backed away. He gave me a sad little wave as I reached the door.

Then, with a bang, he fell to the floor.

Alarmed, I glanced up from the large, wet, crimson stain seeping through the back of his gown to see Big Momma squatting on the edge of the fire escape, grinning like a Cheshire cat as she pointed a smoking gun barrel at my chest.

42

THIS DID NOT COMPUTE.

Big Momma was a patient, a helpless pawn in The Institute's heartless chess game. She was a zombie, a drone, a kindhearted but strange man-woman who had been stoned out of her mind for ninety-five percent of our previous interactions.

But she was not stoned now.

Her bright, vindictive brown eyes glittered with menace in the light of the setting sun as she started to laugh a slow, deep, masculine laugh that bubbled up out of her chest like a long-winded belch, filling the room with the horrible sound of it.

I could barely feel my legs beneath me as I clenched the silver door handle so hard that I swore I heard something crack. I let my blind-sided stare flick down to the old man for just a second, knowing that that one look could mean the difference between my own living and dying.

I could hear the gurgling, bubbling blood sputtering out of the small, black hole just to the left of his spine as well as if I were holding my ear against the wound. I couldn't tell if the sound and the accompanying smell of damp, rusty metal was real, or a creation of my traumatized brain, but it was all I could do not to vomit as I watched him lying there, bleeding to death, knowing that I would now have to choose between saving my life and his.

"Hey there, sugar," Big Momma boomed, stepping inside the window. The floor shook beneath me as she hauled her bulk across the sill and into the now-tainted art museum.

The first bullet hit the door just two inches from my face.

Blinded by panic, I fumbled with the handle and somehow managed to throw the door open just as the next round singed my hair.

Next thing I knew, I was hauling ass down the empty hallway as fast as my lumpy, bandaged feet would carry me. There was no strategy in it now, no self-assuredness; no reckless, half-baked scheme that would somehow miraculously manage to work out in my favor in the end. There was just panic and terror, and the gut-wrenching realization that I had finally lost what little control I had ever had over the situation I was in.

I could hear Big Momma grunting as she chased me, her loose-fitting slippers slapping against the linoleum with every heavy, ground-shaking step she took. Bizarrely, I was drawn back in time to the night I had spent in the restroom crouched atop the toilet tank with Hoagie, trying not to laugh as she moaned about her bowel movements in the stall next door.

I definitely wasn't laughing now. Although she weighed at least twice as much as I did, she was just as fast as I was, maybe faster. I had primitive survival instinct on my side, but I also had torn, tattered, sheet-wrapped feet and the soul-sucking fatigue of three long, horrible days spent trying to cheat death.

A third bullet winged my right shoulder as I ducked into the stairwell. I could feel the warm, wet blood already dripping down my arm, but I was too amped-up to feel the pain. Knowing that I would be a veritable sitting duck in the small, enclosed concrete space, I did my best to leap down several steps at a time, causing more and more damage to my rapidly swelling feet each time they hit the ground. I had hurtled down at least five flights by the time Big Momma banged her way onto the stairs, and I quickly flung open the first door I came to before she could get another shot off.

With a sharp stitch in my side that hurt worse than my bullet wound, I raced down the narrow white corridor with absolutely no idea where I was going. I was hoping that there would be another set of stairs at the other end of it, but I couldn't be sure.

The smack-crackle of a bullet embedding itself in the plaster to my left announced Big Momma's presence in the hall.

"You sure are a quick one, ain't ya, baby?" she called, laughter in her husky male voice.

It was then that I noticed that there was no second set of stairs.

There was no fire escape, there was no window, there was no hole in the floor I could fall through just as Big Momma shot her sixth and last round at me. There was only a blank white wall ahead of me, and sure, certain, inescapable death.

Even knowing that there was nothing there for me, I kept on running, hoping with an insane, desperate, naïve sort of hope that a door would magically appear. The wall was six yards away. Three yards. Two yards. One yard. Two feet...

Suddenly, someone grabbed me around the waist and yanked me out of the hallway and into a small, silver vestibule. I struggled with my new captor, slapping hysterically at his strong, slender arms as a set of doors closed, trapping us inside the tiny steel box as I heard Big Momma call out in surprise and anger.

I was finally crying then, scratching and clawing at the arms that held me while I screamed and screamed inside my own head. There was a jerk and I realized that the box was moving.

The elevator. I was in the elevator.

"It's me!" a voice was shouting as the arms clung to me, not constricting me but holding me; not strangling me but hugging me. "Charlie, it's me!"

I couldn't seem to stop fighting him. I knew I recognized the voice, but my brain was so fried by fear and pain and panic that I just couldn't place it. But the arms didn't let go. They held me close to a taut, sturdy chest, tightening around me until my sodden cheek was pressed against it so close that I could hear the heavy, rapid pounding of someone else's panicked heart.

For some strange reason, this soothed me. Slowly, the world came back into focus as I listened to the strong, steady, slightly erratic beat, gulping down lungful after lungful of thick air that smelled like sweat and blood and lemon Pledge.

"Hoagie." My lips moved soundlessly against his tear-soaked scrubs. I leaned back a bit to look up at his bruised, battered face as I mouthed his name again, wanting so badly to speak it out loud so that he could hear the gratefulness and the relief in my voice.

A storm seemed to be raging behind his ocean-blue eyes as he stared down at me, tears streaking his own scruffy cheeks. "You should have listened to me," he said, his voice hoarse as his bottom lip quivered again. "I tried to tell you this would happen."

I opened my mouth to argue, but remembered at the last moment that it was futile. I sealed my useless lips once more, casting my eyes downward as I resigned myself to enduring whatever other harsh (but still maddeningly factual) words he had for me.

My silence seemed to stir something else in him though, something kinder and softer and more protective. "What did they do to you?" he whispered, reaching out to run a gentle finger across the bruise at the base of my neck.

His touch moved from my throat to the long, shallow gash on my upper shoulder, and I reached up to wrap my hand around his finger, partially because he was hurting me, and partially because I wanted him to pierce me with those big, melancholy blue eyes again.

"Thank you," I mouthed, hoping he could read the words that my throat couldn't speak.

He reversed our handhold and pulled our intertwined fingers over to rest between our close-pressed hearts in a silent gesture so much more meaningful than anything I could have come up with.

"They've got Chase," he said bluntly, his expression weary and angst-ridden. "They know that as long as they keep him here, you won't leave. Not for good, anyway. They said that the more you fight them, the worse it'll be for him."

I don't know if it was battle fatigue or the fact that I had already predicted that outcome, but I was more numb than upset as I nodded in understanding.

"They also said that if I help you, it'll make it even worse when they finally get their hands on *you*. That's why I wouldn't help you before in the cafeteria. I thought if I just did what they said, they might not..." He trailed off, looking a bit broken. As if to distract himself from his inner turmoil, he punched the emergency stop button on the wall panel. A shrill, high-pitched bell began to ring loudly in the tight space, filling our heads with the sound and the bad memories of our last meeting.

"I *wanted* to go with you," he continued, as if I were arguing with him, "but I didn't know what to do! I don't know what they want! I don't know why they're doing this, or how no one knows about it, or how to stop it! All I know is that I shouldn't have let Friedman take you into that tunnel, and I shouldn't have let them get Chase, and I shouldn't have let you jump through that stupid glass door—not without me! Charlie, I just—"

I held a shaky finger up to his lips as I made a low, barely audible "shh" sound. He was breathing hard, his throat clogged with emotion and his heaving chest crushed against mine, wracked with guilt over the fact that he had been trying to save my life (not to mention my brother's). He blinked down at me with dark, deep, desperate eyes, begging me for answers or forgiveness or some sort of affirmation that I still cared about him.

His intensity took my breath away as I realized that, even if I had been able to speak, I wouldn't have known how to put my feelings for him and his sacrifice into words. I lifted my finger from his lips to lightly stroke his cheek and he closed his eyes.

"I just...I just want to know *why*," he whispered, just as tormented by the memories of the past few days as I was—and more. He had had a whole lifetime of experience with the cruelties of The Institute. He had had years of not knowing why people were being hurt and mistreated and used as pawns in someone else's life-or-death chess match. He needed answers. And I had them.

I gently tapped his chin to get his attention and he opened his wet, anguished eyes. I pointed at myself and mouthed grimly, "I know why."

"You know why they killed Hawkes?" he asked incredulously, his eyes brightening with disbelief.

I nodded.

"Why they framed Chase?"

I nodded again.

"Why they drug everyone?"

I gave him one of my patented nod-shrug combos for that one. I wasn't totally sure yet, but I had been working on a theory ever since Sybil had taunted me in our room the second time... and since Big Momma had begun trying to kill me.

He swallowed hard, as if he were choking on all of this new

information. "So...you know who's behind all this?"

That time my nod was heavy, weighted down with the knowledge that would confirm his earlier hypothesis—and his worst fear.

There was a loud, "whooshing" sound as he let out the breath he had been holding. "Geez," he breathed, "you've been busy!"

I gave him a shrug and a sad little smile. Even though I had collected the earth-shattering information, I had no way of conveying it to him. He could try to read my lips, maybe, but that could take forever, and we didn't have that kind of time.

"How good are you at charades?" he asked, reading my mind instead.

I glanced up to see him grinning at me, the storm beginning to calm in his sparkling, azure eyes, as he affectionately brushed a stray strand of bullet-singed hair out of my face.

Just like that it was back again: all the hope, all the confidence, all the belief I had in myself and my boys and our ability to get through whatever horrors The Institute had in store for us. I felt lighter, better somehow, as I realized that, just like in the tunnel, I wasn't alone, and I never had been. With the monotonous buzzing of the alarm bell ringing in my ears, I stood up on my tiptoes to kiss him, cupping his face with both my clumsy, bandaged hands as he used his to squeeze me to him so tight that I could barely breathe.

"Wow," he said after a moment, his voice husky and his eyes still closed as he pulled back slightly, "you really *are* good at charades."

The cheesiness of that line only made me want to kiss him even more, but, unfortunately, there wasn't enough time. I settled for giving him a tiny, light little peck on his puffy, blue-violet nose, and then I leaned back, gently extricating myself from his snug, safe embrace. He was reluctant to let go, so I allowed his arm to linger around my waist as I slipped my left hand into his and pulled it away from the emergency stop button.

"Where are we going?" he asked, nuzzling his scruffy face into the hollow between my neck and shoulder as he stood behind me, giving me goosebumps.

I thought about it for a moment, then I pressed the number seven on the wall panel (seven was supposed to be a lucky number, right?).

"What's on the seventh floor?" He was still apparently under the impression that we were in a car at the drive-in instead of the middle of a highly volatile rescue/escape mission as he kissed a ticklish little spot beneath my right ear, making me shiver.

I waved him away a bit (without really wanting him to go), and pointed at the button labeled "8."

"Eight?"

I nodded.

"I don't understand...I thought we were stopping on seven?"

I nodded again and he took his hand off my waist to run it through his hair in bewilderment. Before he could get frustrated, I pointed at the number seven again.

"Seven," he nodded, "got it."

Still not quite sure he was following, I pointed up at the emergency escape hatch in the back corner of the ceiling. Doing my best to replicate the talents of my pseudo-namesake, Charlie Chaplin, I mimed opening the hatch, then climbing up an invisible ladder to the next floor.

"Wait a minute..." He frowned. "You want to stop on seven, then climb up to eight?"

I grinned and tapped my nose.

"Why?"

I bit my lip, trying to think of a way to describe it with just my worn-out, beaten-down body. I opened my arms wide and pointed upward, as if at someone watching from above.

"God?" he guessed, completely baffled.

I shook my head. I did the motion again, then pointed at the elevator doors.

"Charlie, I don't—"

Getting agitated by my own ineffectuality, I waved my hands as if I were erasing what I had done before. Then, I jabbed at the wound on my arm, my fingers making the shape of pistol.

"A gun?" he tried. "A bullet?"

I shook my head.

"Blood? Hospital gown?"

I slapped my forehead. I puffed out my cheeks like a puffer fish and held my arms out in front of me as I took a few hulking, zombie-like, Frankenstein-esque steps.

"Big Momma!"

I nodded, grasping his hand in encouragement.

"Big Momma..."

I made a talking motion with my hand and pointed up at the sky again.

"I don't..." then his eyes lit up. "You think Big Momma told the doctors what happened and now they're watching to see where we stop!" he exclaimed, fortunately figuring out the last half of the puzzle without any further need of my rudimentary charades skills.

I kissed him on the cheek and he puffed out his chest with pride.

The elevator slowed to a shuddery stop and I pushed the "Door Close" button before it could open.

"But how are we gonna get up there?"

I gave him a sly grin as I pointed to him, then at myself, mouthing, "*You* tell *me*."

43

IT WASN'T A *BAD* PLAN, really…just a dumb one.

Hoagie, more than happy to take over as chief hijink engineer, had pointed out that, in order for the closed doors to stay closed, someone would have to stand there next to the wall panel with their finger on the button, constantly applying pressure to the circuit until we were out of the way. After ascertaining that he had nothing of use in his junk-drawer pockets (aside from a fistful of powdered Fig Newtons, which I ate), he decided that he would hold in the button while I climbed up onto his shoulders and opened the emergency hatch in the top of the elevator.

The ceiling was just under eight feet high, just a couple feet higher than Hoagie's head. Thusly, I had to hold my own head sideways with my shoulder to the steel plating as I perched atop his shoulder blades and tried to contort my aching body into a position in which I could reach the screws on the trapdoor. I could already feel the crick forming in my neck as I attempted to turn the first of four thick flathead screws with the flat end of the plastic dart from Hoagie's pants. My only solace, though, was that he had it even worse than I did.

Unfortunately, the hatch was in the back corner of the elevator cab, a good four or five feet from the wall panel. I tried not to laugh as Hoagie wobbled unsteadily beneath me, holding onto my thighs as he tried to balance us both on one leg, using the toe of his left foot to hold in the button.

"I feel like one of the Three Stooges," he muttered, wiping his sweaty forehead on my bare leg as he sputtered and huffed, hopping comedically in an attempt to stay upright.

I responded by accidentally dropping the first screw on his head.

I covered my mouth in a silent "Ooops!," but he just sighed.

"You know," he grunted, shifting my weight back a bit and making me bang my elbow on the roof, "after you get that off, we should take the elevator up a few more floors before we get out. That'll really throw 'em."

I stopped, struck by his genius. I leaned down and kissed him on the top of the head to show my agreement.

I worked the second screw out of its groove and one side of the door flopped open, making it much more difficult to get to the two remaining screws. Wriggling around to come at it from an even more unnatural angle, I felt like a Cirque du Soleil performer as I held the metal slab in place with one hand and kept unscrewing with the other.

"Hey, Charlie?" Hoagie asked, straining hard to support my weight.

I couldn't answer, so I just waited for him to go on.

"Do you think that maybe after all this is over and Chase is safe and the patients are all taken care of and everything, you and I could do something 'normal' together?"

If we're not both in jail... I thought.

"Something nice and calm, like going to dinner or the park. Or maybe a movie!"

I smirked down at him. A movie was what had gotten us into that mess in the first place.

"Alright, alright, not a movie," he said hastily, trying to shrug but failing to move his shoulders, "but something else, though?"

I gave him a coy smile as I removed the third screw. How could I turn down a guy who had the guts to ask me out on a date when he was hopping around like a sweaty flamingo?

I nodded.

"Yes!" he cheered. Then, embarrassed, he cleared his throat and said, "I mean, hey, that's cool."

I rolled my eyes, still grinning as I removed the fourth and final screw. Careful not to let it fall on my poor, one-legged counterpart, I removed the cover from the small, square hole and tossed it aside with a loud, metallic clang.

"Thank God," Hoagie grunted as he hobbled over to press his hip against the button so he could put both feet on the floor.

I handed him his (now mangled) dart and attempted to slide down his back as gracefully as I could. Instead, though, I got one of my bandaged feet caught in the collar of his scrubs and fell backwards, pulling him down with me as I somehow managed to bang all of my throbbing wounds simultaneously against the cold metal floor.

Miraculously, Hoagie was able to reach his leg up and hold the button in with the toe of his right shoe before the door could open. "Are you okay?" he panted, his eyes wide and worried in his swollen, freckled face as he posed like some perverse ballet dancer in an absurd arabesque on top of me.

My feet were burning, my head was throbbing, and my stinging shoulder was now bleeding profusely all over the stainless steel floor, but all I could do was laugh. I must have looked like some sort of deranged, silent hyena as I shuddered and shook, my shoulders rocking and my chest heaving with soundless giggles as I covered my face with my hands.

"Man, I miss that," came Hoagie's soft, affectionate voice from just inches away.

I moved my hands to look up at him questioningly, my eyes still watering.

"Your laugh," he clarified, his expression tender and nostalgic. "That's the first thing I liked about you. Well, that, and the fact that the first thing you did when we met was call me a smart-ass."

I met his teasing smile with a genuine one, touched once again by how much he had come to care for me in such a short amount of time. I would have given anything to say just one single word to him right then.

Instead, though, there was a loud, earsplitting whistle as something punched a big, round hole through the elevator door.

44

In a selfless act of heroism, Hoagie flattened himself on top of me, shielding me from the barrage of bullets that was now streaming into the tiny space, pinging off the walls and peppering holes in the metal all around us. Unfortunately, though, this courageous act caused his foot to slide off the button he had been trying so hard to hold in.

The heavy door slid open, leaving us completely exposed to the posse of heavily armed orderlies waiting outside. Hoagie bore down hard, as if he were attempting to hide my body beneath his as two of the men stomped inside.

"NO!" he shouted. "Leave her alone!"

"Give it up, man," someone said (I couldn't tell who, since Hoagie was currently obscuring my vision with his smelly right armpit). "Just hand her over and we can all go home."

"No!"

"Listen, if you let us have her now, the boss won't hurt her!"

"Bullshit!"

Through the sea of fear that now seemed make up the permanent landscape of my mind, a completely ridiculous thought swam to the surface. That was the first time I had ever heard Hoagie use a real, bona fide curse word. *Wow,* I thought, feeling a bit dazed, *he really* does *like me!*

I realized then what I had to do. Hoagie would do everything in his power to keep me safe, even if it meant him getting injured or killed himself, but I couldn't let him do that. He, like Chase, meant the world to me by that point, and I would have gladly sacrificed my life to save him. Hopefully, though, it wouldn't come to that.

I tapped on Hoagie's shoulder to get his attention. His eyes were wide and wild as he stared hard down at my face, as if he were trying to memorize it. For a moment, I wondered if I should try to memorize his too, just in case.

No. There would be plenty of time for sentimentality later.

Focusing on his stormy blue stare, I pointed at the guards and nodded.

"No," he said immediately, "no, no, no, not that."

I nodded harder.

"Charlie, no! They're lying!"

I looked up to make sure the orderlies were watching Hoagie instead of me. Then I winked as my lips formed the words, "So am I."

For a second, he was flabbergasted. He recovered quickly, though, and, despite the wary, worried frown on his sweet, boyish face, he climbed off of me.

As I had expected, the guards moved back toward the entrance to the crowded elevator car to give us some room, knowing full well that we were sitting ducks anyway. Gallantly, Hoagie helped me to my feet, his expression grim. I subtly maneuvered him over to stand directly in front of the wall panel as I turned toward the orderlies.

"It's about time," a large, stupid-looking one groaned from the back, his head like a blonde basketball perched atop his steroid-sculpted shoulders.

"Just come on, girl," sighed another, much wearier-looking guard. Dimly, I registered that he was the scarred orderly who had taken me to Friedman's office before.

Aside from those two, there were three more gigantic men clustered around the doorway, all armed to the teeth with firearms and stun guns as they blocked our only viable exit.

I must have been one hell of a threat.

I held up my hands in a gesture of surrender, and the stupid one reached forward and grabbed me by the arm. Before he could drag me out, though, I planted my feet and held up a finger, begging him to wait.

"No, we're going," he said, giving me a yank.

I shook my head vehemently and held up my finger again.

"What does she want?" one of the other orderlies asked, sounding genuinely curious.

"It doesn't matter," the stupid one barked, "she has to go!"

I shook my head again, then pointed at Hoagie, who looked just as confused as they did. I pointed at him, then at me, then made a kissy face (that probably looked more like a fishy face) as I held up my finger one more time.

"What the hell—"

"She wants one last kiss!" Hoagie interpreted loudly, sounding much more confident now that he had caught onto my plan. "One last kiss before she goes."

"This isn't a Ryan Gosling movie," Scarface snarked.

"But we'll never see each other again!"

"So?"

"So, what is it gonna hurt if I kiss her just one more time before you take her with you? It might even make her more cooperative!"

The orderlies frowned in unison, and took a moment to confer upon the matter. I, unable to believe that my latest hare-brained, spy-movie-based scheme was actually becoming plausible, couldn't risk giving myself away by glancing at Hoagie. Instead, I stared intently at the group of guards, my eyes bugging out as I tried not to blink too much.

"Alright, you've got ten seconds," declared the weary one, looking harassed now as he rubbed his scar. "Then we're taking her. No further arguments."

"Deal," said Hoagie.

I smiled like an idiot and clapped my hands in an expression of pure and completely unbelievable girliness and moved forward to shake the hands of all five orderlies, starting with the ones in the back. As I came around to the last two in the front, still grinning as if I had just won the Miss America Pageant, I tripped on an invisible fold in the steel carpeting and fell forward. Instinctively, they both stepped back, unknowingly moving their toes behind the line that separated the floor from the elevator shaft.

Apologizing like a sloppy drunk on mute, I shuffled over and wrapped my arms around Hoagie who, in turn, leaned me back against the wall panel in the interest of privacy. As his warm, scratchy lips met mine, he pressed his palm into the "Door Close" button.

45

The orderlies knew instantly that they had been had, but they were too slow to do anything about it. One of them inserted the barrel of his revolver into the tiny gap between the quick-closing doors, but Hoagie pressed another floor button and we were moving before he could fire it.

The gun clattered down the elevator shaft as we rose up, my stomach swooping as if I were on a roller coaster. We did it. We really did it. *Again.* By all measures of logic and reason, we should have been dead by then, or separated at least, strung up in two different torture chambers or hooked up to the machine in the lab where I'd found Chase. There was no way that we could have been lucky that many times—it just didn't make sense! But I wasn't complaining.

"Oh my God," Hoagie muttered. A loud, slightly deranged-sounding laugh escaped from his lips as he ran his hand through his hair over and over again in complete and utter disbelief. "Oh my God, you're a genius!"

I took a fake bow and then he was kissing me again, passionately, desperately, breathlessly this time, as he pressed me into the wall, filling my swooping stomach with flaming butterflies and sending tingles of warm static electricity rippling throughout my entire body.

We were still completely lost in each other when a bell rang and the elevator stopped, but Hoagie still had the presence of mind to keep the doors closed.

I pulled back a bit and said, "We should probably—"

I gasped, clapping my hands over my mouth as my eyes flew open. I had spoken! My voice had been a raspy, crackly, hoarse little bleat, but that bleat had come from my own throat in my own voice!

"Say it again," Hoagie begged me. His face was flushed as he stared intently at my lips, not daring to believe his own ears.

"We...we should probably go," I croaked, sounding as if I were talking through a staticky old radio from the 1950s.

"HA HA!" Hoagie shouted, literally jumping for joy as he hugged me and laughed, just as happy to hear me speak as I was. "You can talk!"

"I can talk!" I confirmed, beaming as I rubbed my achy throat.

As he kissed me once more, I half-wondered if it had been his last kiss that had awakened my sleeping vocal cords (as opposed to the much more probable passage of time and increased blood flow to the area). Maybe I had been in need of a Prince Charming after all...

"This is amazing!" he exclaimed, pulling back, "This is incredible! This is—"

All of the sudden, Hoagie's delightful string of superlative adjectives was blotted out by a stab of guilt as I thought about Chase. He would have been even happier than Hoagie to hear my garbled old radio voice (assuming he'd known I'd lost it in the first place). He would have picked me up and spun me around like a little kid, laughing as he made me quote lines from old movies for him.

Somehow, in the middle of all the revelations and the injections and the gunplay (not to mention all the ill-timed make-out sessions), I had forgotten why I was there.

"Miraculous! Beautiful! Absolutely—"

"Hoagie, we need to go," I said abruptly, my voice like a car driving down a gravel road or a man from an old jazz band. "That orderly was right. This isn't a Ryan Gosling movie. We need to get a move on."

"You don't think I look like Ryan Gosling?" He pouted, pretending to be hurt by my insinuation.

I put my hands on my hips.

His smile faded slightly, but he understood. "Okay, okay, you've got it, boss."

Then, without preamble, he grabbed me around the waist and hoisted me up through the hole we had made in the ceiling. Before I could notice much more than the still, silent darkness and the eerie coldness of the empty elevator shaft above me, there was a ping of metal on metal as a bullet zinged past my cheek.

"PULL ME BACK IN! PULL ME BACK IN!" I rasped, hoping Hoagie could hear me.

He could.

Without hesitation, he yanked me back in as a shower of bullets rained down on us from a set of open doors five floors up, sounding like b.b. gun pellets smacking against aluminum siding.

"Screw it," Hoagie growled, pulling me with him back over to the button panel. With a punch that made his knuckles pop in protest, he hit a button and sent us skyrocketing up the enemy-laced shaft to the twentieth floor. "When the heck did they get guns, anyway?" he demanded, sounding more indignant than afraid as we heard the clatter of revolvers and stun guns being dropped on the roof as we rose higher and higher. "This is supposed to be a hospital for crying out loud!"

I, having already accepted that the guards (and patients, apparently), had weapons and no qualms about using them, had other things on my mind. Things like what we were going to do if the door opened on the twentieth floor and Big Momma was waiting there to fill me full of lead like a gangster in a mafia movie. I had already proven that I could be scrappy if the occasion called for it, but nothing I could do could stop a bullet, let alone the crazy man-woman who wanted to shoot me with it.

Up until that point, the whole thing had been like a game to me—an odd, scary, dangerous game of skill that I could somehow manage to win if I just tried hard enough and outsmarted enough of the other players on the board. Now, though, they had weapons I couldn't match, soldiers I couldn't compete with, and a deep-running, win-at-all-costs vindictiveness that I could never have tapped into even if I had wanted to. Someone had died and they hadn't cared. Someone had actually, legitimately bled to death (well, two people, if you counted Hawkes), and no one had tried to stop it. If The Institute was that heartless in regards to their own people, I could only imagine what they would do to Hoagie and me once they caught us...and what they were doing to Chase at that very moment.

"What floor is Chase on?" I asked as the cab began to slow again.

"Five, I think," Hoagie replied, looking green as the bell dinged and the doors banged open. "We'll have to take the fire escape down to go get him."

I nodded, only half-listening.

No one.

No one was waiting for us. No one was leaning in from the hallway, ready to stab us with needles or shoot us with handguns, and no one was shouting a warning to announce our arrival.

Still, I hesitated, reaching back behind me to find Hoagie's hand as I peeked around the doorway at the seemingly empty corridor.

"Where are they?" Hoagie whispered, surely feeling, as I was, that the apparent absence of a threat was worse than the real thing. If we could see the attackers, we could at least know when to duck or where to hide, but if they were invisible, we would have no warning until it was too late.

The hairs were standing up along the back of my neck as I stepped out onto the cold, slick white tile. Hoagie pressed a button in the panel and the elevator door closed behind us, sending our bullet-pocked safe haven down to another floor and out of our reach. I hoped that the reappearance of the cab on another level of the building would serve as a diversion, but I wasn't counting on it.

I could barely breathe as my eyes darted around, taking in door after closed, locked door, certain that every single one of them was concealing a deadly assassin just waiting for the perfect moment to strike.

"We need to get to the fire escape," Hoagie said into my ear, making me jump a foot in the air. "It's in room 2012."

My stomach churned. I knew where the fire escape was. It was in the pseudo art museum with the candy and the paint and the kind old man who had been shot to death while helping me. It was also the place where I had learned Hogarth's terrible secret.

And Hoagie's.

"I'm not sure if that's a good idea," I waffled, still scanning for danger.

"We don't really have another choice," he replied, swallowing hard. "The only way to get down to the fifth floor now is to use the fire escape, assuming they haven't blocked it off yet."

I took a few reluctant, tiptoed steps toward the room at the end of the hall, the eerie silence dripping off me like a cold, icy sweat. He would find out eventually. He had to. I couldn't shield him from the truth when it was the only thing that might possibly save our lives. Still, though, my steps were heavy and hesitant as we continued to creep forward.

When we got to the door, Hoagie stopped, tightening his hand around mine as he took in the wooden splinters all over the floor and the large, ragged bullet hole in the narrow white door.

"Were you in there?" he asked me quietly, sounding more scared than I had ever heard him. "Were you in there when that happened?"

I nodded. "But that's not all that happened in there," I replied, as if that vague, ominous statement could somehow prepare him for what he was about to see.

With a tremor in my hand and a pounding in my heart, I pushed open the door.

46

THERE WAS a low choking sound as the door swung open and Hoagie saw what was waiting for us inside. I, too, was taken aback by the grisliness of the scene. I knew what had happened, and I had seen the dead man before, but nothing could prepare me for the clammy, sick feeling I got from seeing his now-stiffened body splayed out across the floor like a victim in an episode of *CSI*.

"Ernie," Hoagie gasped in disbelief, letting go of my hand as he stumbled into the room and dropped to his knees beside the old man.

"You know him?" I crackled, momentarily forgetting my earlier conversation with the old man as I scanned the room for lurkers. When I confirmed that the coast was clear, I quietly closed the door behind us, hoping to muffle the sound of our hushed voices.

"Yeah," he replied, feeling for a pulse in the man's whiskery neck. "Shoot, he's dead."

My stomach fell even further. Apparently, a small, childish part of me had still been holding out hope for a miracle or some magic dust to bring him back to life.

The rusty scent of stale blood filled the air and swirled in the breeze that blew in through the open window, buffeting our faces and tickling our nostrils, ensuring that we would never grow accustomed to the smell. There was another smell, too, one that tickled my spine as well as my nose. It was a cold, musky, stale sort of smell that coiled around me like an old, moth-eaten snake skin and lay down heavily upon my shoulders. With a jolt, I realized that that smell was most likely the scent of a decomposing body: the scent of death.

"How did you know him?" I asked, trying to take my mind off the gnawing fear and repulsion that had begun to eat away at my insides.

"He's been a patient here since I was a kid," Hoagie replied, reaching out a shaky hand to touch the sticky blood on Ernie's hospital gown. "He had the room right next to my mom's. I used to sneak him candy I got from the vending machine downstairs, and in exchange, he would tell me stories. He taught me how to paint, too. He was a pretty famous artist before he had his nervous breakdown in the eighties. I used to spend hours in here with him, painting pictures of patients I'd..." He trailed off as he spotted the portrait on the floor beside the old man. His fingers trembled as he reached for the one painting I was hoping he wouldn't notice.

"He told me that was you," I whispered, tiptoeing over to kneel beside him as he picked up the blood-spattered canvas, "you and—"

"My mom." His voice cracked slightly on the last syllable as I watched him trail a finger up the terrycloth noose around her neck, just as the old man had less than an hour before. "I painted this," he told me, blinking rapidly as he studied the woman's face. "Ernie said he wanted a picture of her and me to remember us by, after she..."

I waited for him to go on, unwilling to supply the word he was looking for.

"She's beautiful," I said into the loaded silence that stretched out between us, "I didn't know you were a painter."

"I'm not, really," he replied gruffly, shoving the picture away and rubbing at his eyes with his clenched fist. "I only ever did it because she liked to see my paintings, she and Ernie both. They said they were the only happy things they ever saw in this place."

"So all these are yours, then?" I asked, feeling a bit choked up myself as I looked around the art gallery with newly opened eyes. Now I understood the look of concentration he had had on his face in the parking lot when he was preparing my make-up for my initial infiltration of The Institute. There really had been something artistic in it; I really had been a living, breathing canvas for him to paint on.

I was strangely honored.

"Most of them, yeah. That one was the last one I ever did, though, and the last time my uncle ever let me hang around with Ernie. I was eighteen at the time. That's when she..." He turned the painting over and got to his feet. An odd, stony, closed-off expression came over his face. "She died in here, you know. In The Institute."

I felt the blood drain from my face as I realized that I was going to have to tell him about the other Hogarth's true character.

"They said she was bipolar. My uncle said she used to have these mood swings where she would try to kill herself when I was a kid. Most of the time she was fine, though, the sweetest woman you could ever meet." He let out a choppy laugh. "You would've liked her. She was funny, like you."

Tears burned my eyes as I stood up to take his hand.

"But, after my dad died, she got worse and worse until my

uncle suggested that we bring her here for treatment." It seemed to be getting harder and harder for him to get the words out as he continued, "I was only four years old at the time, what did I know about psychiatric treatment? So we came to live here, her in the room next to Ernie's and me in the new wing with my uncle. For the next fourteen years, I was as much a patient here as she was. I woke up when the patients did, I went to sleep when they did, I even ate all that crap they serve in the cafeteria!

"As I got older, though, I started to notice that my mom was getting worse, not better. She started trying harder and harder to kill herself, and they kept giving her more and more drugs to try and stop her. It wasn't until she died that I realized that it was the *drugs* that were making her do it, not the disorder. The more drugs they gave her, the worse she got. That's why I was trying so hard to keep you from taking them. By the time I was seventeen, she was frail and bony like a skeleton, with these wide, empty eyes. I don't think she even recognized me most days."

He kicked the painting away as he got louder, his angry voice getting closer and closer to giving away our position. "I kept thinking, 'Why the heck aren't they watching her better?' and 'Why don't they change her medication?' But I was an idiot. I didn't realize that *they* were doing it to her. *They*—my uncle or Friedman or Caleb or whoever else is writing the script for this deranged nightmare you and I are living in—were drugging her to keep her quiet, just like they were doing to everyone else. They were controlling her, they were containing her, they were killing her! But all I could think at the time, the time when it really mattered, was 'Why does she want to kill herself when I'm right here?'"

The tears were sliding down his stubbled cheeks as he stared out the window, looking at the darkening sky without really seeing it.

"Hoagie," I swallowed, still blinking back my own unshed tears, "she didn't kill herself."

He turned to me, his red, freckled face swollen and damp and his sad, sorrowful blue eyes breaking my heart as they bored into mine, as if he already knew what I was going to say. "Who did, then?"

"I did."

We both jumped as Dr. James appeared in the doorway. Like a demon in a bad dream or a phantom in a ghost story, his eyes were dark pools of hatred in his pale face, and his black brows were furrowed as his hand shook with some intense, repressed emotion around the doorknob.

"That's what you were going to tell him, isn't it?" the elder Hogarth snarled through clenched teeth. "That I killed his mother?"

I seemed to have been struck dumb again by sheer shock, so I just gaped at him.

"*ISN'T IT?*" he demanded, rattling the walls with his crazed baritone as a chunk of his finely coiffed hair broke free of its pomade confines and fell across his sweaty forehead.

"Uncle Hogarth, what—"

"THAT GIRL IS A *LIAR!*" the older man bellowed, a dangerous light dancing in his midnight blue eyes. "She lied to you! She seduced you! All she wants is to free her brother by any means necessary!"

I opened my mouth to argue against the first half of that statement, but he cut me off.

"Little Hogarth, she wants you to believe that *I* am the bad guy here, so that you will help her destroy me and this entire Institute. Is that what *you* want? To destroy the place where you grew up? To soil your poor mother's memory by ruining the reputation of your only living relative? And for what? For this girl's worthless, violently unstable brother?"

Hoagie's hand began to sweat against mine as he glanced at me, looking nervous, but not conflicted. Destroying The Institute was exactly what he wanted to do. But he wanted all the facts first. "Tell your side," he said to me, a bit breathless.

"What?"

"Tell me your side of the story," he urged. "I want to hear it."

I swallowed hard, feeling his evil uncle's glare on my flushed face as I tried to find the words. "Ernie told me that Hogarth—the older one—killed your mother, but he made it look like a suicide. He said it was because he loved her, but she didn't love him back."

I could feel Hoagie's skin grow cold and I knew then that, up until that point, at least, he had only known half of the story. He had known about the drugs, but he had never been certain about his mother's fate, or his uncle's involvement in it. I could already tell, though, who he was going to believe.

"*LIAR!*" the elder Hogarth shouted, moving toward me.

I dropped Hoagie's hand to put up my bandaged dukes like an ill-trained pugilist, but his uncle never reached me. Before I even knew what was happening, Hoagie had bull rushed him, tackling him to the ground as he started whaling on him, pounding him with his fists over and over and over again, creating a sick, cracking sound every time his knuckles met his face.

"Why?" he shouted, his voice strangled and thick with pain. "Why did you do it?"

"I DIDN'T!"

"YOU *DID!* I know you did!"

"YOU'RE WRONG! THAT GIRL'S A—"

"DON'T YOU LIE TO ME, UNCLE HOGARTH!" Hoagie screamed, his words broken and his fists covered in the other man's blood. "I *knew* it was you! I knew it was you all along! It had to be!"

Suddenly something shifted and the older, quicker man flipped Hoagie over and onto his back, pinning him down by the neck with his long-fingered hands.

"You know *NOTHING*," Dr. James growled, as I picked up the painting that his nephew had kicked away moments before. "You have no idea what sort of things I have had to do to preserve our family and your mother's memory!"

Hoagie's eyes were full of hate as he glared up at his uncle, his face contorted by a rage that made him almost unrecognizable. "Liar," he gasped, scratching at Hogarth's knuckles, "Charlie's right. You did love her, I know you did!"

"She was my sister-in-law!"

"Not that kind of love!" Hoagie spat as I paused, mid-swing, with my stretched-canvas weapon held high. "You loved her like Dad loved her! I could see it every time you looked at her!"

"So what if I did?" his uncle snarled back. "If I loved her, why would I kill her?"

"Because you couldn't have her. Just like you can't have Charlie or Chase or any of the other patients here, not anymore. I won't let you." As Hoagie finished, his gaze flicked up to me.

I knew a cue when I saw one. With all the strength I could muster, I brought the wood frame of the painting down against the back of Hogarth's head and he fell forward, crashing down onto Hoagie's chest.

Repulsed, Hoagie shoved him off and got to his feet. I rushed to him and he pulled me into a shaky, one-armed hug, massaging his neck with his free hand.

"Let's go," he said grimly.

I nodded. With his hand at the small of my back, we headed for the open window and the darkened fire escape that lay beyond it. Just as I was stepping up onto the windowsill to climb out, a soft, sinister voice called to us from across the room.

"You've made a big mistake, Little Hogarth." We turned in unison to see the deranged doctor sit up slowly, calmly, carefully, as blood streamed down his once-handsome face and dripped from his disheveled hair. "You should have left it alone. You shouldn't have helped her. Now you know too much, just like everyone else."

My stomach tensed up as terror tickled the back of my scratchy throat.

"You were right, though," he went on, his voice deadly calm and quiet, "I *did* want your mother. But I couldn't have what I wanted. Now, neither will you."

Then, before I could breathe or think or react at all, someone grabbed me by the hair from behind and yanked me out the window and over the railing of the fire escape.

47

I was dead.

I had to be dead. There was no other plausible outcome.

The wind stung my face as I free-fell hundreds of feet toward the hard, concrete ground below. There was a screaming in my ears that couldn't drown out the shouts of my name or the horrible, vindictive laughter from above as I sliced through the burning, empty air, my eyes blurred by tears and an asphyxiating terror that wrapped itself around my heart and squeezed it tight.

I expected my life to flash before my eyes, pointing out with perfect clarity all the mistakes I had made and all the opportunities I had missed along the way; all the times I had laughed and loved and cried and succeeded at something, but all I could see was a bright, blinding nothingness as the only words that had ever meant anything to me echoed in the emptiness:

Chase and Charlie.

48

The smack came sooner than I expected.

It wasn't even a "smack" at all, really. It was more of a "snap" or a "thud," or some sort of weird twitchy, lurching "pow" as my stomach caught on something hard and the rest of my body wrapped around it like a folding chair, knocking the wind out of me.

For a second, I couldn't make sense of anything. I couldn't figure out why I had stopped moving or why I wasn't dead, or how I was suddenly moving sideways instead of straight down when I could still see the parking lot fifty feet below me, waiting to collect my guts when they splattered across the pavement.

It wasn't until I was flat on my back on the cold steel fire escape that I realized that someone had caught me.

I took one look up at the big, bruised, blonde-stubbled face staring down at me and burst into loud, sloppy, obnoxious-sounding tears, reaching out for my brother as he reached out for me.

"Charlie," he croaked into my hair as he scooped me up to press me against his massive chest.

"Chase," I croaked back stupidly, so overcome with relief and joy and pain that I couldn't think straight. "How did you—"

"I'm so sorry," he gasped at me, his own voice garbled and thick with tears, "I'm so sorry, Charlie."

"What do you mean? Why are you—"

"That'll be quite enough, Mr. Chapman."

My entire body froze as the voice of the wicked witch made its way into my muddled mind.

Chase squeezed me tighter, but then pulled away. His face was haggard. His eyes were wet with emotion, and dark with regret.

"I had to do it," he said, as the devil woman stepped up to pull him out of my reach, "I had to do it to save you."

"You had to do what?" I panted, suddenly finding it impossible to breathe as I caught sight of a small, silver gun in the doctor's hand. "Chase, what did you have to do?"

"He made me a deal," Friedman informed me, with a wicked, wicked grin, "His life for yours."

"*NO!*" I screamed, but the bullet was already out of the gun.

49

THAT'S when my life flashed before my eyes.

That's when I remembered all the laugher, all the tears, all the secrets I had shared with my big brother; all the things we had been through, all the things we had done. I remembered all the summers we spent at Grandpa Max's house, learning magic tricks and camping out in the living room under forts made of bed sheets and tablecloths. I remembered all of our mini golf games and our road trips and our all-night movie marathons. I remembered how he taught me to drive and to fish and to care about people, no matter how odd or different or off-putting they seemed at first glance. I remembered how he had patched me up when I was hurt, how he had checked my homework every night until college, how he had listened to all of my pointless jokes and stories no matter how stupid and long-winded they were, and how he had always been there with a hug when life's pressures got to be too much.

Who would be there for me now? Who could ever take his place?

How could I get through the rest of my life without him?

Chase's brown eyes widened and he slumped forward onto

his knees, blood gushing out through the gaps between his big fingers as he held them to a hole in his stomach. He tried to say something to me, but I had snapped.

My body was not my own as I vaulted over him and he fell across the landing. All I could hear was the pulse pounding in my ears and the wicked bitch's shrill, savage cackling as I reached out with both hands and grabbed the gun from her. The barrel burned my skin, but it barely registered in my brain as I turned it around and squeezed the trigger once, twice, three times into her chest in quick succession, pausing only to adjust my grip before sending one more bullet into her rapidly-deflating lungs.

Like a puppet cut from its strings, she collapsed just inside the room adjacent to the fire escape. I clambered in after her, ready and willing to pump what I assumed would be the last of her bullets into her cold, black heart, but one look at her told me that that wouldn't be necessary.

Dark, brackish red blood poured out of her chest like burnt marinara sauce from a pan, full of chunks and grit and gore that glistened in the empty room's dim fluorescent lighting as it pooled on the floor around her. Ragged, wet, choking gurgles were bubbling up from her throat as I knelt over her, surveying the damage I had done, the results of the terrible, horrible, irreparable act I had just committed.

My stomach churned and my head was spinning. I had killed someone. I had taken someone's life.

I was no longer detached from the situation. I could no longer convince myself that I was in a movie, or that I hadn't been in control of my own actions. I couldn't pretend that everything would be fine, and I couldn't keep the burning, nauseating guilt from filling my chest as I tried to close my eyes and block the image of the dying woman from my mind.

Friedman emitted a more lucid-sounding gurgle and my

gaze found her face, blood-spattered and grey. Her eyes were wide, rolling around and around behind her thick, cracked glasses as she parted her rouge-painted lips and released a stream of fizzy red blood that ran down her pointed chin.

Her feeble right claw rose up from the floor, beckoning me to come closer. Against my better judgment, I leaned down close enough to smell the gore and the sweat and the fear as it leaked out of her.

"You...you'll never...get...out of here..." she wheezed, choking on air and her own vile, sticky fluids. "No one does. No one...gets...what they...want."

As she dissolved into loud, raspy, whooping coughs, I turned around and darted back outside, where I threw up over the side of the fire escape.

50

Once the candy bars and the Fig Newtons and the sick, cloying guilt had all left my system, I squatted down next to Chase, turning him over onto his back so that I could see his face.

"Chase!" I shouted, "Chase! Can you hear me?"

His eyes fluttered behind his swollen lids as I moved to put pressure on his wound. "Stop yelling..." he slurred, as if his tongue had gone numb, "I'm right here..."

A strange, yelpy sort of sob left my throat as I pressed hard against the hole in his gut. Maybe it wasn't too late. Maybe I could fix him. Maybe I could come up with a way to plug the bullet holes and—

"Charlie...I think this is it."

My blood ran cold as his coated my hands.

"No," I said, "no, we're gonna get out of here. We're already so close!"

"Do you remember...at the end of *Saving Private Ryan*... how Tom Hanks got shot trying to save Matt Damon?"

I squeezed my eyes shut, silently begging him to stop talking. "If you tell me to 'earn it' right now, I swear to God—"

"Tom Hanks knows he's dying...and he's okay with it, right? Because he saved someone's life..."

"Chase, please don't—"

"Well, I'm okay with it too."

He wove his slick fingers between mine as he opened his eyes. There were no tears in them now, no pain. Just a calm, melancholy resignation that killed whatever tiny spark of hope I had been fanning before that moment.

"Charlie, I am so, so proud of you," he told me, squeezing my hand as the tears cascaded down my burning cheeks, "not just for what you did here, but for who you are. You said before that I was your hero, but you got it backwards. You've always been the reason I've been able to do what I love and be who I wanted to be in this life. You made me who I am. And there is no possible way that I could ever repay you for that."

"Please," I whispered to him, my throat tight as I put even more pressure on his wound, "please, Chase, don't."

"It's not really up to me," he replied, a somber sadness coloring his voice now. "You know I would stay if I could."

"You can!" I sobbed, "You can! You can do whatever you want to do! You can fight this, I know you can! And I'll help! I'll pick you up and carry you down all these stairs if I have to, just please, please, *please* don't leave me!"

The tears finally found his eyes as he blinked up at me, lifting his hand to touch my chin.

"Don't you *want* to stay?" I asked, my voice small and weak and childish, as if I were a little girl he had threatened to leave behind at the park.

"You know I do."

"Then do it!" I cried. Then, before he could stop me, I freed my bloody hands and dove back through the window. With shaking, fumbling fingers, I ripped the clothes from Dr. Friedman's corpse, wadding them up into rags I could use to stopper the holes in my brother's belly and back. I felt like a pervert as I left her there, naked except for her pointy beige bra and matching granny panties, but there was no time to dwell on it.

With my arms full of her half-soaked business attire, I scrambled back out onto the scaffolding and knelt back down beside Chase.

"What're you doing?" he asked, sounding tired or drunk as he continued to slur his words.

"Fixing you," I replied curtly, pulling up his new hospital gown and stuffing one of Friedman's nylons into the two-inch hole just to the right of his belly button. He winced and hissed with pain, but I ignored him.

After thinking it over for a second, I replaced the already-sodden stocking with Friedman's blood-dampened white blouse, folding it up into a neat, crisp little square as I placed it over the bullet wound.

"Can you roll over a little?" I asked, holding the shirt in place with one hand as I tried to fold up the black pencil skirt with the other one.

It took him a few tries, but eventually he was able to turn over onto his side, lying with his left hip against the criss-crossed metal platform. Sticking my tongue out between my teeth like a slow student trying to work a math problem, I stuck the wadded-up skirt to the matching hole in his back above his right buttock.

"Hold this one," I instructed, waving my elbow to gesture at the compress on his stomach. He grunted, but did as I told him.

I let the fabric fall from his back wound for a moment as I picked up the pantyhose again, tying the two single stockings together this time with a knot and a whole lot of faith. Then I wrapped the stretchy material over the shirt square on his front, sticking the excess beneath him for the time being. I used the remaining leg of the nylons to hold the other compress in place as well, and turned Chase over onto his stomach. He grumbled and swore under his breath, but I was almost done. I took both ends of the stocking rope and tied them together at his hip, making a hideous (but surprisingly effective) belt that would hold the makeshift bandages in place until we could find something better.

"Okay, done," I announced, wiping my bloody, sweaty palms on my gown before I pulled his back down over his goofy boxer-briefs.

I helped him into a sitting position as he grumbled in protest, clearly still ready to check out on me.

"I let you watch way too much *MacGyver* when we were kids," he groaned, squeezing his eyes shut to try to block out the pain.

"You can thank me later," I told him, patting him on his clammy brow before I put my arms under his shoulders and gave a large, upward heave.

I screamed in agony as my upper abdomen seemed to split in two. I could feel the bones grinding against each other beneath my skin as I dropped Chase and fell backward onto my butt, writhing in pain as I wrapped my arms around myself.

"What? What is it? What happened?" Chase demanded, much livelier now that it was my life he was worrying about.

"You broke my ribs," I puffed, probing them with my sticky fingers and trying hard not to throw up again, "before, when you caught me around the middle. I thought maybe they were bruised or something, but they're broken."

"We've got to get you to a hospital."

"We've got to get *you* to a hospital!" I returned, getting a grip on myself and attempting to stand up again as I wondered how in the world I hadn't noticed my shattered skeleton earlier. The pain intensified as I got to my feet, but I didn't scream this time. "Come on, I'll help you up."

"No, I'll do it," Chase said quickly, waving away my helping hand as I came at him like a hunchback who had just been kicked in the jewels.

At first, nothing happened. He huffed and he puffed and his face turned all red, but he couldn't seem to get his footing. Then, though, he grabbed a hold of the railing and dragged himself up to half his full height, crouching and slumping even lower than I was.

"You're ridiculous, do you know that?" I told him, watching his face turn from red to white to green as he clutched the metal bar at his back.

"Why's that?" he panted, sweating like he was in a sauna as he stood up a bit straighter.

"When it's just about saving *your* life, you just lay there like a slug and whine about Tom Hanks movies. But when it comes to saving mine, all the sudden you're Superman!"

"Well, what can I say?" he grunted, a bit of his normal color coming back as he flashed me a smile. "I guess I just need to get my priorities straight."

"You will," I assured him, looping my arm through his as he held onto the rail and we slowly began our descent down the rickety staircase.

We hadn't taken three steps, however, when suddenly something big and black and loud screamed past us, banging once against the fire escape before colliding with the pavement below with a crunching, gut-wrenching splat.

"What the hell was that?" Chase exclaimed, trying to stop and look over the banister.

"Let's just go," I replied hastily, trying to get him to move faster. I had seen enough movies to know that when bodies start raining down from the sky, it's time to leave.

It took us forever to reach the last platform of the fire escape. We had only been five stories up, but without a single functioning abdomen between us, we could only move along at a snail's pace, cursing and wincing and hissing in pain with almost every step.

"Let's rest for a minute," Chase suggested, the sweat from his gaunt, white face dripping down onto my shoulder blade.

"Okay, but just one!" I wheezed back, secretly glad for the chance to let go of him and massage my throbbing ribs.

As we both breathed in the cool evening air and wondered, once again, how we were both still alive, a low, rumbling groan floated up to us from the parking lot below.

Chase's entire body went rigid. His eyes were round and frightened as he reached out to grab my arm.

"What?" I whispered, not sure why he was reacting that way. We had known someone had fallen just moments ago, so it shouldn't have been so odd to hear their last, ragged death rattles as we got closer to them, should it?

"That voice," he said, his own voice hard and tight and quiet, as if he were afraid of alerting a malevolent ghost to our presence. "That's the voice I heard when they were killing Hawkes. That's the murderer!"

It was my turn to try to learn over the rail, but he pulled me back. "Forget it," he said firmly. "It doesn't matter now. We need to get as far away from here as we can—fast."

I hesitated, knowing that that person could clear Chase's name if we ever got free (assuming he lived past the next few minutes, of course). Then, as I felt Chase's sweat soaking through my gown and the blood seeping through his own, I realized that he was right, it didn't matter. If we didn't hurry, he would have no name left to clear anyway.

I nodded and we moved on, wasting several long, painful minutes trying to figure out how to climb down the metal-runged ladder that led to the ground without ripping our collective guts apart. Eventually, we both gave up on gracefulness and just slid down the ladder as if it were a fireman's pole, scraping our hands on the rusted steel and jostling our injured organs as we dropped onto the sidewalk below.

The groaning was louder now; it was a wretched sort of sound that reminded me of a wounded bear or a dying hippo. It was more sympathy than vengeance, more curiosity than anger, that compelled me to shuffle across the empty lot to the body that lay before us.

"You be careful, Charlotte," Chase warned, too shaken from the descent to follow me.

I nodded wordlessly as I approached the dying man, wondering if there was anything I could (or should) do to help him. This was the person who had been dispatched to kill Hawkes in order to cover up Dr. James' lies. This was the person who had made my family's life into a living hell. This was the person who was responsible for putting Chase in that terrible place, the person who had almost had him taken away from me for good.

I leaned down to get a better look at his face and bit my lip as a flower of pain bloomed in my torso. Suddenly, just as my watering eyes were focusing in on the killer's broken, battered countenance, I realized that Chase wasn't the only one who should have recognized the low, deep moan that was still issuing from the dying man's throat.

"Big Momma," I gasped, completely taken aback.

Obviously, he had never been the person he/she had first appeared to be, but I had had no idea just how deadly she really was. She had tried to kill *me*, yes, but I had just assumed that that act had been a byproduct of mind control or a mental instability that had been exploited and manipulated into an overwhelming loyalty to The Institute by Hogarth and his henchmen. But could a person really, truly be brainwashed to the point of becoming a hired killer, tasked with bludgeoning people to death in the middle of a crowded movie theater miles away from the influence of the alleged brainwasher?

Just as my foggy mind was filling up with all of the possible explanations and ramifications of this discovery, there was a loud, wet, splintering sound as a second body smacked down next to the first.

I jumped back, clutching my ribs.

"Charlie?"

"I'm okay!" I yelled to Chase, creeping past the massive pile of broken limbs that was Big Momma to get a better look at the sky's second victim:

Wolfman Norman.

The hairy, gangly sex addict from the cafeteria was now lying in a heap of shattered bones on the pavement, and I had no idea why.

"That must have been the other one," Chase told me grimly, his voice hoarse with exhaustion as he made his way over to me.

"The other what?"

"The other guy at the movie theater. The tall, strong guy that held me back while the other one killed Hawkes." He cringed. "I can still feel those hairy arms around my neck... Whoever put them up to it must be trying to cover his tracks. He must know we got out."

I looked back at the building. It looked taller and more macabre than ever in the pale moonlight, with its dark, sinister towers piercing the midnight blue sky, the same color as the evil Hogarth's eyes. He would kill them all, every single one of them. Every guard, every patient, every doctor, every nurse—every single living soul in that building would have to die in order to keep his secret safe.

"I think I have to go back," I said, feeling the blood drain from my face and form a knot in my stomach as I realized what I needed to do.

"What? No," Chase said, grabbing me by the shoulders and squeezing them roughly. "No, you're not doing that. I'm not losing you *again*."

"Chase, Hoagie's in there." There was a desperate sort of pleading in my voice as I got ready to make the second most important decision I had ever made in my life. "And the patients, too. Someone has to—"

"Hoagie wouldn't want you to die for him!" he shouted, his hands actually hurting me now.

"I know that!" I shouted back at him. "That's why I have to go back..."

"That doesn't make any—"

"This whole thing started with me trying to save you, so we could be 'Chase and Charlie' again, like we used to be," I said heatedly, "but somewhere along the way, it became about something even bigger than that, bigger than us! Hoagie saved my life in there, more than once. Yours too! He's a part of the team now, he's a part of us, a part of me. And I'm not leaving a piece of myself behind."

Chase stared at me for a long, tense moment, his fingernails making ten moon-shaped divots in my rigid shoulders. Then he sighed, releasing his grip as he dropped his hands to his sides.

"That idiot better earn it," he said gruffly.

Then he pulled me into a hug so tight and so fierce that it made us both cry out in pain, but we didn't let go. He knew, just like I did, that that was it, the end of Chase and Charlie. Things would never be the same again, no matter what the outcome. We would be forever changed, forever broken by what had happened at The Institute, and by what was still to come.

"I love you, you know that, right?" Chase hissed through gritted teeth.

"I love you too," I squeaked back.

With that, we broke apart, now two separate beings instead

of one, no longer a single soul sharing two bodies. With a short, sad wave, my big brother turned to walk out to the road, where he would try to flag down an emergency responder or someone with a cell phone. He wanted to come in with me, I could tell. But he knew as well as I did that he was too injured, too crippled by pain and blood loss to be of much help.

So I went in alone, just me, just Charlie, ascending that damn fire escape for the last time as flames began to spill out of the building's top floor windows.

51

As I was pounding my way up the fire escape, barely able to breathe through the suffocating pain in my ribcage, I was struck by a thought:

I was running into a burning building to save a guy I had known for less than 72 hours.

I had gone crazy. I was insane—completely nuts! I had had the chance to escape with both my brother's life and my own intact (well, mostly), but I had thrown it all away. I was an idiot, I knew, but I had never felt so sure of anything in my life. What I had said to Chase was true: Hoagie was my partner now too; he had been since the moment he had offered to help me.

And every good action hero knows that you never leave your partner behind.

By the time I reached the fifth floor, I was dizzy and disoriented, but determined. Without wasting a second to catch my breath, I climbed in the open window. Careful to step around Friedman's dead body, I picked up her gun from the floor where I had dropped it. I didn't know enough about guns to say what kind it was, but it was silver and feminine, and it only had one bullet left in the chamber.

I really hoped I wouldn't have to use it.

I snuck over to the open door and peeked out into the hallway, leaning around the doorjamb like a cautious cowboy in an old Spaghetti Western. I could hear some faint screams in the distance, but the corridor in front of me was empty.

The fire hadn't spread to my floor yet, but I could feel it burning in my chest and stomach as I sprinted toward the staircase. I was Hoagie's last hope, the patients' too. It was a lot of responsibility. Too much. And how could I tell a good patient from a bad one after what I had seen? How could I trust anyone but myself? Should I just assume that everyone I came across was an enemy? That didn't seem fair...but if they were all bad (which I highly suspected they were), how would I ever make it past all of them anyway?

"HEY!" someone shouted from behind me.

Without a backward glance, I took off running, racing toward the concrete stairwell. A bullet smacked into the banister as I fell down the first flight of stairs, but I rolled up onto my feet and kept running. With the adrenaline blocking a good portion of my pain for the moment, I was able to keep up a good pace until I reached the second floor. Once there, I threw open the door and burst into the well-windowed hall, where I was met with a rush of cool air and another explosion of gunfire.

I ducked down just in time to avoid taking a bullet to the brain, but one clipped my thigh as I dove onto the floor, sliding onto my stomach as the shells rained down around me.

"STOP IT!" I shouted, trying to keep the note of desperate, frenzied pleading out of my voice, "I'M TRYING TO HELP YOU!"

I don't know why I said it. I had no intention of helping anyone but Hoagie and maybe a few patients. Nevertheless, someone called for a ceasefire and the hall went silent.

"What are you talking about?" called a male voice, sounding dubious.

I tried to think of a good answer as I lay flat on the floor, covering my head with my hands like a kindergartener practicing a tornado drill. "He's trying to kill you!" I squawked finally, wishing that I was as smooth as I was crafty.

"Who is?"

"The boss, Hogarth James! The older one. The doctor! He's trying to get rid of all of you to cover up his crimes!"

As I said it, I realized that what I had said before was true. On some level, I really did want to help them. The patients weren't the only ones at risk at that point—everyone in the building was a target, even Dr. James' henchmen.

The shooters must have realized this too.

"Go get John," the lead voice ordered authoritatively, "then get the patients."

There was a smattering of heavy footsteps as several of the gunmen rushed off, but I could sense that I wasn't alone.

"Get up."

My legs felt like jelly once more, but I lifted my head and peered up through my fingers at the remaining orderly. It was the big black one, the one who looked like The Hulk. The one the boys had stabbed in the back with a syringe the night before.

I put my head back down.

"Get up," he repeated, more forcefully this time.

I mentally begged Hoagie's forgiveness for my failed rescue attempt as I slowly sat up, then got to my feet, my wimpy little gun dangling uselessly at my side.

"Were you telling the truth just now?" The Hulk asked, squinting his dark eyes as he pointed a much bigger, much less embarrassing gun at my head. "Is he really getting rid of everybody?"

"Yes," I told him, puffing out my chest in a grand display of false bravado. "He's already killed Big Momma and Norman, and he's set the top floor on fire."

The Hulk blanched. "What about Friedman and Caleb?"

My stomach squirmed, but my gut told me to be truthful. "I got Friedman…" I said slowly, not sure how he was going to take that, "but I haven't seen Caleb."

"*You* got Friedman?"

"She shot my brother!" I said defensively, my former rage and guilt returning, along with a flash of frustration. We were wasting too much time. "They made some sort of deal, his life for mine. But she was going to kill me anyway, just like Hogarth's gonna kill you! They've been using you this whole time—they've been using everyone!"

His face hardened, but the look in his eye said he knew more than he was letting on.

"You know it's true," I said, more softly now, "otherwise you wouldn't have sent your guys out to free the patients."

"I didn't send them to free the patients," he replied, with a strange, somber tone to his voice now, "I sent them to kill 'em."

I had just enough time to raise my gun before he fired his. He missed me by two inches, but my aim was true. He didn't make a sound as he stiffened and fell backward onto the floor, soaking the white tile with blood from the hole I had just put in his chest.

I swayed, suddenly on the verge of fainting for the second (and most likely last) time in my life. I took a deep breath, though, and pushed on, wading through a sea of shame and disgust as I plunged back into the death tunnel.

<h1 style="text-align:center">52</h1>

"Patients or Hoagie, patients or Hoagie..." I muttered to myself as I sprinted across the carpet of rats and bugs and spider webs in the dark, eerie passageway. My heart was screaming "HOAGIE!" but I knew he would never forgive me if I didn't try to save the helpless patients on the first and second floors first.

But *were* they helpless? Big Momma and Wolfman Norman had been ruthless killers in disguise (or drug-addled, brainwashed assassins at the very least) and Sybil hadn't seemed very innocent the last time I saw her either. Was everyone a cog in Dr. James' death machine? Was the entire Institute full of confederate agents charged with the single task of burying Hogarth's terrible secret?

I paused at the mouth of the tunnel, paralyzed by indecision. If I fell for one more trick, both Hoagie and I were dead. If I didn't at least check on the patients, though, I could end up with even more blood on my already drenched hands.

I could smell smoke as I tiptoed out into the abandoned break room. Either the top floor fire had spread, or another had been started somewhere else. Either way, there wasn't much time.

"Good evening, Jane Doe." I didn't even jump as Dr. Caleb sauntered into the room, looking much less haggard than he had the last time I had seen him. "I've been expecting you."

"Really?" I said airily, wishing I had another bullet in my stupid, girly gun.

"Yes. Scuttlebutt is that you killed my colleague."

"Which one?" I returned, slowly moving toward the doorway he was blocking, waiting for an opportunity to skirt past him. "I've killed a lot of people today."

"Really? Good for you. I didn't think you had it in you."

"What?"

"Killing." He grinned, holding up yet another bigger, badder gun as he stared down his long, hawk-like nose at me, his former stern solemnity replaced by what appeared to be some demented form of glee.

"Well, I'm just full of surprises, I guess."

"I'll say."

"You know Dr. James is going to kill you, right?"

"Dr. James only kills people who are no longer useful to him," he replied, a prideful purr in his slow voice.

"And you think you're still useful to him?"

"I will be." He smiled, lifting his gun to aim it at my chest. "Once I bring him the girl he's been waiting for."

"Over my dead body," I growled. I had nothing to lose. Why not go out with a bad cliché?

"That's the plan," he assured me.

Suddenly, there was a high-pitched, aboriginal-sounding scream and a wild woman with crazy, wispy brown hair grabbed the crooked doctor from behind, climbing up his back like a rabid spider monkey as she straddled him, plunging a huge, muck-filled hypodermic needle into his jugular vein.

I jumped back, alarmed, as he fell forward, taking the monkey-girl with him. I watched with my mouth hanging open as the young woman dismounted, yanking the syringe from his neck as she got to her feet.

"Sybil!" I gasped, not sure whether to be relieved or terrified.

"We're busting out," she informed me, her once-lifeless eyes now full of a raw, primitive sort of excitement. "All of us. We're getting the guards before they get us. You in?"

I felt a wide, slightly delirious smile spread across my face as I finally realized whose team she was playing for. "Later," I promised, reaching out to hug her. "I've still got work to do."

<h1 style="text-align:center">53</h1>

WITH THE PATIENTS' lives in Sybil's capable (if not mildly deranged) hands, I was free to focus all my energy on finding Hoagie. The last time I had seen him had been on the twentieth floor of the shorter of The Institutes' three massive towers, but I doubted that he was still there now. I had trouble reading the elder Hogarth, but I felt certain that he would have planned a much more artful end for his nephew/nemesis than leaving him to burn in the fire he had set.

Still thinking, I limped out into the hall and was immediately run over by a fat, naked inmate wielding a deployed tazer gun as he screamed something that sounded a lot like "MARSHMALLOW SKY!!!" The rolls of fat around his stomach and waist flopped like Hefty bags full of vanilla pudding as he bowled over several other people, most of them patients, and most of them flinching in disgust as his blubber-covered junk flapped in their faces.

It was total anarchy.

At least two dozen patients were screaming and yelling absurd-sounding obscenities and battle cries as they ganged up on ten or twelve confused-looking guards, using everything from guns and needles to golf pencils and cafeteria trays as weapons. I even saw one woman use a chunk of her own hair as a garrote to choke out a Mexican orderly from behind as he sobbed and fell to his knees, praying to God in Spanish.

There was blood everywhere, and it was clear that most of it had once belonged to the guards. I wasn't exactly sure what had spawned the uprising (perhaps the patients sensed a weakness or distraction in the orderlies or had discovered their plans to murder them all, or perhaps the mayhem had just caused them all to miss their meal-time medication), but the inmates definitely had the upper hand. They were not the prettiest soldiers, with their wild, crazy eyes, ratty, tangled hair and flabby, naked bodies, but they were determined to take back the lives that had been stolen from them by Hogarth and his henchmen.

I felt a strange sense of pride as I threaded my way through the war zone. It was as if just by having been one of them for a few days, I was a part of their oncoming victory. Their enthusiasm and success gave me hope, and I could just picture the look of horror on the mad doctor's face when he found out that all of his carefully controlled peons had escaped.

Then I had it. I knew where Hoagie was.

Dr. James would have taken him somewhere secluded, somewhere he could torture him with lies and false information until he broke him, all from the comfort of the one place where he surely felt the most powerful.

I hobbled to the elevator as fast as my sore feet and punctured thigh could carry me. A few of the savages waved cheerfully at me as they tazered another huge guard, and I gave them a salute as the Swiss-cheesed elevator doors opened and I stepped inside.

Panic choked me for a second as I remembered the last time I had been in an elevator; trapped in that cold steel box as the enemy surrounded us on all sides, just waiting for an opportunity to poke in their guns and strike us down.

I shook my head to clear it.

"This is no time for an anxiety attack," I told myself as I scanned the buttons on the wall panel. There was a loud thud as a body crashed into the doors and I stood up on my tiptoes to press a long, thin, rectangular green button near the ceiling.

My stomach lurched as the cab moved upward, making a worrisome screeching sound as it went.

"Someone needs to get some WD-40," I muttered, feeling a bit feverish as I paced around, unable to stand still.

As the deathtrap crept toward the highest, most lethal floor in the building, I decided to distract myself by taking inventory of my wounds. I touched all of them in turn as I counted them off in my head. Broken ribs? Check. Chunk of flesh missing from inner left thigh? Check. Bullet wound in right shoulder? Double-check. Glass cuts, bleeding scrapes, bruised shins, purple neck, aching back? Check, check, check, check, check. I couldn't find one single part of my body that didn't hurt. I only hoped that I was still strong enough to take on Hogarth in our final battle.

Although the elevator had been moving like a salted snail, it reached the top floor long before I was ready. The green light glowed in the panel as the heavy doors slid open, revealing the now-familiar wide, empty white room.

I took a deep breath and stepped out, wincing at the pain as my lungs pressed against my cracked ribs. The door brushed the back of my heel as it slid closed much too quickly, and I cursed as I realized that I should have found something to prop it open with.

The room was just as eerie and ominous as it had been before, with its blank, unadorned walls that all surely concealed much more than they let on. The air seemed to buzz with an odd, electrical energy that prickled my skin and made the hairs on the back of my neck stand up. I felt like a woman about to be struck by lightning, but there was no cover in sight.

Walking faster than I cared to (in order to hide the fact that my legs were shaking), I crossed the void and approached the unmarked door that I knew was hidden in the back wall. At first glance, there was nothing at all to signify an entrance or a portal or a threshold of any kind. But then, as I leaned in so close that the tip of my nose touched the slick plaster, I saw a long, thin crack in the wall. It was barely the breadth of a human hair, but it was there.

I followed the line with my finger as it framed the hidden door, wondering how on Earth I was supposed to open it. Just as I was considering that it was a magic door that only opened with a tap of a wand or a whispered spell spoken by its master, I pressed my right palm against its cold surface and the whole thing gave way beneath my hand.

I jumped back, aiming my unloaded gun at whatever monster was waiting inside to jump out at me, but nothing happened. With my legs quivering beneath me, I took a step closer to the darkened room.

The blue lamp was off now, leaving the black, sinister shadows to play to their wicked hearts' content. The darkness seemed to pulse, to throb, to shimmer around me as I tiptoed into the dragon's den, completely unprepared for the challenge I was about to face. I knew in my heart that this was the darkness I had always been afraid of, the darkness that couldn't be escaped or avoided or chased away by a mere flash of light. It was deeper than that, scarier than that, more powerful than that. But I had to press on.

I was two feet into the room when the door slammed shut and someone grabbed me around the neck from behind.

Immediately, I swung my arm upward, meaning to bash his

head in with the butt of my girly gun, but he was too quick. Like a ninja, he caught me by the wrist and twisted my arm behind my back, making me grimace but not cry out. I wouldn't give him that satisfaction.

He tightened his hold on my throat, squeezing my sore windpipe until I let out a thin, raspy croak. Left with no other option, I bared my teeth and bit down hard on his sweaty forearm until he let go, howling in pain. Spitting, gagging on the coppery taste of his blood, I turned around to grapple with him face to face.

"You...you...monster!" he growled, trying to grab me by the throat again.

"WHAT DID YOU DO WITH HIM?" I shouted, dropping my gun and clawing at his whiskery face with my nails.

He stopped struggling.

"Charlie?" he whispered, sounding completely astonished as the rage and the hatred left his voice.

"Yes it's Charlie, you son of a—"

Next thing I knew, he was kissing me, folding his fingers around my wrists, much more gently this time, as he made a choked, strangled, sobbing sound.

I pushed him away. "What the—"

"Charlie, it's me," he said with a ragged, stuttering breath, "it's Hoagie."

54

"You were dead," he was murmuring over and over into my hair as he pressed his lips to my temple, "I thought you were dead..."

"We need to turn the light on," I said roughly, trying to make him stop.

This was wrong, it had to be. It shouldn't have been so easy to find Hoagie, let alone free him. I had expected to discover him lying half-dead on an operating table or bound and gagged in an electric chair as his uncle stood by and laughed. Instead, though, he was free and strong and full of life...and apparently lying in wait for someone else.

"Oh, Charlie—"

"Turn the light on!" I repeated, more forcefully this time.

He felt like Hoagie, he smelled like Hoagie, and he certainly kissed like Hoagie, but a dark, aching feeling in the pit of my stomach was telling me that it was a trap.

Finally he moved away, stumbling over something on the floor as he made his way to his uncle's desk. There was a small click and the room was illuminated by a bright, blinding blue light from the colored desk lamp.

We gasped in unison.

It was Hoagie alright, but just barely. His nose was like a flattened red velvet cupcake, squashed and chunky and mashed across his face, and his left eye was completely swollen shut beneath a baseball-sized knot on his forehead. Four long, jagged claw marks dragged their way down his cheeks from where I had scratched him, and the entire right shoulder of his shirt was blacked with crusty, half-dried blood. He walked with a limp even worse than mine as he stepped toward me, his face white as chalk as he pointed a shaking finger at my stomach.

"Is...is that..."

I glanced down and saw that the front of my mint green gown was soaked through with rust-red stains and for a moment I panicked, fearing that my broken ribs had somehow manage to cut through the skin that bound them. I quickly realized, though, that the blood (well, *that* blood anyway) wasn't mine.

"Chase got shot," I told him, glancing back up at his face, trying desperately to find just one little freckle in the mess of gore and bone.

He blanched even further. "Is he—"

"He got out," I interrupted, noticing then how hard I had been trying not to think about Chase and his possibly fatal belly wound. "He's going to get help."

He closed his good eye and let out a long, relieved-sounding sigh. "You did it then," he said, "you did what you came here to do."

"*We* did it," I corrected.

He opened his eye again and I felt the long-suppressed butterflies flutter weakly in my stomach. "I thought you were dead. You fell twenty stories."

"Eh, I only fell fifteen," I said with a shrug, waving my hand dismissively. "Chase caught me on the fifth floor."

"Thank God."

"No, thank *Chase*," I amended. "If he hadn't have caught me, I'd be—"

"Don't say it anymore," he begged me, wrapping his arm around my waist and pulling me to him. I winced as he crushed my burning sternum and he jumped back. "What is it? What's wrong?"

"My ribs." I grimaced, still trying to rub the pain away with my hand. "Chase broke them when he caught me. But I guess that's the price you pay for living, right?"

He was not in the mood for jokes. His face darkened with angst as he asked me the one question he should have already known the answer to. "Charlie, why did you come back?"

"For you," I answered, without a millisecond of hesitation.

"Why?" he persisted. "Why would you come back in here for me when you had already saved your brother? That's who you came here for, and he was in the clear—you both were! Why come back for me when you knew what was waiting in here for you if you did?"

I stared at him for a long moment, finding it hard to speak. There was too much emotion, too much history, too much meaning to be summed up in just a few words. I remembered the laughter he had shown me when I needed it most, the way he had been loyal to me since the beginning, the way he had fought for me, had risked his life for me, had taken care of me when I was at my weakest points. He was like Chase, but different somehow. He hadn't been obligated to protect me because of blood or family or past experiences. He had done it because he had wanted to, because he wanted me.

"Because...because I think maybe I might love you," I said lamely, dropping my eyes in embarrassment. "That's weird, right?"

"No, it's not weird," he replied, a smile in his voice as he reached out to take my hand.

"Really? Because it's only been like two days. That's not really enough time to get to know a person, let alone develop feelings for them. I mean, crap like that only happens in the movies, right? And not even good movies. I'm talking like *Twilight* or that one with the guy from—"

"Charlie?"

"What?"

"I love you too."

I finally met his eye again and found him smiling his sweet, boyish smile at me, giving me the familiar swooping sensation in my stomach that I knew now was much more than just the thrill of adventure.

"Good," I said, blushing harder than I ever had in my life, "I'm glad I'm not the only crazy one here."

"Well, we *are* in an asylum," he pointed out, leaning down toward me.

"Just so you know, though, I'm not talking about the 'throw me down on this table and ravish me right now' sort of love," I clarified.

He grinned. "Of course not."

"Or the 'let's get married tomorrow and have ten kids' kind of love."

"Sure. That's a lot of kids to have in one day," he replied, leaning in even closer as I continued to interrupt his attempt to put the moves on me.

"I'm just talking about the kind of love where I can't really picture my life without you in it anymore, that's all."

"Charlie?"

"Yes?"

"Would you just kiss me already?"

"Oh, *that's* what you were doing," I teased, pretending to be oblivious as to why his lips were now just inches from mine. "I thought I had something on my face."

"You do," he replied with a roughish wink, "me."

I laughed at his ever-present cheesiness as he pressed his lips to mine, and for a moment I could almost ignore the gnawing, ominous feeling of paranoia that was still swirling around in my gut.

55

"So, what happened after I left?" I asked Hoagie, picking up my empty handgun and searching the room for booby traps or concealed escape hatches.

"You mean, after you got thrown off the balcony?"

"No, after I left to go on that snack run."

He smirked at me and I stuck my tongue out at him. We were way too cute to be stuck in the middle of such an ugly mess.

"Not much," he said heavily, kicking down the pile of textbooks he had tripped over in the dark. "Uncle Hogarth beat the snot out of me, then he threw Big Momma over the fire escape. I passed out after that and woke up here alone. I was waiting for him to come back when you got here."

"I smell a trap." I frowned, my ominous feeling intensifying with every passing minute.

"Definitely," he agreed, helping me to pull books off the floor-to-ceiling shelving unit as we tried to find some sort of switch or camera or recording device. Hogarth must have had a plan. He wouldn't just leave Hoagie alone and unbound when he was still fully capable of thwarting his plans. That would just

285

be stupid. No, he had to have brought him to the office for some reason...but why?

"What happened after Chase caught you?" Hoagie asked, his voice quiet now, as if he could feel the rippling, prickling feeling of dread that must have been emanating from me in waves at that point.

"Friedman showed up and shot him," I said, blinking hard to try to clear away the image that had been burned into my brain. "She said they had made a deal, his life for mine."

"Geez..."

"Hoagie, don't ever make that deal," I said suddenly, turning toward him.

He looked guilty, as if that had been exactly what he had been planning to do, if given the opportunity.

"Promise me!"

"I can't promise that," he replied somberly, as if he would have given anything to tell me otherwise. "If I'd been in his shoes, I'd have done the same thing."

I made a frustrated sort of growling sound and went back to pulling books. Why did guys always think that trading their life for a girl's would make her like them more? It wasn't a gift or a compliment, it was a burden—one that she would have to carry with her for the rest of her life! And she would have to carry it alone, because the guy who gave it to her was gone.

"You're being a tad bit hypocritical, don't you think?"

I bristled. "What is that supposed to mean?"

"Charlie, this whole thing has been about you risking your life for Chase, and then for me! You didn't make a verbal agreement with anybody about it, but the end result is the same. You'd trade your life for ours, and we'd have to deal with it. Just like you'd have to deal with us doing the same for you if it comes to that."

I dropped my gaze to the floor. He was right. That was exactly what I had been doing.

"You're not the only one who can risk everything for the people you care about, Charlie. We can do it too."

"You're right, I'm sorry."

"Don't be sorry," he smiled, reaching over to stroke his thumb across my hand. "Just know that Chase and I care about you just as much as you care about us, that's all."

"Very touching, Little Hogarth."

I groaned inwardly as the dragon reentered his lair, his black, snakeskin dress shoes barely making a whisper against the tile as he crossed over to stand behind his desk. I almost made a lunge for the door, but it snapped shut with an unnaturally loud, electrical-sounding click that assured me that any attempts at escape would be futile. We were trapped...again.

Man that was getting old.

With the exception of a few puffy blue bruises on his cheekbones and along his chiseled jaw line, and a small cut just above his perfectly formed nose, the elder Hogarth was as dapper as ever. His suit, though spattered with blood in some places, was unwrinkled, and his boyish brown locks were neatly slicked back now, unruffled by his previous scuffles and firestarting. His tie was straight and his hands were clean, as were the bright, dazzling white teeth he was baring at us.

I wondered if he had gone to the restroom to pretty himself up before our meeting.

"Miss Chapman, you look very well for a person who just fell twenty stories to her death!"

"What can I say? I'm resilient." I shrugged, feigning nonchalance.

I had figured out the trick now. It was the same as all the ones that came before it: the old bait-n-switch. Kidnap Chase or Hoagie and I would inevitably come to rescue them. Then, voila! Two suckers for the price of one. What I didn't get, though, was why he was wasting his time meeting with us when he should have been evacuating the building and leaving us to burn. He was obviously toying with us, but why? There was nothing left to gain—The Institute had been liberated and the evidence was surely being destroyed as we spoke, so why not kill us right away? Why put himself in danger?

"I said it once, and I will say it again," Hogarth told me, with a humorless, barracuda-esque grin, "You are quite a clever girl."

"Thanks, your opinion means the world to me."

He clenched his fist on the desk.

"You have almost single-handedly destroyed the entire institution—the entire *life*—that I have tried for so long to maintain. You killed my best doctor. You allowed patients to break free and attack the guards that once contained them. You seduced and used my own impressionable nephew against me, and you forced me to kill all of my protégés and apostles just to preserve the secrecy of my Institute and its activities. You made me set the building on fire—you are making me burn my beautiful castle to the ground! And for *WHAT?*"

He screamed this last word with a shrill roughness in his crazed voice that sent Hoagie and me jumping back into the bookshelves behind us, grabbing for each other's hands as he banged his fist on the desktop.

"Your brother? Is that it? You had to save the majestic, gentle giant from a death that could have been quick and painless if you had just left well enough alone? Well, congratulations, Miss Chapman, you did it. You saved your beloved brother. Unfortunately, I cannot say the same for the dozens of other people that are going to die when this building explodes in thirty minutes."

The stricken expressions on our faces made him smile even wider, his teeth like a shark's beneath his hungry black eyes.

"I planted a crude explosive here years ago," he continued, more calmly now that he had regained the upper hand, "as a sort of fail-safe, just in case I ever found myself in this type of situation. I activated it ten minutes ago, and there is no way to stop it from detonating. What do you think of that, Miss Chapman? Clever enough for you?"

A bomb? Really? What was he, a Bond villain?

"When that bomb goes off, you'll die too," I said, my throat dry as my mind raced, trying to come up with one last solution.

"I am quite aware of that," he replied, sitting down and leaning back in his big leather desk chair as he crossed his arms over his chest, clearly enjoying the melodrama.

"And that doesn't bother you?" Hoagie asked, his nasally voice tight as he squeezed my hand so hard that it hurt.

"Not at all. We all must die sooner or later. Why not go down with your ship? And, even better, why not take down your adversaries with you?"

"You're insane," Hoagie muttered, running his hand through his hair in agitation as he broke our handhold to pace back and forth in front of me, "completely insane!"

"You know Chase is going to tell someone about this, right?" I said, wishing Hoagie would just stand still for five seconds so I could think. "Even if you kill us, he'll know it was you. Everyone will know."

"Will they?" the dragon sneered, delighted, as always, by his own superiority. "Do you really think that people will believe a brutal 'murderer' like him? His face was all over the newspapers, all over the news! There is not one single person outside of this room who believes he is innocent. I bet your parents don't even believe him, do they?"

I glowered at him and he laughed, sounding like a hyena on cocaine. He was slipping, that much was certain. On the outside, he may have appeared as unruffled and unflappable as ever, but on the inside he was coming unhinged. His eyes were wild, darting around the room like a trapped animal's, and his big hands shook with something like rage or fear as he tried to keep his cool, keep his composure, keep the upper hand. His barbs were all tinged with desperation now, and his self-assured tone had descended into something more like the high-pitched ramblings of a movie villain's barely stable toady.

"Tell us about Mrs. James," I suggested thoughtfully, hoping to buy us some time to come up with a possible escape strategy.

Hoagie froze.

"You mean Virginia?" Hogarth asked, his eyeballs bulging like a frog's as he tried to maintain his air of equanimity.

"If that's her name, then yeah."

"Why?"

"Why what?"

"Why do you want to know about her?" he snapped, loosening a clump of hair from his impeccable part.

I shrugged. "Just curious, I guess. I figured a story might be more entertaining than just sitting around watching each other die. Plus, you're a villain, right? Villains love monologueing. So go ahead, lay it on us."

"You're trying to shake me up." He squinted warily, getting truly uncomfortable now. "It won't work."

Suddenly Hoagie spoke up. "I—I'd really like to hear it," he said quietly, sincerely, "if you don't mind."

The elder Hogarth glared at his nephew for a long, tense moment, weighing the pros and cons of sharing his final secret. I could hear the seconds ticking away on the clock in my head, each one bringing us all closer and closer to an ever more inescapable death.

"I met Virginia in college," he began, a hard edge to his low voice, as if he were divulging the information against his will, "before my brother knew her. She was in my English class."

Suddenly, the edge softened and his voice took on a nostalgic, dreamlike tone as he went on. "I remember, because I would always find a way to partner up with her when we did peer reviews of each other's work. Her writing was so beautiful, so painfully tragic. She wrote about things like death and loneliness in a way that made them seem almost as worthwhile as life itself. My favorite piece, I think, was a short story she wrote about a rabbit that was killed by a cat. At first, the cat was portrayed as evil, as dreadfully, mercilessly cruel. But by the end of the story, Virginia had turned it into a sad, misunderstood being who had only murdered out of necessity and out of a compulsion to belong with the other members of its feline clan. In her story, the cat regretted his actions, something that I had never believed a murderer was capable of. But she made it seem so honest, so real, so much a metaphor for human life and suffering that I asked her to make a copy of it so that I could keep it on my bookshelf next to my Poe collection. She agreed, of course. She was never one to disappoint someone.

"So, we arranged a meeting in one of the gardens on campus. She would bring me a copy of her story, and I would provide us with a picnic lunch. It was supposed to be our first real date—the one where I told her how much I admired her and her work, and how much I had longed to kiss her since the moment she had entered that classroom.

"But then your father showed up."

Hoagie, transfixed by the story, limped closer to his deranged uncle and sat down stiffly on the hard, straight-backed chair across the desk from him. I, unwilling to let him out of arm's reach, hurried to his side, and he pulled me gently onto his lap as Dr. James went on.

"It was supposed to have just been the two of us—Virginia and me—but Vincent came over to 'say hi.' He sat down on the bench next to me while I was waiting for her. I told him that I was meeting someone, that I would talk to him later, but he kept pestering me about the suit and tie I was wearing in the eighty degree heat."

I physically flinched as an unwelcome sensation stung me: sympathy. Compassion for a killer. The thought of a younger, nerdier, more pathetic Hogarth James in a full-on dress suit in the middle of a summer day, waiting for the love of his life to meet him for a homemade picnic lunch, was so painfully awkward and sad that I could hardly bear to picture it.

What the hell was happening to me?

"And then she was there," he said, his eyes distant as a nostalgic, all-too-human smile spread across his bruised face. "She was beautiful. She had dressed up too, I could tell. She was wearing a light, billowy little sundress and white sandals, and there was this big, bright yellow flower tucked behind her right ear—a lily, I think—that stood out like the sun against her long, soft, silky brown hair.

"My heart stopped. I couldn't speak. All I could do was stare at her, basking in the glory of her perfection, drowning in the sparkling gold of her hazel eyes. Until Vincent spoke."

His face darkened as Hoagie wrapped his arm around my waist.

"He was always the articulate brother, the one who always had a joke or a compliment or the perfect word to say at the perfect time. Right then and there, he swept her off her feet. 'Love at first sight,' he told me later, as if his love was anything compared to the desire that had been burning a hole in my chest for months! And she loved him too, that much was clear. From the moment she saw him, she was blinded to me. She never looked me in the eye again, unless she was telling me some story about how wonderful my brother was. The bitch!"

He picked up the small picture frame from his desk and hurled it at the door, sending hundreds of tiny shards of powdered glass sprinkling down upon the floor like snow. His face was red and he was breathing hard, but after a few deep, unsteady breaths, he was ready to speak again. "Vincent used to tell me about her mood swings," he said, still staring blankly off into the distant past. "He wasn't sure if he could marry her, wasn't sure if he could handle her 'emotional instability.' That's what he called it, *'emotional instability,'* as if she were just a moody woman acting upon her hormones. He didn't understand her *or* her illness, not like I did. Once I found out about her bipolar disorder, I changed my major to psychology, got a degree in psychiatry, a residency at Bellevue. I was going to help her, I was going to be there for her like Vincent never could!

"But while I was working on that, your parents eloped. Before I knew what happened, Virginia was pregnant. I thought I had really lost her then, I thought she had finally, truly slipped through my fingers for good.

"Then your father was killed in that accident at the mill four years later."

Hoagie's hand clenched into a fist atop my thigh, and I gently pried it open to slip my fingers inside.

"I thought to myself, '*Now* is your chance, Hogarth. *Now* is the time to tell her how you feel. She named her son after you, for Christ's sake!' So, after the funeral, I pulled her aside and told her how I had loved her for so many long, painful years, and that I would love her forever. I told her I would give her the life she deserved, the love she deserved, the understanding she needed to live a long, happy life.

"But she said no."

I waited for him to go on, but he didn't seem to be able to. His midnight blue eyes glittered with angst as he stared down at his open hands, as if he were still wondering why hers weren't in them.

"She said no because she loved Dad," Hoagie said softly, a

strange reluctance in his voice that might have signaled an oncoming lie, "not because she didn't love you."

Hogarth seemed to snap out of his daze. He looked across the table at his nephew with wide, curious eyes, as if he had never seen him before.

"I gave her time," he told him, "I told her to take as much time as she needed, but she said that she could never love another man as long as she lived. She said she was sorry, but that Vincent was her one true love.

"Then she got sicker, too sick to work, to function. So I bought The Institute so that I could give her a home, a place where she would be safe, a place where she could heal. I found other patients to keep her company. I helped to raise her child! All the while thinking that eventually she would see how much I loved her and give me a chance.

"But she wouldn't." His face was shadowy now, and sinister, and I could feel the cold tongue of terror licking its way up my spine in a way I never had before. "Around that time, an old classmate of mine, Doctor Benjamin Hawkes, was working on a drug in his lab at the university that would help control the behavior of children with ADHD. He said that it wasn't going well, that there were too many side effects—one of which was the complete inability to think for oneself while under the drug's influence. Whatever the scientists told the patients, they would believe it, as long as the medication was in their system. They had taken the drug too far; they had only intended to control the patients' behavior, not their minds.

"But I had other ideas. I procured some of this highly unstable drug and I tested it out on some of my own patients. Sometimes, nothing happened. Sometimes the patient had a seizure and died. Other times, however, the patient fell into a stupor in which they were completely open to suggestion—to doing anything I asked them to do. They stole for me, fought for me, did disgusting, degrading things for me, all the while believing that their own brains were telling them to do it. Hawkes was so intrigued by my results that he came here to work for me, along with Jill Friedman and John Caleb. Together, we created an army of lethal, well-crafted machines that we used to settle old debts and even old scores, never taking any of the blame if the patient was caught.

"But that wasn't what I wanted. I wanted Virginia, and I was finally going to get her. After all those years, after all that trying and failing and begging her to love me, I had finally found a way to make her mine.

"I gave her the drugs. At first, nothing happened. Then, slowly, steadily, over a period of years—YEARS!—I increased the dosage until she was not only subdued, but pliable, ready for anything I might suggest."

Hoagie was barely breathing as he dug his nails into the side of my palm.

"So, as a test, I asked her to kiss me. Just a kiss, nothing too sensual. Just a quick peck on the lips. And she did it.

"But that wasn't enough. The touch of her soft, beautiful lips on mine unleashed something inside of me, awakened a hunger that couldn't be sated by just one platonic exchange! So I kissed her harder, deeper, more passionately, but she pulled away. Her eyes were wide and her words were completely lucid as she screamed 'Leave me alone! Leave me alone, Hogarth!' I said that I couldn't leave her alone, that I loved her more than any man had ever loved any woman, and she stepped back, crossing her arms over her breasts, tears cascading down her beautiful, pale cheeks as she whispered to me, 'I told you, I told you I will never love you.'

"So I killed her. I grabbed the belt from her robe and wrapped it around her neck and I killed her!" His voice crackled and shook, then it shattered completely. "I killed her, just like the cat killed the rabbit! But worse! Because the cat didn't love the rabbit. Nothing loved anything as much as I loved that woman. I had saved her from a life of misery, I had given her a home! I had created an entire world—an entire universe!—with her at the center of it, but *still*, she didn't want me!

"When Hawkes came in, I was lying beside her on the floor, hugging her dead body to me as I sobbed into her hair, asking over and over again, 'Why didn't you love me? Why?' Hawkes helped me to fix up the scene to make it look like she had committed suicide, and he helped me to give her a nice funeral. But he couldn't help me get over the grief and the guilt. For four long years he tried to help me, to keep me in check—to control me, the same way I was still controlling the patients—but then he couldn't take it anymore. He said he was going to go to the police and tell them what we'd done. He'd 'developed a guilty conscience,' he said. So I told him that I would stop, no big deal. Then I waited until Thursday night, the night he always went to the movies to unwind, and I sent two of my best drones to take him out. Tyrone and Norman killed him while I switched off the lights in the control room, then I came back here to set up a false estate in his name, an estate that would will all of his money to me and The Institute. This came in handy for framing the Chapman boy as well. With Hawkes gone, my secret would be safe, as long as I could control the witnesses. But then Miss Chapman here showed up, and you know the rest. None of it matters anyway, though. No matter what happens, no matter what I hide or who I kill or how I choose to live my life, I will never have what I truly wanted."

The room was silent. Hoagie seemed to have turned to stone, and I was completely speechless. As we sat there, staring at the broken man before us, he stood up and walked over to the door. He knelt down and picked up the photo he had thrown, brushing the broken glass off the waxy paper as he began to weep openly.

"Here." He sniffed at Hoagie, his voice jerky and strangled with emotion. "She'd want you to have this."

With shaking fingers, Hoagie took the picture from him and held it out in front of us. Together, we took in the long, soft, silky brown hair, adorned by a single, bright, sun-yellow lily, as it fell around the angelic, smiling face of a young Virginia James.

56

"Uncle Hogarth, why didn't you tell me any of this before?"

Dr. James shot his nephew a look of pure sarcasm as he responded, "Gee, could it be so that you wouldn't know that I killed your mother?"

"No, not that part, the first part. About you and Mom, about you being so in love with her. Why didn't you ever tell me that?"

"Why would I?" Hogarth snarled, sneering through his tears as I got to my feet. "So you could mock me like your father did?"

"No, so I could be there for you!" Hoagie shouted. "Don't you think that I knew what it was like to want my mom to love me like I deserved?"

The doctor and I both froze, startled by the painful edge of honesty in Hoagie's fractured voice as he crumpled up his mother's photo in his fist. "She was never right after Dad died, you know that! Do you know how many times I asked myself why she couldn't be happy with the son she had left? Why I wasn't enough for her? Why she didn't love me? We could have talked about it, Uncle Hogarth! We could have helped each other! But, instead, you just went psycho and threw away the only real family you had left."

Hoagie's chest was heaving as he glared at his uncle. I hadn't realized how betrayed he had felt by him, and I never would have suspected that it could be the absence of an uncle that had hurt him worse than the loss of a mother.

"I...I never thought of it that way..." Hogarth said, the anger leaving his voice as his once black, once evil eyes shone clear and blue in the lamplight, "I'm sorry."

"Yeah, well, it's too late now," Hoagie grumbled, turning his back on him as he struggled to hold himself together.

"What if it's not?"

Both Hogarths cocked their heads at me, their incredulous expressions as eerily similar as their Zac Efron-ish faces.

"What if you could make it right?" I suggested, moving over to lean on the desk in front of the elder James as I spoke. "What if you could fix it all right now?"

He frowned at me, understandably suspicious. "How?"

"Let us go," I told him. "Let Hoagie and I leave here, unharmed, and it'll all be square. You'll have made up for not being there for him all those years, and you'll have made up for taking Virginia's life by sparing her son's...and preferably his plucky sidekick's."

Hogarth's frown deepened as he thought it over, trying to find a flaw in my logic as our remaining seconds of life ticked by in our heads, each one coming faster than the last.

"Please," Hoagie whispered, his plea barely audible over the thudding of my heart, "do it for Mom."

Hogarth's eyes had never looked bluer as they met those of his nephew. Both of them stared at each other for what felt like hours, each trying to read the other one's mind as I struggled not to lose mine. Then, after what seemed like a year of unspoken words and thoughts passing between them, Hogarth broke their gaze and dropped his to his desk. There was an odd, electrical buzz and Hoagie and I jumped as the door opened behind us.

"Go."

Hoagie nodded gratefully and put his hand on the sore small of my back, attempting to lead me out.

But I couldn't move.

As I watched, paralyzed by some insane, self-destructive brand of empathy, the elder Hogarth's handsome face crumpled in misery and he buried his face in his hands.

"Charlie?" Hoagie urged, "What's wrong?"

I had to swallow three times before I was able to get the words out. "We have to take him with us."

"No," Hoagie said firmly, shaking his head. "No. No way, there's no time for this. We're getting out of here, you and me. Quickly."

"I'm not leaving without you," I called to Dr. James, planting my crudely bandaged feet as I crossed my arms stubbornly.

"What are you doing?" Hoagie exclaimed, running his hand through his hair in anxious frustration as he looked back and forth between me and the door.

The doctor's face was visible now. He was squinting at me, calculating me, trying to figure out my game. But I didn't have one, not that time.

I hated Hogarth James. I loathed him for what he had done to Chase and to Hoagie and to Virginia and to all of his other patients, and for what he had done to me. I hated what he had turned me into: a desperate, panicked killer. But he was human, just like everyone else.

And he was Hoagie's family.

"Hoagie, he's your uncle," I said, imploring both of them to listen. "He's a bad one, sure, and he deserves to be punished, big time, but he's the only blood relative you've got, as far as I can tell. You can't leave him behind. You can't let him die here like this. If you do, you'll regret it. Trust me."

Hoagie's jaw was clenched as he continued to search my face in disbelief. Then, as if against his will, he sighed. "Fine," he conceded, "but he's going to jail."

"Definitely," I agreed. Then I turned to Hogarth. "What do you say, Doctor? You wanna call a truce?"

A deep, heavy silence fell over the office, eating up at least one of our remaining few minutes. I kept waiting for Hogarth to respond; to smile, to shrug, to scoff, to push me down and make a mad dash for the exit, but he remained still, solid, as unmoving as a perfectly chiseled statue. He just stared at me, with an odd, enigmatic sparkle in his midnight blue eyes that I couldn't even begin to interpret.

"You have one weakness, Miss Chapman," he said finally, drumming his fingers against his fine oak desk. "Just one. You know what it is?"

"What?" I replied as I stiffened, bracing for the impact of the following words.

"Loyalty."

"Loyalty?"

"Loyalty." He grinned, bearing his teeth as he stood up. "Most people in your...'situation'...would just run away—they'd take their boyfriend and their brother and escape while they had the chance. But not you. You are the perfect personification of the phrase 'loyal to a fault.' You would do anything—including risking your life and your sanity—to save your brother as well as my nephew. You are driven by such an overwhelming sense of allegiance to those whom you consider to be family that you don't realize that not everyone is driven by that same ideal.

"You think that, since Young Hogarth is my nephew, my only living relative, I would want nothing more than to save his miserable, meaningless, pitiful little life. You think that I have repented, that I have now seen 'the error of my ways' and have formed a familial bond with my true love's only offspring. But really, I am just intentionally wasting your time."

I tensed up as he came around the desk, towering over both Hoagie and me as he approached us, an expression of smug arrogance written all over his dark face.

"You see," he continued, running a long, velvet-skinned finger down the line of my clenched jaw, "I am driven by something much deeper than loyalty, and much more powerful. *I* am driven by hatred."

He let his words hang in the air as he circled around us like a cobra, searching for signs of weakness as he waited to strike.

"It is a beautiful thing, hatred," he went on, his voice softer now, more sensual, as if he were whispering to a lover. "It is born from love, born from the pain and the anguish and the vengeance that forms in response to the travesty that *is* love, and once you are armed with it, you can do anything you want. You can destroy buildings, destroy lives, even murder the woman whom you once loved more than anything else in the world. And then, once that is done, you can trap yourself in a tower and greet your death with open arms and no regrets, as you watch your most formidable opponent die with you."

"You're crazy," Hoagie whispered, barely breathing as he wrapped his sweaty fingers around my wrist.

"Perhaps," Hogarth acknowledged, taking a step back to smile at us, savoring our crushed, panicked expressions, "but not as crazy as Miss Chapman. It takes at least seven minutes to reach the ground using the fire escape from this level, three if you use the elevator. Thanks to her attempts to 'rescue' me, you now only have sixty seconds. Well, maybe sixty-five, if I must be precise. Tell me, Charlie, my clever girl, do you have any more tricks up your sleeve?"

"Just one," I growled in reply, as a savage thirst for revenge coursed through my veins.

Then I sprang at him.

57

The dragon laughed as I wrestled him to the ground, not even fighting me as I grabbed at his arms.

"You idiot girl!" he cackled maniacally, his eyes watering with mirth instead of crocodile tears now. "Don't you realize that killing me will only accomplish my goal even faster?"

"Yes, I do," I grunted, pinning him down with my knees as I shouted at Hoagie, "Take off his belt!"

Hoagie looked confused, but did as I said.

"What is this?" Hogarth giggled, squirming like a drunken sorority girl as his nephew removed his expensive leather belt. "Are you going to molest me now?"

"You wish," I muttered, taking the belt Hoagie handed me. With fumbling fingers, I wrapped the leather strap around his wrists, binding them together and buckling it so tight that his hands turned red.

"Wait a minute..." he said slowly, his good humor and sense of crazed superiority slipping away. "What are you doing?"

"Saving your ass," I smirked, getting to my feet and grabbing a hold of his right leg as I proceeded to drag him out into the enormous white room beyond, "whether you like it or not."

304

It was my turn to feel superior as Hoagie grabbed his other leg and we rushed toward the elevator, pulling the struggling doctor across the pristine tile floor.

"No. No!" he cried, trying to wriggle out of our grasp. "This is *not* how it is supposed to end! This is *not* the plan!"

"Well, plans change," I told him, hiding the excruciating pain in my ribs and leg with sarcasm as I punched the button on the wall beside the elevator.

I could have killed Hogarth then. I would barely have even felt bad about it. But that was too easy. If I made it out of that hellhole, I was taking him with me, and he would get the punishment he deserved, not the quick, self-inflicted death he wanted.

"Charlie," Hoagie said softly, leaning in closer to me as the elevator began to rattle up toward us, "what if we don't make it?"

I looked at him for a second, trying to memorize his adorable, swollen facial features one last time. I knew it was over, I could feel it. We would never make it out in time. There was no way. Our struggles had been for naught, but I wouldn't admit it, not out loud. But I couldn't just let his question hang there in the air between us, along with all the other unspoken thoughts and feelings we'd never have time to share.

The elevator doors opened as I stepped over to kiss him on the cheek, lingering there for a moment, cherishing the feel of his scratchy stubble against my lips. A single, silent tear slid down the bridge of my nose as I whispered, "Then I guess I'll see you on the other side."

At that moment, as if on cue, there was a rumble and a bang and we leapt into the elevator cab as the building crumpled like paper and collapsed around us.

58

THE DOORS DIDN'T EVEN HAVE time to close before the elevator broke loose from its main cable and sent us plummeting down the shaft, hurling us toward the afterlife. Sparks pinged against the walls and burned holes in our already-tattered clothing as the unimpeded metal cab scraped against the reinforced steel. There was a loud, squeaky twang as the last few wires broke loose and we picked up even more speed, our feet barely touching the floor as the sheer force of the descent sucked us upward.

Hogarth was screaming like the spineless coward he was, begging for it to stop. I guess he hadn't planned on suicide being so painful.

After thirteen or fourteen floors of straight freefall, there was a jerk and a crash and a ripping, roaring, cracking sound and the entire shaft shifted sideways, flinging me into Hoagie as the elevator continued to slip downward at a forty-five degree angle.

As Hoagie wrapped his arms around me, squeezing me so tightly that I couldn't breathe (as if I had been breathing anyway) I could hear him muttering something under his breath. After a moment, I realized that he was praying.

I hoped he had enough pull with the man upstairs to spare both of us, because I couldn't seem to form a single coherent thought myself. The only thing I could feel was fear; the only thing I could see was Hoagie's bloody collarbone as I shoved my face even deeper into the hollow beneath his chin. This was it, the real thing. No more strategies borrowed from fictional action heroes, no more daring escapes, no more lucky breaks. This time it was really over, we were really dead.

Suddenly I could see Chase in my mind, smiling, laughing, enjoying the life he would lead now, the life I had helped to return to him.

What we had done had not been for nothing. We had not failed. *I* had not failed. I had saved my brother, and that was all that mattered.

As I closed my eyes tightly, breathing in the smell of Hoagie's aftershave and the cloying, sharp scent of our mingled terror, I had no regrets.

Suddenly we crashed into the ground and were thrust upward by the elevator's leftover momentum and too-sudden stop. We all banged our heads on the ceiling before dropping back down in a tangled heap, where we barely had time to inhale before the steel cage gave one last, shuddery lurch and tipped over onto its back. Rocks and debris rained down on us as we coughed and sputtered and winced with pain, wondering if the torture was ever going to end.

Then it was silent.

Buried beneath pounds of bricks, sharp, jagged hunks of plaster, and mounds of other wreckage, I realized that it really *was* over.

And I had survived.

"Oh my God, Oh my God, Oh my God," came Hoagie's muffled voice in my ear, saying the words over and over and over again as he hugged me tight, "Oh my God! Charlie, we're alive!"

"We're alive!" I shouted back, relishing the cottony taste of insulation dust in my mouth and the throbbing pain in my ruined ribs.

"Impossible," came the voice of the slain dragon from a few feet away, "Impossible!"

Hoagie shoved a particularly heavy block of concrete off my back and pulled me onto his chest as he laid back against the steel wall of the elevator. "We did it," he whispered in awe, grinning dazedly up at me as if he couldn't quite believe his own words, "we really did it!"

"We really did." I grinned back, taking in his sweet, boyish smile and his beautiful blue eye more slowly and more carefully this time, knowing that I now had all the time in the world to memorize them.

Suddenly, as if he couldn't hold it in any longer, he burst, "I love you!"

"I love you too!" I burst back, giggling.

As we dissolved into a deep, passionate, heart-stopping, earth-shattering kiss, I could hear Dr. James mumble, "Disgusting..."

I also heard something else.

There was a loud, smacking sound as I broke the seal between Hoagie's lips and mine and sat up, cocking my head to the side like a hunting dog trying to capture the sound of a fox tiptoeing in the distance.

"What is it?" Hoagie asked, grasping my fingers in fear as he held my bandaged hands to his heart.

"Shhhh," I urged him, listening intently to the barely perceptible sounds coming from outside our concrete cave.

Then I heard it.

"CHARLIE!"

My stomach soared up into my throat as I scrambled to my feet, pushing aside boulders and pieces of tile and plaster to dig myself out of our would-be grave.

"*CHARLIE!*"

I cut my hand on a broken pipe, but I didn't care. I was shoving, shifting, kicking things out of the way as I got closer and closer to the surface, closer and closer to the voice I thought I'd never hear again. Hoagie was helping me now, tossing rocks and hunks of building onto his uncle, who cursed and spat at us like an incensed tabby cat.

"CHASE!" I screamed as the cool night air hit my face and I could finally make out the glittering stars in the sky above me, "CHASE!"

"Thank God," he choked, from across the parking lot.

Red and white emergency lights lit up the scene, pulsing and strobing dizzyingly as I managed to climb up to the top of the rubble pile. I stopped and turned to Hoagie, proffering him a hand to help him out of the hole, but he waved it away.

"Go." He laughed, shooing me off.

I grinned.

Then, limping like a half-lame racehorse, I slid clumsily down the mountain of wreckage and shot off across the lot. My head was pounding and my ribs and feet were on fire, but I could feel no pain as I leapt into Chase's arms, throwing mine around his neck as I sobbed into his ear, "Chase, we did it!"

"*You* did it," he sobbed right back, squeezing me tight, as he kissed the top of my matted hair.

I don't know what I had been thinking before. Chase and Charlie hadn't ended. Nothing had changed. We were still two halves of one whole, two parts of one person, and nothing could ever change that.

"Please tell me you're not going back in there for anyone

else." Chase grimaced, wiping his slick cheeks as I glanced back at the pile of debris where the three ominous towers of The Institute had once stood.

"No, I got everyone I came for," I assured him.

"Good." He nodded. "Now let's get the hell out of here."

59

"I KNEW SHE COULD DO IT," Chase told Hoagie for the hundredth time, puffing his chest out proudly, as he moved our enormous Chuck-E-Cheese doll to plop down next to me on our lumpy living room couch a few weeks later. "And that's not just because she looked like a female Die Hard the last time I'd seen her."

I laughed as I reached across him for the DVD player's remote, wincing slightly as I scraped my still-smarting ribs on his still-bandaged stomach.

"I knew she could do it too," Hoagie replied, just as proudly, as he popped a handful of red Skittles into his mouth, banging his hand against the hard plastic guard over his newly-reconstructed nose for the umpteenth time. "I never doubted her for a second."

He winked at me and I laughed harder. I never know what to say when they talk like that. Sure, I saved them both, cleared Chase's name, freed over two dozen mental patients and put the true criminally insane murderer behind bars (with the help of the de-zombified patients' testimonies and Hoagie's smuggled pills, of course), but I'm no hero. I'm just a girl who has watched enough movies to know that there's a way out of any situation, as long as you have the guts and the brains to keep believing in yourself.

As I settled back into the squishy couch cushion, holding Hoagie's hand and resting my head against Chase's shoulder, I grinned as I realized that I had definitely given Colonel Hogan and his Heroes something to be proud of.

Chase turned down the lamp next to the sofa (I never let him turn it all the way off anymore), and I pressed play. Hoagie snuck me a kiss on the cheek in the semi-darkness as the t.v. screen lit up with the opening scene from the original *Star Trek* movie, and I plunged my hand into our big, communal bowl of sticky, candy-filled popcorn.

"Damn," Chase muttered, wincing as he wriggled his way up off the couch. "We forgot the napkins."

"I'm coming with you!" I shouted, dropping the remote and the bowl onto Hoagie's lap as I sprang to my feet.

"Charlie, the kitchen's like three feet away," Chase sighed, feigning exasperation as he waited for me to catch up.

"I don't care," I told him, looping my arm through his, "I'm not taking any chances!"

A Note from the Author

I hope you enjoyed reading this book as much as I enjoyed writing it!

As you probably know, reviews from readers like you can mean the difference between success and obscurity for authors like me. If you have a moment, please consider sharing your thoughts about this book on Amazon or your other favorite book review websites. This would not only help me as a writer, but it would help other readers in their search for their next book as well.

If you'd like to learn more about me and my books, visit www.jessicascottromano.com.

Thank you for reading!

About the Author

Born in Louisville, Kentucky, Jessica Scott Romano has been writing since she was three years old. After reading far too many books about grand adventures in faraway places, she was inspired to go on a few of her own.

She now lives in Italy with her husband and two cats, where she spends her days writing, traveling, and sampling every delicious dish the country has to offer.

You can find Jessica online at www.jessicascottromano.com.

To learn more about her adventures in Italy, you can also visit her blog at www.anamericaninitaly.com.

www.ingramcontent.com/pod-product-compliance
Lightning Source LLC
Chambersburg PA
CBHW032216050726
47591CB00001B/141